Breaking Away

ALSO BY KRISTIN LATTANY
Published by Ballantine Books

Kinfolks
Do Unto Others

Breaking Away

Kristin Lattany

ONE WORLD

Ballantine Books • New York

A ONE WORLD BOOK

Published by The Ballantine Publishing Group

ISBN 0-345-44249-0

Book Design by BTDnyc

Manufactured in the United States of America

Acknowledgments

My gratitude and appreciation to the following "water buffalo" victims who are members of Delta Sigma Theta Sorority and the University of Pennsylvania class of 1994: Colleen Bonnicklewis, Nikki Taylor, Denita Thomas, and Suzanne Jenkins, for their bravery and strength, and especially to Ayanna Taylor, for sharing her experiences so generously.

My thanks, also, to their classmate, Ericka Blount Danois, for facilitating our meetings and bearing true witness.

Thanks, in spite of everything, to the University of Pennsylvania, my alma mater and erstwhile employer, for providing me with many lessons—the most important ones unintentional, the rest the basis for a lifetime of learning.

Breaking Away

Chapter One

Life was good.

Dr. Bethesda Barnes finished the last of her ten laps, rolled over, and floated on her back contentedly in the warm peace of the pool. Surrounded by blue light, breathing chlorinated air, she counted her blessings.

A job I love. Thank you, Lord. She did not have tenure, but she did have a sense of security. Her four-year contract had only a year to run, but it had been renewed once almost automatically, and she did not anticipate any problems this time. Her class comparing male and female American writers with similar regional backgrounds was almost as full as last year's Black Literature and Music. Overflowing, like Beth herself in last year's purple bathing suit.

Black Literature and Music was successful, but it had been a mistake. She had been inspired to create the course when she was teaching Black Women Writers and learned that most of her students knew even less about music than she did. When they read Paule Marshall's sublime *Praisesong for the Widow*, and she found out that they had never heard of "After Hours" or any of the other great recordings with which the Jay Johnsons pleasured themselves in private, she felt something had to be done. Avery Parish's great piano blues, her father had told her, had once been so popular people called "After Hours" the Negro National Anthem. Many people of her generation, he'd said, would not have been born at all were it not for that record played for slow dancing at dimly lit basement parties.

She had taught the course with the help of local musicologists, and it had been a blast. But she could never repeat it, because over the summer one of her two guest lecturers had died, taking his knowledge of big bands, folk music, blues, and boogie-woogie with him.

Among her other blessings Bethesda counted being born in the fifties, and not before. With her gifts and drive, she felt, she would have succeeded anyway, but when she emerged from grad school, Ph.D. in hand, at twenty-eight, the barriers were down and the doors were open.

She had put in seven years of teaching at a state school, during which she published her book on Ohio writers, a sardonic study of Himes, Paul Laurence Dunbar, Morrison, Giovanni, and Dove called *O. is for Other,* and then landed this plum spot at one of the Ivy League schools. The world was hers. Now, to paraphrase another of her favorite writers, all she had to do was keep her oyster knife handy.

Beth still felt oddly distanced from this institution where she had spent four years as an undergraduate and seven as a teacher, but her popularity with her students and her close relationships with a few of them made up for that. There was something about the place that kept people apart. Tall buildings blocking the sunlight. Communication via mailboxes and e-mail instead of face-to-face conversations. She had only one friend on the faculty, Irene Levinson, a Shakespeare scholar who kept warning her that she ought to do more to shore up her position. Irene said that she should read all the faculty newsletters carefully, cultivate relationships with full professors and department heads, and go to faculty meetings even though her attendance there was not required.

Beth ignored her friend's advice because she was diffident about reaching out to her white colleagues. She saw no point in attending meetings when she was not a voting member of the faculty. After preparing for her classes, conferring with her students, and reading their papers, she had no time to socialize or go to meetings, anyway. So, instead of cultivating friendships with other faculty members, she kept her distance, just as they kept theirs, and she became close to her students. Instead of reaching out to her peers and asking questions, she preserved an air of independence and aloofness.

It had taken Beth two years to locate the ladies' room on her floor of the Humanities Building, years during which she borrowed the secretaries' keys to use the facility on the first floor. Once she had said to herself, "Beth, this is ridiculous," and stopped a female colleague in the hall to ask the location of the ladies' room on her floor. The woman simply stared at her with eyes like pus-filled gray sores. She never answered. Later Beth learned that she was from South Carolina. After that encounter, rather than ask directions around the fortresslike campus, whose new buildings turned blank faces to the street, she carried a map in her purse.

The warnings of her parents, Curtis and Delores Barnes, must have registered deeply on her childish consciousness. They had said repeatedly as they sent her off to various white schools, "You going to be around *them*, and you supposed to know everything *they* know. If you don't know, don't show your ignorance by asking. Find out the best way you can."

Her mother was part of that generation of women who always dressed in their best to go shopping downtown, wearing hats, pearls, silk dresses, and white gloves so they would not be insulted or refused service by some prejudiced, minimum-wage clerk. They were often humiliated, anyway.

Still, Bethesda, having begun her career in the years when Blackness was in and doors were opening to the qualified, did not attribute the poor communication on campus to racism. The place was just cold, she thought.

After all, Black Literature and Music had been one of the most popular courses ever offered in the department, enrolling almost an equal number of black and white students. It was still being talked about by undergraduates, who often came to her office asking when she would offer it again. But besides the death of one of her guest lecturers, she had no grant this year with which to pay visiting speakers. Instead, she'd had to think up a course that she could do all by herself. She had come up with one that compared male and female American writers from similar backgrounds, an easy shoe-in as a women's studies class that allowed her to enter the entire twentieth century through the side door. Bethesda had begun Man's World/Woman's World in Twentieth-Century American Fiction with the obvious comparison, James and Wharton, both upper-class New Yorkers, and moved forward in time to Zora Neale Hurston and Erskine Caldwell, who were from the neighboring states of Florida and Georgia. She would attempt to prove that region was at least as important an influence on their work as race or sex before moving on to Faulkner and O'Connor, who, though from different states, were both Southern whites. She planned to end with Richard Wright and Margaret Walker, a pair of black writers from Mississippi.

She was enjoying her new course, though it required a lot of close reading, and she was enjoying her students. Two of them, girls named Rhonda and Dana, were especially quick and responsive. A boy called C. T. Jones was mostly quiet, but he had made a couple of razor-sharp comments. The brightest and the best came to this school. She had been one of them. *Thank you, Lord.*

Propelling herself with a lazy yet powerful frog kick, she continued counting her blessings. *A man who loves me. Thank you, Lord.* Her other guest expert on music, Lloyd Bounds—a postal clerk by day, a disc jockey by night—had filled her classroom with his vast knowledge of jazz. Now he filled Bethesda, too, quite adequately and quite often. She had no complaints about their life in bed. But, though he brought her groceries and cooked for her like a Cordon Bleu chef and played new records every weekend for their private finger-popping fun, something was missing.

Lloyd didn't really get what she was about; that was it. They inhabited different worlds, and sometimes they seemed to be on different planes. That was why she had refused to move in with him. One weekend at his house with his loud recordings breaking into her thoughts had been enough. Lester Young's "Lester Leaps In" had charged into her consciousness, commanding attention through five speakers while she was trying to concentrate on Baldwin's great first novel. It was followed by Charlie Parker's "Bird Feathers," a bright blast of male exuberance breaking the mood of the somber organ symphony that was *Go Tell It on the Mountain.* Then Lloyd played another Parker song, this time with strings: "Just Friends"— a rhapsody of soaring, fluent notes. By now the music had Beth's full attention. Next Lloyd played a Mariah Carey cut, "Hero." Carey's voice, almost too ornate, cascaded and tumbled and decorated the melody much like Parker's playing.

"Ah," Beth had said.

"Ah," Lloyd had echoed, smiling because he knew she understood the connection he had made, so much like the connections she made among writers' works when teaching. But her reading had been hopelessly interrupted, and she never returned to it that day.

Beth had assumed that someone with Lloyd's knowledge of music would also love to read, but she had never seen him crack a book.

Stop complaining, Beth, she told herself as she kicked more energetically, moving herself toward the edge of the pool. Lloyd loved her, and he was good to her. She could teach him to respect her work, if not to appreciate it. *Thank you, Lord, for Lloyd.*

She added good health and a healthy family to her list of blessings. When Beth made and kept appointments for checkups, her doctor looked at her as if asking, "Why are you wasting my time?" He did want her to lose weight, though. She always politely accepted the diets he gave her, folded them, and put them in her bag, where they stayed until she changed pocketbooks. She was comfortable with the lush padding under her skin that made her resemble a sleek brown seal in the water, and since Lloyd liked it, too, she had no plans to change.

Sometimes, though, carrying thirty pounds of extra weight around, along with her course load and her concerns about her family, made her feel as overburdened as a mule or an ox. That was why she loved swimming. The water buoyed her, made her weightless and free. She stared at the patterns the pool's underwater lights made in the water, white streaks in turquoise, ducked underneath to see them better, and came up coughing. She hated swimming underwater because she could not hold her breath long enough to stop the water from going up her nose, but sometimes she did it, anyway. She did a few slow, luxurious spins on her back, using one arm as a rudder, and then a couple of extra laps with her powerful backstroke before she resumed floating. Yes, she was heavy, but she was healthy. Just in case, though, it was good to have the best health insurance and the availability of one of the city's—no, one of the world's—greatest teaching hospitals. *Thank you, Lord.*

Coming back to this pool at night was a way of coming home, a way of touching base with her past self. She had learned to swim here under duress. If she squinted, she could go back in time and see her classmates, Sherri, Laura, and Margaret, bobbing in the pool, clinging to the side with heads like balloons from the strips of chamois wound round them under their caps. The chamois was supposed to keep their heat-straightened hair dry. It hadn't worked for Bethesda; she always had a wet head and a cold that lasted all winter. Since her hair was naturally near-straight, Beth hadn't really needed the chamois. She just wore it not to be different from the others.

Four of them had been close friends—four black girls of the class of '75 who called themselves the Foxy Four—Beth, Sherri Davis, Laura Mills, and Margaret Brown. The quartet had hated the swimming requirement and had vowed to lobby for its repeal, once they became rich, powerful alumnae. Beth, especially, had feared she would never pass the swimming test and would never graduate. But after two continuous years of swimming, she became expert and learned to love it.

Beth was one of the lucky survivors of the Foxy Four. Sherri Davis was another—still unmarried, but successful. The fates of the other two were heartbreaking. Laura Mills had married right out of school and died of complications from pregnancy the following year. Margaret Brown had become a social worker, moved to California, and been murdered by one of the disturbed teenagers who were her clients. That was the trouble with tokenism, Beth thought. If half the tokens died prematurely, the community that had struggled to put them in place ended up right back where it started. Things were better now, she thought, with more minority faculty and open admissions for all capable students.

Beth's thoughts returned to her family. Bonita and her little girl, Della, were fine, though she had written with the news that she and James were definitely divorcing. Beth loved her kid sister but was baffled by the metamorphosis of that sweet, dimpled little girl into a gun-toting, ass-kicking policewoman. Their father, Curtis, seemed unchanged, except that since his retirement from the school system, he had more time to sit in his La-Z-Boy chair reading periodicals and muttering obscurely motivated curses at politicians and perpetrators.

It had been three years now since their mother's surgery, and the cancer had not come back. Delores had not even needed to lose a breast. *Thank you, Lord.* She supposed Neet would move back with their mother if the need to care for her ever arose.

Beth felt a sudden chill. She began treading water to get warm.

Edwina, the locker room attendant who had been there forever, appeared by the side of the pool nearest her with an armful of towels and held one out to her.

"Ain't you been in there long enough?" she asked.

"No," Beth said, though she had begun to shiver. Edwina had been an attendant here since Beth's undergraduate days. She was one of the reasons Beth always swam at the nearly abandoned women's gym. The peace and the emptiness were another, and a third was that she was old enough not to want to share the pool with loud, rough boys. Let the young girls have all the pleasure.

But Edwina, a slim woman of medium height with an ageless, speckled face the color of walnuts, was able to reduce her to a teenager with a few words. When that happened, Beth got rebellious, like any teenager.

"Why are you telling me when it's time to get out of the pool?"

"Because it's my job," the homely older woman said. She spoke with the authority of someone who had known Beth practically since infancy. "Come out, now."

"Yes, ma'am," Beth said meekly, and climbed the four tiled stairs, accepting the large towel the older woman draped around her shoulders.

"You going straight home, ain't you?" This was more an order than a question.

"Yes, Edwina. I'll wait till I get there to shower and wash my hair."

"And suppose you see a friend on the way? Suppose you see a store window with something in it you just got to have? Suppose that jazzy little man of yours crosses your path, looking sharp and whistling one of the tunes he plays on the radio? You made me a promise to go straight home and shower, but you expect me to believe you going to keep it if something like that happens?" The questions were rhetorical; Beth was not expected to answer.

Edwina turned to Lincoln, the ancient security guard who as usual was perched on his stool in the shadows, witnessing their nightly game. "Some people believe their lives belong just to them, you know what I mean, Lincoln? Some of our young people believe they got that education all by themselves, on their own, free and clear, without strings or obligations."

"Mm-hmm," he responded, like he was sitting on the deacon's bench in church and hearing a call in the sermon.

Edwina was working up to a feverish climax. "Soo, they believe they can throw their lives and their educations away any time they want. Don't believe they got connections or obligations—"

"Mm-hmm, no, they don't."

"Don't believe they owe anything to the ones who went before them, or the ones who are coming after. No, they can take their degrees and their positions and throw them all away in an instant—" She snapped her fingers. "—going out in the cold air with wet heads or walking barefoot in the rain or doing any other foolishness that takes their fancy."

Beth finished drying her hair with the towel and took another from Edwina to wrap around it. "My boyfriend is working tonight," Beth told her. "The stores are closed. Even if they weren't, I don't have time to go shopping. I have thirty papers to grade before I fall asleep. So, whether you believe me or not, I *am* going straight home."

"Listen to her, will you, Lincoln? Did she get me told, or not?"

"Sure did."

"These young ones are getting just too uppity for words, ain't they?"

"Sure is."

Beth exited the pool to the sound of Edwina's cackling laughter and entered the locker room. She stepped out of her wet bathing suit and rubbed herself as dry as she could. Then she took the towel off her head, dressed, jammed a beret down on her hair, and walked out past the booth where Edwina presided over stacks of towels. It was a sort of three-sided cage built of opaque glass that was strengthened with chicken wire. Through it, the long watchful shadow of Lincoln could be seen, pacing the perimeter of his territory.

Sometimes Beth chafed at Edwina's dictatorial fussing, but mostly she liked it, knowing it was an expression of love. On impulse she leaned across the counter to plant a kiss on the older woman's cheek.

Edwina ducked out of the way, just beyond Beth's reach. Beth was reminded of another time in the pool, when she had tried to splash water on the older woman to get back at her for some bossy remark or other, but had failed. The water had puddled all around Edwina's feet, but she did not get wet.

"Go on with you," she said now.

As Beth left the peaceful, nurturing aqueous world for the noise and confusion outside, she heard Edwina call, "Go straight home, now, before you catch a chill!"

Stepping onto the westbound street, she noticed to her surprise that some of the campus stores were still open. United States Sportswear, a candle shop called Incandessence, and a jewelry store called Jewels of the East were all open. She stopped to inspect a tray of silver rings in the jewelry store's window. Beth had been into rings lately. She wore them on as many fingers as possible, but lacked one for the second finger of her right hand.

A silver ring wrought of yang and yin symbols, with blue and gold stones for eyes, attracted her. Maybe it was just the wish to defy Edwina that pushed her inside the store to try it on.

The Asian Indian woman behind the counter seemed reluctant to take the tray out of the window, probably because it was closing time and she wanted to go home. Nevertheless, she showed Beth the ring and quoted an impossibly high price. It didn't fit the finger Beth wanted to wear it on, anyway. Beth left the store.

She had reached the parking lot and her little white Mustang convertible when she heard running footsteps behind her.

"Hey, lady! Lady!"

It was the East Indian saleswoman and, just behind her, a man, probably her husband. She stopped, and they caught up with her, panting, the extraordinary whiteness of their eyes and teeth gleaming even in the dark.

"Lady, there is a ring missing from that tray. We want it back."

"I didn't take anything," Beth said in a small voice.

"That ring was worth a hundred dollars. Pay for it, or give it back."

It was a scam, Beth decided. Now she felt like going upside the woman's head. She balled up her fist. "I don't have any of your rings. I don't want any of your junky merchandise."

"We want the ring or the money," the man said, "or we will call the police."

"Do that," Beth said, getting into her car. "But first, you better go back and check your stock. I took nothing." She felt more confident now. They would have to call campus police, and once the campus cops saw her faculty ID, they would get respectful and apologize. She started her engine.

"No, no, you're not leaving till we see some ID. Who are you?" the man demanded.

"I don't have to do this," she informed him, but passed her driver's license and her faculty ID through the window.

The foreign man did not seem impressed. He took a long time copying the information from her cards and then went around to the back of her car, probably to write down the letters on her license plate. *He better hurry up, before I back this car over his skinny foreign ass,* Beth thought.

By now Beth was aware of her damp body and felt chilled clear through. She started her heater, but the engine was not warm yet.

The Indian man came back. "You will hear from us shortly," he said, wagging his finger in her face as he returned her ID.

Beth felt scared, humiliated, and then enraged in rapid succession. Her heart was racing, and her face was hot as she rammed her accelerator. "You will hear from my lawyer!" she screamed as if she really had one.

Chapter Two

Whilе mentally listing her blessings, Beth had neglected to include a loyal and understanding girlfriend. She and Sherri Davis had been tight ever since their sophomore year at the university, when they started spending study weekends together and hanging out on the phone for hours when apart. There were many things they did not agree on—among them the persistence of racism since the civil rights reforms of the sixties and their tastes in men—but there was no doubt that they were friends for life.

Beth was inclined to think that the race problem had gotten better since the sixties; Sherri thought the opposite. Neither of them cared terribly whether their men had college educations, which gave them a broader field to choose from than the other professional women they knew; but Beth liked guys who were trying to do something positive with their lives, while Sherri was drawn to dangerous men—hard-core criminals and hoodlums.

There was no accounting for tastes, but sometimes Sherri got guilty enough to try to defend hers. "Ain't no options out here for a really ambitious black man but crime," she had said. "If he tries to operate inside the law, he gets shot down."

"Girl, that is the biggest load of bullshit you ever dumped on me," Beth had replied. "It's just a lame excuse for liking gangstas."

"No, it's the truth," her friend had said. "Look what they did to Adam Powell. Slapped him with a bogus charge as soon as he got close to being Speaker of the House. And look how they pulled that sting on Marion Barry just to keep him from meeting that ugly old bitch, the Queen of England. As for poor old O. J., he just had to be guilty because he matches the image of the vengeful nigger in their heads."

"Sherri, you know there are opportunities out there for our men. All they have to do is be prepared and learn the rules."

"And be mediocre. That's Rule Number One. They can't be so smart they outshine the white boys. Look what they did to that genius on Wall Street, Joe Jett. They made him a fall guy for the entire firm, then put him out. And if our men really threaten them, the way Martin, Malcolm, and Medgar did, you *know* what happens." Sherri had made the gesture of cutting her own throat. "And don't forget Ron Brown."

"Sherri! That plane crash was an accident. Surely you don't believe—"

"I surely do."

"I still think you're making too many excuses for the brothers," Beth said. "There are plenty of opportunities for them out here today, and you know it." She shook her head, remembering that conversation. Sometimes her best friend really tried her patience. Once Sherri's racial paranoia got rolling, there was no point in trying to haul it back.

Beth was glad to get home tonight to her warm, cozy apartment. She had bought several pieces of fifties furniture at a second-hand store for their solid, durable wood. One of them, a bright yellow dresser that held linens and clothes, caught and magnified the light. A copy of *Shotguns,* a painting by John Biggers of pregnant women in front of their shotgun houses, dominated one living room wall over a brown sofa with animal-print and kente cloth pillows.

When the phone rang, she knew it had to be Sherri. They hadn't talked in two whole days.

"Fox Number One here. Is this Fox Number Two?"

"Fox Number Two speaking."

"How they hangin', Professor-baby?"

Beth settled into her favorite high-backed armchair, kicked off her left shoe, and used her toes to drag the chair's matching footstool into place. "High, wide, and handsome, thanks to my Eighteen Hour Bra, but my eighteen hours are almost up. I just got back in the house, and I've been gone since seven this morning."

"That bra must be hollerin', 'Have mercy!' "

"So is my chest," said Beth. She pulled up her sweater and unhooked her bra. "I just let 'em out. What a relief."

"I know what you mean," Sherri told her, dropping her bantering tone. "I'm dragging, too."

"Those little knobs of yours couldn't drag if you hung twenty-pound twins on 'em," was Beth's rejoinder.

"Hmm. I like that idea," Sherri said. "I'd feel sorry for the twins, though. They'd have to root like pigs or die poor. Still, wish I could go shopping for a pair. Of twins, I mean."

"They're giving babies away, from what I hear, especially Chinese girls and black boys." As their biological clocks sped up, she and Sherri had discussed adopting, but neither of them had pursued it.

"No kidding. I'll look into it." Sherri sounded serious. "I couldn't support any kids right now, that's the problem. I'm about to lose my job."

Sherri had created a successful neighborhood arts program in the toughest part of the city and run it for nearly ten years. Children and adults in the community came to study dance, theater, art, and music at her center, and their productions regularly received good reviews.

Beth kicked off her other shoe and rubbed her toes against each other in friendly communion. This was going to be a long conversation, she could tell, one demanding a lot of commiseration. "Oh, no. What happened? Problems with the funding?"

"Yes, but that's nothing new. I've been through that before. Something always comes through at the last minute."

"What, then?"

"I'm about to be superseded by Miss Anne."

"You don't mean your assistant." Sherri's assistant, a blank-faced blonde, really was named Anne. Anne Lawrence. Sherri had been inclined to dismiss her as a lightweight, but Beth had caught a remark or two of Anne's that suggested she was not as stupid as she seemed. "You know, Sherri, I always felt you should keep an eye on that girl, and not get too complacent."

"Well, you were right," her friend said. She paused. "You know she was sent here by the Ross Foundation."

"Your biggest patron."

"Yeah, and she's the director's bimbo. He has the clout. So if he wants her promoted over me, what can I do?"

"Sabotage her," Beth said promptly. "Sign her name to dumb memos. Leave idiotic messages from her on important people's machines. Send her boyfriend a bunch of dead flowers from her, along with some Red Rooster pills for his flagging potency. Some Viagra. Isn't that what Red Rooster pills are called these days?"

"You have a really evil, sneaky mind, you know that, Beth Barnes? It's what I admire most about you."

"Thanks for the compliment. Put a pack of condoms in her purse, with one missing."

"Cool, Beth," Sherri replied. "Really fiendish. I'll do it."

"Put a pregnancy test in there, too. And a pack of love letters. I'll help you write them."

"You really cheer me up, girlfriend, you know that? Now that you've helped with my problem, how are things with you?"

"Okay, except I had a bad experience tonight." And she went on to tell Sherri about the incident in the campus jewelry store—getting chased, accused, and threatened. As she recounted it, she felt as if she were drowning. All the bad emotions she had felt then were piling up again and pushing her under.

When Beth had finished, Sherri said, "Welcome to the club, kiddo. You've just been profiled. Did they follow you around the store?"

"Um, let me think." The man, whom she had hardly noticed at first, had come sliding out from the back of the store and had found an excuse to mess with the merchandise on the shelves behind his wife. "Maybe. I'm not sure. Probably."

"Profiled. Definitely," Sherri said.

"Oh, no, I don't think so," Beth said. "They weren't white. They were brown people. East Indians, I think."

"You kidding? They're the worst. Some of them may come here without prejudice, but they catch on quick. They're so anxious to be honorary white folks, they'll do anything. Look at that guy who wrote *Inequality in Education*, Dagunga Dinza, or whatever his name is."

"Dinesh D'Souza," Beth corrected automatically.

"Whatever. He tried to get ahead by putting us down and climbing up on our backs."

"No one takes him seriously, Sherri. That book is full of lousy scholarship."

"No one in *your* world takes him seriously, Beth. Outside of the ivory tower, he confirmed a lot of ignorant hunkies in their prejudices and did us a lot of damage. He's another nail in the coffin of affirmative action. So are those people who wrote *The Bell Curve*."

"Do you think we really still need that?"

"Need what?"

"Affirmative action. I mean, look at you, look at me—"

"Girl pull-leez. I cannot talk to you about this tonight, except to say, look at us, indeed. Look at you, working like a slave without any hope of tenure. Look at me, about to be displaced by a minimum-wage ho I just trained. It's late, let me change the subject before I go ballistic. How's Lloyd?"

"He's all right, I guess."

"What's that mean?"

"He's fine. I'm just not sure he's right for me."

"Is he breathing? Does he wear pants? Does he know to eat his pie with a fork and stir his coffee with a spoon?"

"Yes to all of those."

"Does he know a grace to say before meals?"

"Yes—in fact, he knows several."

"Can he fuck?"

"Oh, yes."

"Then he's right for you; in fact, he's better than you deserve, you dumb bitch. You haven't been out there lately, you don't know how limited the choices are."

They had had this conversation several times before. This time, Beth took a daring new tack. "Who says I need a man, anyway?"

"Girl, pull-leez. Come off it." Sherri paused for several seconds and then added in a shy whisper. "I met somebody."

"What's his rap sheet like?"

"He doesn't have one."

"What?" This *was* news. "You've got to be kidding, Sherri Davis. Men without criminal records don't interest you. Besides, there are only ten men in this town who've never been in jail."

"He's one of them."

"I take it he's white, then."

"Don't you know me at all, Beth? I don't mess around with white boys. They're suicide. I love myself."

Beth had dated white men, off and on, ever since high school and saw nothing wrong with it, but she knew better than to discuss that with Sherri. "Why are they suicide?" She was genuinely curious.

"Oh, you know. They never take you home to meet the family, so you know there's no chance of marriage, not that you'd want it. They don't introduce you to their friends. They're afraid to be seen with you in public. They take you to dark, creepy little places off the beaten track, and if they see somebody they know, they duck and run. All this backstreet shit puts your self-esteem down in the sub-basement. No, thank you."

Beth would have to think about whether her interracial relationships had followed this pattern. If she were honest, she might have to admit that it was true. The last white man she had dated, a New York editor named Russell, had promised to visit her on a weekend about two years ago. She had made restaurant reservations and all sorts of plans, but he hadn't shown. When she called his house, a woman answered. A white woman, Beth judged from her flat, uninflected finishing-school accent. Russell had been her last white boyfriend.

"Tell me about the new man."

"He's just a decent, law-abiding brother. No bad habits. No criminal tendencies."

"Sounds boring. Where did you meet this paragon?"

"At the church where we have the sculpture class for seniors. Remember I told you we were starting one? He teaches it."

"Oh-ho," said Beth. "Not boring. A fascinating, romantic artist. Has he asked you to pose for him yet?"

"No," Sherri said. She hesitated. "The hard thing for me is, he's celibate. He wants to save himself for marriage."

"Bad news," Beth pronounced. "You're a hot-blooded, horny woman, just reaching your prime. He's a weird, withholding kook."

"No, he's not. He's just into health in a big way. Herbs, exercise, bottled water, teas, no meat, no exposure to diseases."

Beth took a chance on a long shot. "If he's celibate, how does he explain his four kids?"

She was right.

"They happened before he became enlightened about health and spirituality."

"Girlfriend, I repeat," Beth said, "you are a hot-natured woman. What will you do about the physical problem?"

"Um . . . he asked me to marry him."

"And?"

"I'm considering it."

Beth was about to say something on the order of, "I think I'm going to faint. I'll call you back when I regain consciousness." Instead she gave in and let out the voluminous sneeze she had been trying to hold back for a couple of minutes." 'Scuse me. I been swimming," she apologized, and let out another ripsnorter. She dug around for a tissue for her runny nose.

"Then get a hot shower and go to bed. I'll call you this weekend. You'll meet Solomon soon, I promise. Bye."

Muttering curses and complaining about how her best friend was about to ruin her life, some people couldn't be left alone for five minutes, Beth undressed and obeyed the orders she'd been given by both her female friends.

At least this Solomon sounded better than the number Sherri had brought to Beth's birthday party last August. Red leather suit, red suede shoes, platinum and diamonds twinkling at his wrist and in his ears—the whole pimp getup. Sherri had been entranced with Nathan until he tried to enroll her in his escort business. Now she seemed to be falling for his opposite. The dumb ho.

Another sneeze convinced her to put thoughts of Sherri aside. Getting warm, dry, clean, and fed was her first order of business.

"All that hair," Edwina had said, with a touch of envy. There *was* quite a lot of it, Beth conceded after using up three globs of shampoo and another three of conditioner. A lot of women her age were cutting theirs. She had considered it, but then decided that whatever it was about her hair that made other women, even the eternal Edwina, jealous was something she wanted to keep. It was long, lush, abundant, and a motherfucker to dry.

She was plump, of course, but tonight her body seemed more bloated than usual. Once a month, just before her period, a single blemish popped out on her face. Beth wiped a window in the fog that clouded her mirror, and peered through it. Yep, there it was on the left side of her nose, glowing like a headlight, marring her otherwise perfect mocha skin. She would have to sleep in her stained old period panties tonight.

Beth often amused herself by laughing at all the propaganda about feminine daintiness. A woman was nothing more than an open sewer, with all the fluxes of blood, sweat, semen, and her own juices that kept pouring through her. You just had to learn to deal with it. The antiperspirants, sprays, douches, talcs, and colognes were all out there to help you, so there was no excuse for being funky. She often wondered how her parents had made it on their old-fashioned once-a-week bathing schedule. Religiously, they observed National Negro Bath Night—Saturday night, so you would be clean for church, except that they never went. Daily, they raised hell with Beth because she wanted to bathe more often. All over the tiny cost of a little hot water.

Beth also wondered how her friends had gotten along in the old days without washing their hair between twice-monthly salon visits. If Beth didn't wash her hair every other day, she got physically ill. Rashes, fatigue, itching—the whole nine yards.

Before she wrapped herself in a bath sheet, she wiped the fog off the full-length bathroom mirror and inspected herself.

"Beth Barnes, you are one fine bitch, you know that?"

Beth was built like a V—large bust, small butt. At five feet seven and 175 pounds, she was overweight, but Lloyd liked her that way, and so did she. She had boobs like overripe melons, narrow shoulders, slim thighs, and small, plump hands. She couldn't remember what it was like to have a waist. Her face was as full as her chest, with cheeks so round she had forgotten what her bone structure was like, too, but with her large, tilted eyes and satin skin, it looked marvelous. To accommodate her inverted-triangle shape, she had become expert at snatching size 20 tops off the rack to pair with size 16 bottoms when buying two-piece outfits, and felt no compunction about doing so. In the stores where she shopped, everything was overpriced, anyway.

Her color was medium brown with an underpainting of glowing red—a light mocha. Her wide, naturally purple mouth and abundant, coarse black hair gave her an Indian or *mestiza* look, which she had come by honestly. There was American Indian in her family, as in almost every African-American family, and on her, it showed. Curtis, her father, had some Choctaw people mingled with his African ancestry down South.

Beth thought her eyes were her best feature. They were large, dark and liquid, almond-shaped, with brilliant whites and thick lashes. She was skilled with makeup and wore it every day, but she knew better than to gild the lily by applying mascara. *Thank you, Lord,* she murmured, *for not making me ugly.*

The pale tweeds, sensible shoes, and mousy colors worn by the rest of the female faculty were not for her. Beth had been a standout all her life, and she saw no point in changing now. When the undergraduate chair, a grim mouse named Cornelia who taught the Victorians and looked as if she lived among them, had hinted that Beth's look was not appropriate in a university setting, Beth retorted that she had a right to look any way she damn pleased, and that her critic was probably jealous. Cornelia backed off. Beth went right on wearing her brightly colored suits with tight sweaters or bright blouses, high-heeled pumps and fishnet stockings, and, in a fury the next morning, had darkened her lipstick, added liberal splashes of her heaviest, muskiest perfume, and topped off her outfit with one of her wild collection of church hats.

Then there were the fingernails. Beth had hers regularly augmented and enameled into works of art. At one faculty party, Cornelia was heard to say, "No serious woman paints her fingernails." Beth's response had been to cover her mouth with the palm of one hand to hide her grin, and peer at the undergraduate choir through splayed fingers tipped with shiny navy-blue nails. She thought her nails were conservative. At least, they matched her conservative navy dress, which she had bought for funerals and faculty parties.

Compared with the other women at school, maybe, Beth was flamboyant, but at church she was drab next to the rest of the female flock. Brocades, furs, metallics, a palette of wild colors— no raiment was too fine for them to wear to glorify the Lord. As for the hats—no fantasy was too wild or too expensive for them to plunk down on their heads on Sunday mornings.

Beth smiled, thinking of the hat store that supplied the women of her church. She loved to go shopping there. It resembled an observatory or a bird sanctuary, with some styles that resembled ringed planets and others like birds in flight. It was amazing what some women would perch on their heads—fruit baskets, crowns, cartwheels. Many hats in the store appeared to defy gravity so completely she thought the shop ought to supply sandbags to its customers.

Beth was not a regular churchgoer, missing more services than she attended, but she showed up at least once a month to hear a guest preacher or the choir in concert, and for those days, she kept a spectacular hat collection in her closet. Being a backslider did not trouble her. Black preachers used death as a means to terrorize their congregations, and while Beth liked being exhorted and moved, she did not like being frightened. She did not want anyone to die for her, either. She wanted only to be shown how to live. She believed in a God who listened to her and who had blessed her since birth, but she was not sure what else she believed. She had promised herself that she would use her next vacation to examine and clarify her fuzzy religious beliefs.

During the week Beth mostly went hatless, with her hair pulled back and anchored by a large comb attached to a bow that matched her clothes. She also wore large, dangling earrings and heavy makeup like a showgirl's. Except when she pulled her reading glasses out of her bosom by their gold chain, she did not look like a scholar.

But she was.

Stretched across her bed in a leopard-print terry robe, fine-point pen poised over a student paper, she ticked off grammatical and factual errors as well as brilliant insights, pausing only to snatch a bite of the pared apples and cubed cheese she had placed at her bedside. "This is not my reading of the text," she wrote on one paper. "Selden does not fail to propose to Lily Bart because he does not love her. He refrains because he *does* love her, but he cannot afford to support her. Read more carefully."

"Thank you for extra reading and careful research," she wrote on another uninspired but thorough paper about Edith Wharton. On a third: "Sloppy, sloppy work! Do us both a favor. I will allow you to drop this course." The drop-add period was over, but she had the power to make exceptions, and this paper clearly called for one. There was no chance that this student would ever perform up to par.

She picked up the next paper with anticipation. Dana Marshall's work was always a joy. This paper was no exception. She understood and cited nearly all the connections between Jews and black Americans in Hurston's *Moses, Man of the Mountain* as well as— boldly and brilliantly—the connections between Moses and Jesus. "A plus. Superb!" she wrote on the back, with flamboyant underlinings. Then she added, "P.S. We're not sure who the parents of *Jesus* were, either." Always ask for more, was her motto. Always push them toward perfection. That was what her parents and teachers had done to Beth, and it had worked.

Beth's stomach growled its dissatisfaction. The apples and cheese were not satisfying her hunger. Beth rose, poured herself a cup of coffee from the pot that had been plugged in all day, added cream, sugar, and an inch of amaretto to the ink in her cup, and dug out a raspberry-filled chocolate bar from the freezer. Her eating habits were terrible, but who had time to cook?

The phone rang. This late, it had to be Lloyd. "'Lo," she said, with a large chunk of candy in her mouth.

"How's my sweet stuff?" His rich, mellow baritone made something turn over inside her.

"Warm and mellow," she answered.

"Keep it warm for me," he said. "Better yet, heat it up till it melts."

"Lloyd, you know I can't see you tonight, it's late and I'm exhausted and maybe catching a cold and—"

He gave a deep, wicked chuckle, and the imp down inside her did flip-flops. "Just talking trash, baby. Just messing with you. I can't come over; I'm working till six tomorrow morning."

"Awww," she complained. Lloyd's segment at the radio station was usually 10 P.M. till 2 A.M. "How come?"

He chuckled again. "I thought you just said you didn't want to be bothered with me tonight. Larry asked me to take over for him. His wife's at the hospital having Baby Number Four. Got your radio on?"

She reached over to her bedside radio and turned it on so she wouldn't be lying. "You know it," she told him.

"Good. The next one's for you."

It was Teddy Pendergrass crooning, "Close the Door."

Damn Lloyd. Damn him.

"Close the door / Let me give you what you've been waiting for," Teddy sang. Dammit. Now she was hot. Her hand moved under the covers while she thought of Lloyd; and then of Frank, who had

screwed her in his living room while his wife slept in their bedroom; and then of that sinister white boy, Jeff, who had done things
to her no one did to nice girls. *White or black,* she thought, *a man
is a man. They have different personalities, different cultures, but
the same physiology, the same urges. People are just people, men
are men, and I sure wish I had one here with me tonight.*

Chapter Three

It was a gray, rainy morning, so Beth dressed in her brightest fuchsia suit—and then wasted twenty minutes looking for the matching hair bow that was attached to a comb. Finally she found it in the wrong drawer, under some old bras and stockings. Her hair was showing its colors, too. Dampness always made it frizz up and rise, but she didn't want to straighten it. Hair that was straightened once in a while soon came to need it on a regular basis. She slicked hers down with some mousse, muttered "Behave yourself," pulled a rain hat down over it, flung on her gold lamé raincoat, and took off.

After buying a cup of coffee from a street vendor, she rushed into her building. She was late for her office hour again. Other people, she had discovered, did not take their office hours very seriously, but she was not other people, she was Beth—a woman who was careless about many things, but terribly conscientious about her job.

At least she had no definite appointments this morning. She dug her mail out of her box, stuffed it into her briefcase, and replied

"Fine" automatically to three or four colleagues who asked routinely, "How are you?" and whose faces she had yet to attach to names. She asked Eloise, the junior secretary, about the quizzes she had put in the copying box for today's class.

"They'll be in your box by noon," Eloise promised. She was a shapely, dark-skinned Venus who needed someone to tell her not to wear low-cut necklines to work, or bright red lipstick ever. Considering her own flamboyance, Beth felt she was not the right person for the job.

"Dana Marshall was looking for you. I told her to go up and wait," Eloise said.

"Thanks," Beth said, and went clacking on her three-inch heels to the stairs, since the elevator was slow. *At least,* she thought, *I know the secretaries' names and something about them.* Eloise, the lowest on the totem pole, drank and partied all weekend and usually came in on Mondays with bags under her eyes. She had been known to get into barroom brawls with her boyfriend, sometimes fighting with him, sometimes against him.

Margaret, the senior secretary, who looked white but was not, was plump, calm, and settled. She lived with a man whose two children she was helping to raise.

Laverne, the chairman's secretary, was brown as an oak, skinny as a stick, and married, with a ten-year-old daughter who looked as if she had been cloned from her mother. The child, who was frighteningly perfect and poised, already knew she was headed for this university.

At least Beth knew the department chairman by sight. He was a short, balding white man who wore rumpled gray suits and rimless glasses. All she knew about him was that he was from Texas, his name was Dr. Richard C. LaRosa, and his specialty was Victorian literature. Most of the other faculty all looked and sounded alike to her, and she did not know them, except for another Americanist named Charles O'Donnell, who had to be the sexiest man alive,

Irene Levinson, and the other black faculty. They included an unpleasant character with a fat, roll-circled neck named Joe Morgan, and Vincent Addison, a good-looking genius who had a joint appointment and wrote and taught poetry as well as a history course. Vincent also coached men's tennis.

"Our all-purpose nigger," Joe Morgan had called him snidely out of the side of his mouth. Joe had a joint appointment himself, in Folklore and in English. But he did not have tenure, and Vincent did. It probably bothered him that, like Beth, he was one of the part-timers on the faculty that Beth had seen described in one memo as "paraprofessional help." Joe was a short, fat worm who slithered from class to class, always with a grin stuck on his face. His motto was "I demand excellence!" So did Beth, but she was impartial about it. Her black students had confided that Joe was harder on them than he was on the white kids. He was so sneaky she thought he might sneak up on himself someday and stab himself in the back.

She was chuckling at the thought when a small shape detached itself from the wall outside her office. Beth stifled a scream.

"Sorry, Dr. Barnes," Dana Marshall said. "I didn't mean to scare you."

"My fault," Beth said to the girl. "I didn't see you. I keep forgetting to tell Maintenance to put in a new lightbulb up here. Sorry I'm late."

Her heart was still beating rapidly while she fumbled for her keys. *I should have these out before I come upstairs,* she thought. *It's dark in this hallway. Could be dangerous.*

When she had opened the door to her office and turned on the lights, everything seemed bright and safe again. Beth had furnished the small room with a yellow swivel chair, an orange side chair, a fake zebra rug, and a couple of bright William Johnson reproductions, one of street musicians and another of country people going to church in an oxcart. She had also brought in an electric heater and a coffeemaker, because the central heating was unreliable and the department coffee tasted horrible.

"Close the door and make yourself comfortable," she told Dana, indicating the chair beside her desk. She divested herself of her shiny gold raincoat and matching rain hat and hung them up. Then she opened her briefcase and rummaged inside it until she found Dana's paper. She was grateful that it was one of the group she had gone over last night. She hoped there would be time before class to read the rest of them.

"Dana, this is a wonderful paper," she said, handing it to the girl. "You really understand the connections Hurston makes between blacks and Jews. And you put it so poetically, and with so much humor. I really think you could be a writer."

This would be heady praise to most students. But Dana did not seem terribly interested. "Thank you," she said, and put the paper away without even glancing at the comments Beth had written.

Beth took a closer look at Dana. She had been crying. There were streaks on her pretty heart-shaped brown face.

"Dana," she asked, "what's wrong?"

"Can I ask you something, Dr. Barnes?"

"Certainly."

"Did you pledge a sorority?"

"No, I didn't. Why?" The Greek organizations had not been in vogue in the seventies. The revolutionary fervor of the recent past had made them unpopular. Now the fraternities and sororities were back in style, along with all of the other conservative rituals like proms and formal weddings. From what Beth had seen of the pledging process over the years—the all-night hazing sessions, the pledges falling asleep in class, the missed assignments, the fiendish cruelties inflicted on male pledges—she wished they were still out of favor. Last year a boy had died from overexposure during pledge week after being left out in the woods overnight. This year, two others had killed themselves at fraternity parties by drinking too much. One had died of alcohol poisoning, and the other had tried to fly out of a twelfth-story window.

"I was hoping it might help you understand. Last night, a horrible thing happened." The girl's voice was so low, Beth could barely hear her. *My God,* she wondered, *has Dana been raped?* Rapes and attempted rapes were fairly common on campus—so common that a female security officer had been appointed just to deal with them—though they usually occurred at the parties held by white fraternities. Beth leaned in close, expecting the worst, and tried to remember the security woman's name in case she had to look up her phone number.

"Tell me about it," she said. Parker, that was it. Capt. Ruth Parker. She reached for her copy of the campus directory to look up Capt. Ruth Parker's number and then drew back her hand. She was getting ahead of herself, and she needed to give Dana her full attention. Students often confided in Beth, and she had a special list of emergency contacts in the front of her directory: a gynecologist, an internist, and a counselor at Student Health, a loan officer at Financial Services, a social worker in the School of Social Work. Today she would add Ruth Parker's name and number to her list.

"Well, I'm a Gamma Pi Gamma, and we have a program every year to celebrate our Founder's Day. Last night, we were rehearsing for our program on the green outside Hopewell, practicing steps for our step show and rehearsing our song. It was late, but it was the only time the four of us could get together. We had to practice, because we only had two days to get our routine right. You understand."

Beth nodded, but she really didn't understand. To her, studying and exams were the main business of college. She thought the whole clubwoman thing was a waste of time, but if a woman were inclined that way, as her mother was, it could and should come later—after degrees were obtained, careers launched, marriages celebrated, and children raised. But she nodded again as if she were sympathetic.

"How late was it?" she prodded.

"It was eleven-thirty when we got started. Four of us—Rhonda, Cynthia, Harriet, and me. Too early for those rednecks in the dorm to say we were disturbing them. They were probably up cutting eye-holes in their sheets."

Dana's sense of humor was still plugged in. Good. Beth could not hold back a chuckle. To her delight, Dana smiled back. "So, they complained that you were disturbing them?"

"They did more than complain, Dr. Barnes. They insulted us and called us all the horrible names you can think of. They threw things at us, too. Food and bottles and trash. They even threw a balloon filled with urine. They told us we belonged at the zoo, not at *their* school. We ran inside to get their names—"

"You ran inside a boys' dorm?" Upperclass dorms were coed, unless students specified same-sex housing, but Hopewell was a freshman dorm, and freshmen were always segregated by sex.

"Yes. Harriet led the way."

Ah, yes. Harriet would, Beth thought. Harriet Tubman Taliaferro. Beth had taught her last year. She was bright, but when she got fired up (and she was fired up often) she was incapable of reason.

"She was so angry, she didn't care. She would have run in there if the building were on fire. Naturally the rest of us followed."

"Naturally," Beth echoed, though she would not have followed Harriet Taliaferro anywhere. The girl was crazy, she thought, always raging about racial injustice, seldom talking about anything else.

"We found those ignorant white boys, but none of them would admit to saying anything, except one freshman, a foreign guy who admitted calling us a word in German that meant 'water buffalo.' "

"Water buffalo?" *How odd,* Beth thought.

"Yes. He used a word that sounded something like *behemoth.* It means a big, ugly black beast, a cow, a monster, something like that. And when he said it, the others hollered 'Moo, moo!' Harriet got all up in his face, but the rest of us dragged her away before she could hit him."

"Was that all?"

"All?" Flames ignited in the girl's eyes. "I think that's quite a lot. Professor Barnes, if you had been there and heard what they said to us, I think you'd agree." She paused and then added, "While we were outside, someone threw a Coke bottle and hit me in the leg. I forgot about it, but it was hurting me this morning." She drew up her long skirt to reveal an ugly, livid gash.

"My God," said Beth. "I want you to go over to Student Health right now and get that attended to. Have them call Security so you can report this incident while you're over there. I'd prefer that you be seen by Dr. Henry Butler." Henry Butler, an internist who was a lecturer in the medical school, was one of her resources. He had his flaws, but professionally, he was a cool, competent brother. "I'll give you his phone number. Or would you like me to call him for you and get you an appointment?"

Dana nodded. "Please."

Already Beth was wishing she hadn't offered to make the call, but she knew it would get the girl immediate attention. "If I reach him, he'll probably want you to come right over. Can you?"

The girl nodded again.

"Is there anything else you would like me to do?"

"Dr. Barnes, the cops came, and we signed a complaint. We're charging those boys with harassment under the University's new policy."

Beth must have looked as blank as she felt, because Dana hastened to explain, "It's some old thing they just got up because too many people were insulting other people. Some of these white kids will say anything, you know. Kike this and nigger that, plus all the cuss words they can think of, because their parents let them get away with it at home. So the University wrote a rule against racial harassment into the charter of the student judicial system. We think we can hold them to it. We want you to be our faculty advisor."

Beth was silent.

"If it's not too much trouble, Dr. Barnes," Dana said apologetically. "See, the girls put me in charge of our case. We're not sure we can count on Dr. Morgan to stand with us, and with Dr. Addison leaving, you're practically the only faculty left that I know."

Vincent leaving? She hadn't heard about it. Nobody ever told Beth anything.

"All you have to do is advise us on what to say and stand up with us at our hearing."

"How did you hear about Dr. Addison?"

"It's in *Letters* this week. He's going south, to Duke, I think."

How many times had Irene Levinson urged her to read the faculty paper, *Letters?* How often did she actually read it? Hardly ever— it was so boring, and she was so busy. And how did this child get her hands on it?

"It's on-line now," Dana said as if she had read her mind. "Anybody can read it."

"Dana, I'm already your academic advisor."

"Yes, but that's—"

"Just a formality. I know." Students like Dana seldom had any academic problems, unless they got too ambitious and signed up for more courses than they could carry. It was Beth's role to prevent that.

"I hope so," Beth said. While she talked, she had been dialing. First she got the receptionist at the University Medical Center; then Henry Butler picked up. He was a weird guy: polite in person, but dirty-mouthed on the phone. "Ah, the beautiful Dr. Barnes," he said. "How delightful. What can I do for you today? Could you use ten inches?"

"Henry, please be serious. I have a young lady here who's been injured. I want you to take care of her."

"For you, I'll do anything. Send her over right away. Then take your drawers off and wait for me."

"There might be legal implications. Be discreet, will you?"

"I am always very respectful and discreet with our children," Henry said. "You, on the other hand, are not a child. You are a fine, sexy woman, and I have exactly what you need. When are you going to let me give it to you?"

She ignored his nonsense. She believed that all Henry wanted was to talk obscenely on the phone; if she ever took him up on one of his lascivious invitations, he would probably run away from her as fast as possible. One way to stop his foolishness was to put a screen of formality between them.

"You'll see her right away, then, Dr. Butler? Thank you. Her name is Dana Marshall." She hung up.

Dana stood and hoisted her heavy backpack to her frail shoulder. She limped to the door, the backpack making her appear even more lopsided. She was so small, she seemed still a child—a wounded one. She reminded Beth of Neet, her little sister, at about seven years old, on the day she had been knocked down while skating. Her leg would not support her, so Beth half carried her sister home, where she vowed to beat up the large boy who had pushed her.

"I'm gonna kick his ass," she had declared through her tears. "I'm gonna kick that ole Roy Harrison's ass. Wait and see." The blood flowing from Neet's knee had been copious, but the wound had been minimal, and the next week she made good on her promise. She had flown at the Harrison boy like a seventy-pound missile of concentrated fury and left him weeping and bleeding.

Beth sighed. *I'm going to regret this,* she thought. "And Dana?"

"Yes, Professor Barnes?"

"You can tell the other girls that I'm on their team."

A triangular, kittenish smile lit Dana's face.

When the girl was gone, Beth sighed again. Her tendency to re-gard her students as her children, and to define her relationship to them as the old-fashioned in loco parentis, sometimes made her overresponsible. But she couldn't find any other way to relate to them that was comfortable. If she hadn't believed that Henry meant it when he said that he observed the same restraint, she would never have sent Dana or any other female student to him.

Some faculty had less healthy ways of being involved with their students, she knew. Some academics and administrators abused their positions and got intimate with these children, even though they could lose their jobs if caught. Beth didn't under-stand how they could violate their trust or how they could even be attracted to such young adults, though she knew college stu-dents were all horny as toads, reeking of hormones, and actively screwing each other.

Well, now she had extra work. First she would have to bone up on this new speech code that she hadn't even heard about. She took a nasty sip of her cold coffee, leaned back, and opened her copy of this week's *Men and Women of Letters*. Yes, Vincent was leaving, according to an article on the back page. *Why not on the front?* He had accepted a full professorship at Duke University. She would miss him, but she couldn't blame him. This backward place had never given him more than an assistant professorship in either department. She studied his handsome face in the photograph that was blurred by a cheap print job and permitted herself a few brief minutes of daydreaming, remembering his animation as he recounted his experiences, picturing his fine, expressive hands. Yes, she would miss him, and she would probably regret not flirting with him, though it was hard to penetrate all that dignity and reserve and get to know the man. It was silly to be so rigorously faithful when she was not even married to Lloyd, but so far, her infidelities existed only in fantasy. She suspected that was the case with Vincent, too, and with most of her other colleagues.

Remembering her present purpose, Bethesda filed her daydream for later. A note in this week's *Letters* on the new harassment policy referred her back to an issue of three weeks ago. She searched for it in the jumble of papers on her desk, then gave up, and found it online. Thank God for the Web. It was a boon to disorganized people like Beth.

Like everything in *Letters*, the racial harassment policy was long-winded and boring. It was also contradictory. Its preamble stated in paragraph two that "the University must be ready to protect the expression of ideas, opinions, information, and knowledge that may, be deemed objectionable to some members of the University community."

Exactly.

Only last week, she had hesitated to discuss the theory Hurston had advanced so subtly in *Moses, Man of the Mountain*—an almost throwaway hint at the end of the book that Jesus was a reincarnation of Moses—lest it offend the Christians in the class. Then she had said to herself, "Hell, this is a university, not a seminary. Let it rip." Protected by academic freedom, she had proceeded with her lecture as planned.

Then, in the third paragraph of the preamble, the policy statement said, "Words that are intended only to inflict pain and suffering are no more legitimate in our community than physical actions intended to inflict bodily harm . . . abusive utterances . . . should not be tolerated any more than violence itself."

She thought it contradicted the previous paragraph, and read it again. The qualifier *only* saved the document from contradicting itself in adjacent paragraphs, Beth decided. She also thought, *This is smoke that suggests a fire*. She really had no idea of what was going on on campus, because she was always so focused on her job, but she figured that some of the beer-swilling frat boys must have been expressing themselves too vividly.

The next paragraph came down hard: "No member of the University may engage in racial harassment, regardless of time or place. Racial harassment is a violation of University policy and may be the basis for disciplinary action."

Pretty strong, she thought, except for that shifty *may* in the last sentence. She scanned the rest of the document, then printed it and stuffed it in her briefcase to study later. If it was as hard on sexual harassment as it was on racial slurs, she could haul Henry up on charges, she thought. Not that she would; he was just a harmless verbal erotic, and his presence on campus was essential. But phone sex was creepy, and sometimes she didn't feel like playing Girl Six for him.

Chapter Four

Beth's four brightest female students crowded into her office as soon as she opened the door. Two of them, Dana and Rhonda, were English majors; the other two were prelaw students who were taking her course as an elective. Dana, Rhonda, Cynthia, and Harriet reminded her of the long-ago Foxy Four. Except that she wondered, looking at them, if she and her classmates could ever have been that young.

Or that dumb.

Supporting them would be a tough assignment, because she was not fully sympathetic to their cause. She didn't even like all of them. Harriet was a wild-eyed radical, and she thought Rhonda was pretentious, with her designer clothes and the fancy elocution she had learned in some suburban drama class. Cynthia Forrest was a spoiled, privileged brat who was always angling for an advantage. Last year she had actually asked Beth for a letter of recommendation before she had even taken any of her courses.

Besides, what were they doing out in the courtyard late at night, stomping their feet, clapping their hands, and belting out songs when they were supposed to be in the library preparing to be tomorrow's leaders, getting ready to challenge the masters of their universe? Their parents were not sacrificing to pay for this sort of incident.

"Are your parents upset with you?" she asked.

"Ye-es," Cynthia Forrest said, drawing out the single syllable into a long sigh. "My father said, and I quote, 'We ain't laying out all that money for you to be a fool.' " She was the smallest of the foursome, about ninety-five pounds soaking wet, and the cutest, with baby fat, dimples, and the soft, indulged air of a daddy's darling. Beth would not have been surprised to see her carrying a teddy bear. Cynthia was fastidious about her appearance. She wore sweats today, but they were pink, and styled with a zipper and a tiny monogram on the pocket. Her nails were a matching shell pink.

"My mother said the same thing," Rhonda reported. She waved the fringes that dangled from the cuffs of her long, flowing black tunic. "What she said, basically, was, 'Stop bothering those white folks and get back into your books. You're there to learn, not to stir up trouble.' "

Privately, Beth agreed.

More than a week had passed since the incident. Dana was healing, but she still had a serious limp. In consideration of her injury, Beth motioned Dana into her only extra chair.

"I've started a file for you," she told the group. "All this opposition must be terribly discouraging. Have you considered giving up your plan to press charges?" She rather hoped they had. She felt she might be joining them on a suicide mission.

In unison, they answered, "No."

"It's too late to give up, anyway," Rhonda said. "The campus police came. We told them what had happened and signed a complaint. That means we've already charged those boys."

"We have to fight back. You can't imagine their insults, Dr. Barnes," Dana said.

"Oh, I think I can. I've been insulted once or twice. What did they call you?"

"It's too embarrassing to repeat," said Cynthia.

Rhonda took a deep breath and pulled herself erect, bracing herself. "They called us black nigger bitches." As she said it, Rhonda seemed to grow taller.

"Ugly black monkeys," Harriet chimed in.

"Fat-ass cows and worse," Dana said.

"Worse? You mean there's something worse?" Beth exclaimed.

"How about two-bit, dirty black whores?" Rhonda queried. She pronounced the words with great care, as if her perfect diction could distance her from them. She gave the vile word two syllables, and her *wh* was beautifully enunciated, like Jessye Norman attacking the first phrase of "Un bel di" from *Madam Butterfly.*

"I would certainly object to the two-bit part," Beth said. "I know I'm worth more than that." Her remark brought the release of laughter to the tension in the room.

" 'Black water buffalo' is bad enough," Dana said, and held out a picture of a fat, slimy, horned beast with the caption, "An African water buffalo wallows in the mud." "I got this out of my on-line encyclopedia. Professor Barnes, water buffalo are black animals that live in Africa."

"And after he called us that, the others yelled 'Moo, moo' at us," Cynthia added.

"Ugh," Beth said, and handed the disgusting photo back. "I wouldn't mention the 'moo, moo.' That sounds too much like boys-will-be-boys stuff."

"Boys will be boys? Are you serious?" Rhonda asked indignantly. "They were insulting us! They told us to go to the zoo!"

"I mean, that's how others might see it," Beth said hastily. "Otherwise, it sounds to me like you've got a strong case. Did you have any witnesses?"

"No, Professor Barnes, that's the problem," Harriet said. "And none of those skinheads would admit to saying anything except the foreign boy."

"And *he* only admits to calling us 'water buffalo' and saying we belonged at the zoo. Which is bad enough, when you think about it," said Dana.

"Yes, it is," Beth agreed. Even before that vile book of pseudo-anthropology, *The Negro a Beast,* white Americans had compared blacks to animals and used that as a justification for slavery and then second-class citizenship. She jotted some notes on a pad and then looked at the petite girl seated across from her. "Dana, how's your leg?"

"It's stopped hurting, but it's infected. Dr. Butler put me on anti-biotics. He says I'll be scarred for life."

"I'm sorry. I suppose none of the boys would admit to throwing things."

"No, of course not," Dana replied.

"Did anybody think to take a picture of the trash they threw?"

All four shook their heads.

"You seem to have a strong case, anyway," Beth said, "but of course, I'm no expert. Have you seen a lawyer yet?"

"We have to wait for them to appoint a prosecutor for us," Dana said. "But my uncle's a lawyer, and he said that unless someone saw who threw that bottle, we can't prove anything."

"Tough luck," Beth said. "Will you be seeing Dr. Butler again?"

"Tomorrow," Dana said. "Meanwhile, I'm supposed to stay off this leg and keep it propped up. But that's not always possible."

Beth promptly overturned her wastebasket, letting the trash roll out, and shoved it toward the girl so she could put her foot up on it. "Yes, it is," she said. "You have to look for ways. This is one I used when I had a broken ankle."

While she was on crutches, Beth had also moved her classes to the black residence, Evers House, because all of its classrooms were on the ground floor. Not long ago, a petition had been circulated around the faculty to close Evers House, couched in the sort of persuasive, silky language that must have been used by the snake in Eden. It had almost convinced Beth to sign. It had said, as she remembered, that segregation was not something that belonged at a democratic institution like the University, and that diverse associations were an important part of higher education.

"Then let them integrate their fraternity houses," Sherri had said when she called her to discuss the issue. "Let them open their precious Greek doors to us. And their boardrooms, and their country clubs." Sherri was Beth's touchstone on political issues. She had a way of cutting as precisely as a razor to the heart of things.

Beth remembered something. She wanted to be sure she had heard it right. She looked at Harriet. "Did I hear you call those boys skinheads?"

"That's what I said," the girl replied.

"Real skinheads, or is that just a generic term you use for bigots and people with bad manners?"

"Their heads were shaved," Harriet said calmly. "They had a swastika on the wall in their room."

This was getting serious. Beth didn't know much about skinheads, but she had heard and read enough to know they were scary. "Skinheads can be dangerous," she said slowly.

"There are a lot of them on this campus," Rhonda said. "They want to start a race war. They've got some crazy notion that minorities stand between them and everything they want."

"They want an excuse to destroy all blacks. Period," said Harriet, twisting her upper lip in scorn. "Not some miscellaneous people called minorities, whoever they are. *Us.*"

"Jews, too," Rhonda observed.

"They only act out what the rest of the white people want," Harriet said. "Which is, to get rid of us. We are at war with these goddamn mean-ass white people, and anybody who doesn't know that is in pitiful shape." When Harriet said things like this, her eyes stared defiantly, her chin jutted forward, and her mouth became twisted. *Her ugly thoughts make her ugly,* Beth mused.

"Harriet," she began, "I really don't think it's quite that bad."

"It is that bad, Dr. Barnes. It is! The goal of most white folks is the total extermination of black folks. The skinheads are just the ones who make the most noise about it—that's all." She stared defiantly around the room at her peers. "While the rest of you are listenin' to that stupid rap mess and wavin' your hands in the air, I'm checkin' out the Internet. And I'm tellin' you, these people ain't playin'. They want an all-white country. They plannin' to kill us all so they can have it!"

"She trippin' again," Cynthia observed.

"Yeah. Let's go, yawl," said Rhonda.

"You just don't want to believe me. Pitiful, that's what you are. Sleepwalkers who won't wake up. Ostriches sticking their heads in the sand. Well, you don't have to believe me. Just check out the sites on the Web. White Pride World Wide. The Church of the Creator. Stormfront. The Aryan Nations. Find out for yourselves."

"Boy, she *really* trippin' today," Dana observed.

"Yeah. Why can't you chill, girl?" Rhonda added. "Professor Barnes gonna think we're a bunch of total snap cases." One of the things Beth loved about her black students was their fluent use of slang as well as King's English; another was that the well-raised ones consistently promoted her to Professor. Bestowing titles on one another was a way, her father had explained to her once, of achieving the respect they were denied elsewhere. He had taught her to call everyone ten or more years older than she Mr., Mrs., or Miss and to elevate all pharmacists to Doctor, all reverends to Bishop, and all teachers to Professor.

"Harriet's views are perhaps more alarmist than they should be," she said cautiously. "Nevertheless, I want all of you to be very careful. Stay alert. Don't go out alone at night if you can help it, and avoid lonely places. Skinheads are violent, lawless people."

"They want to exterminate us," Harriet said calmly with that self-satisfied, ugly twist in her lips. "In case they can't, the government is getting the jails and concentration camps ready."

Was the child crazy? Beth wondered as Rhonda and Cynthia edged toward the door.

"Harriet," Dana said calmly, "give it a rest, will you?"

"They have guns, fool," Harriet stated. "We have to get guns, too."

"And what exactly is that going to accomplish?" Cynthia asked.

"It'll show that we aren't afraid to stand up to them."

"We're outnumbered. We'd be annihilated," Rhonda pointed out.

"Maybe, but we'd take some of them with us." Harriet's stare was so bright and intense, Beth had to look away. She was reminded of a wolf she had seen once, an animal whose fierce gaze said, "Keep your distance."

"If you girls plan to arm yourselves or take any kind of violent or direct action, I hope you'll come and discuss it with me first."

Rhonda snorted. "We ain't listenin' to that crazy fool Harriet, Professor. She be all the time trippin'." This from a girl who wrote such elegant English sentences they had sometimes brought tears to Beth's eyes. Rhonda was tall, cool, and an elegant dresser in a style a bit too sophisticated for a college student. She liked to wear long, flowing tunics and jersey turbans. Today she was sporting a copper cuff bracelet and matching polish on her long nails.

"Yeah, but we love her," said Dana. "Don't we, sorors?" After a struggle, she managed to get to her feet and limp out behind the first two. She wore denim-colored leggings today, and a thick nasty-green sweater. Dana usually looked as if she had grabbed whatever she had that was clean and thrown it on. So did Harriet, whose choices in clothes were so awful, it sometimes seemed she deliberately tried to make herself unattractive. They all seemed terribly young with their thin bird legs and barely developed bodies.

Harriet, who lingered, looked like a refugee from the nineteenth century in her granny glasses and her long, shapeless gray flannel skirt and sweater. She took the chair Dana had just vacated and wrapped her skinny calves in their itchy-looking blue stockings around one of its legs. All through the discussion, even during her ranting, Beth had noticed the girl staring at her.

If she pulls out a gun, I'll scream, Beth thought nervously. *But who will hear me? I should have asked the others to leave the door open.*

"Professor, can I ask you something?" Harriet asked abruptly.

"Yes, Harriet, what is it?" Beth asked nervously. She wanted to say, "No, unless it's important, and if it is, make it quick. I don't have all day." But the girl's eyes burned with a need so great she could not deny it.

"I like the way you dress, Professor. I think you look cool."

With her face relaxed now, the child was not so ugly. Her pert nose and bow-shaped mouth were almost cute. A little tweezing of her heavy eyebrows and some curls to soften her high forehead could work wonders.

"Would you mind telling me where you buy your clothes?"

Chapter Five

That evening Beth became aware of them for the first time. They were a small, quiet presence on campus, but a visible one: boys with shaved heads and cold eyes, always in groups of two or more, who seemed to march instead of walking. They wore khaki shirts, camouflage pants, and high boots, and they did not smile. Maybe their army-surplus look had made her overlook them. Military surplus clothing was frequently worn by college students, and it was not necessarily a fashion statement or one about politics, but often a reflection of their poverty.

Perhaps, also, she had previously mistaken this crew for punks, though the punk kids had hair, usually bleached or dyed, and this bunch did not. Punks also displayed a lot of facial hardware and were said to crave suffering. These Nazis wore only Iron Crosses for jewelry and looked as if they would enjoy beating up people. Someone ought to introduce the two groups, she thought, but she did not smile at her idea.

She did, however, smile about her exchange with Harriet Talia-ferro. Harriet the Harried, Harriet the Harassed, Harriet the Harridan was a human female, after all. She wanted to wage revolution, or at least arm herself for self-defense, but she wanted to look pretty while doing it. Beth, who liked to invent song parodies, added a line to the old black nationalist rallying cry, and sang it as she threaded her way through traffic: "The revolution has co-ome / Time to pick up the gu-un / And some stockings that will not ru-un."

Harriet had confided that she had grown up without a woman's guidance. Her mother had died when the girl was thirteen, and she had been raised by a widowed father and a militant older brother, both grimly serious souls who thought feminine vanity was frivolous. Beth should have guessed.

She had told the girl that she would take her to her favorite store. If there was time, she would also introduce Harriet to her hairdresser. Beth was friendlier to her students than most professors were, but they filled the void left by a bunch of distant colleagues, and this girl had reached out to her. They had agreed on a shopping trip the coming Saturday. Some new clothes and a bit of makeup might brighten Harriet's grim outlook, especially if someone also combed and styled her matted hair.

Tonight, traffic was thinner than usual, and she tooled along in her Mustang with an exuberance that matched her vanity license plate, PROF DIVA. She continued to smile over the converstion with Harriet as she climbed the thirteen steps to her second-floor apartment, glancing at her neighbor Herbie's familiar cartoons that decorated the stairway walls with likenesses of local characters. Herbie, who earned his living cartooning for several small weeklies, had done Beth flatteringly with a big mouth, a purple suit, and big hair, and had hung her at the tenth step—his favorite, he said, since he'd joined Narcotics Anonymous. She had no idea what he was talking about, but she was pleased.

Her good mood lasted through her evening meal—a solitary bowl of lentil soup with half a buttered baguette, topped off with chocolate pudding eaten in front of the television with the evening news for company. She even hummed happily after dinner as she laid out the night's paperwork—Doctorow's novel about the Rosenbergs, and the pile of papers she should have finished reading last night.

The evening would have gone better if she had not gotten curious when she turned on her computer and decided to give in to the usual thief of her time—her wish for distraction. Instead of bringing up her course notes, she went on-line searching for the sites Harriet had mentioned.

In less than an hour, she was sick.

The White Pride site offered a selection of frankly labeled "Racist Cartoons," including one in which a section of a black man's brain showed 50 percent of it devoted to "Craving for Watermelon," 40 percent allocated to cravings for "Liquor, Drugs, Gold Chains, Drumbeats, Criminal Activity, and Pussy," and the miniscule remainder to "Intelligence, Creativity, and Responsibility." In another cartoon, Michael Jordan, on whom she had nurtured a secret crush for years, was shown in an apelike posture with his wrists touching the floor.

The site also offered false statistics on black crime and a phony survey in which black men, in crudely rendered dialect, confessed to their lust for white women. There were links to other sites with similar preoccupations. Fascinated as a woman staring at a poisonous snake, Beth clicked one of them. Then another.

The worst site she found gloated over the murders of Martin Luther King and Malcolm X, and promised unspecified rewards to the slayers of such "enemies of the white race" as Jesse Jackson, Al Sharpton, O. J. Simpson, and Sidney Poitier.

Sidney Poitier? When had that nice, purring old tomcat ever done anything to upset white people?

Ah, but he had a white wife, the site explained with twisted logic. He, Montel Williams, and Harry Belafonte should be made examples of, lest other "insolent black bucks" try to imitate them.

As for poor old O. J., it seemed white people would never get tired of beating up on him, even though his arthritic joints made it impossible to believe that he had killed two healthy young people simultaneously. How had he managed it? Beth always argued when confronted with righteous folks who knew better than the jury. Had he asked one of them to wait while he finished killing the other?

The site offered scanners with which to eavesdrop on the enemies of white people and track their movements, instructions for building and stocking shelters in which to survive the coming race war, and gas masks to neutralize the "horrible stench" of black perspiration. It also had links to other sites offering guns for sale and instructions for making bombs.

Another site informed her that blacks possessed inherent mental deficiencies and suffered from a natural indolence, which must account, Beth thought, for their popularity as slaves.

"He lives!" another site proclaimed in flaming banners of Adolf Hitler, with all the fervor of Christians proclaiming signs of the Second Coming. As a matter of fact, these folks declared themselves to be Christians and direct descendants of Adam, while nonwhites were "mud people," wallowing beasts at water holes. The appelation "water buffalo" took on a more pointed racist meaning after that.

Except for a couple of dating episodes, Beth had not associated much with whites, but they had been kind to her on her educational and career climb. Her white mentors and benefactors might have encouraged her because they found her exceptional. Perhaps they thought of her as a special black, but decent white folks were the only kind she had known.

Who, then, were the people who thought like these Nazis? Where were they? Were they hiding behind the friendly smiles of those who seemed to be fair, even liberal? Or were white liberals tolerant of extremists because at least they, too, were white? Beth did not know, and she did not know whom to ask. If Harriet stared at those hate sites all the time, no wonder she was paranoid.

She hadn't noticed the skinheads on campus until today, but

there was a boy in her Political Fiction class with a shaved head who wore olive drab army shirts and high-topped Timberland boots. She did not know him; he was one of those students who never talked in class. Was his clothing an innocent fashion statement, or was it an expression of something more sinister? She would ask him questions and try to draw him out.

One thing was certain—Beth could not, now, read any of the term papers that were stacked on her desk. In a day or two her normally balanced sense of reality would return, her habitual optimism might even resurface, but tonight her mind was incapable of calm, critical judgment. Scorched by all that hatred, she craved escape.

She tried turning on the TV for relaxation, but there was nothing on it of interest except those black sitcoms populated by incredibly loud and vivacious people. After a few minutes of their outsize gestures and loud, hyper talk, she felt as if she had wandered into a carnival sideshow and were being entertained by extreme geeks. She had never seen people like this, and hoped never to do so. Who, she wondered, did want to see them? Because someone certainly did.

Even the actors, she imagined, must find their roles obnoxious. After a raucous taping ("Girrl! Child! Whassup!") that was punctuated by canned laughter, they would probably relax with conversations about summers in Italy, graduate school at Columbia, or their offspring, who would be the only ones referred to as "child." Imagining the low-key, urbane speech the performers might use among themselves, she giggled. Then she felt a twinge of fear. There were people out there who hated her.

Beth had never been uncomfortably conscious of being alone in her apartment until this minute. Usually she luxuriated in her solitude and the freedom it offered: she could scratch her most intimate itches, walk around in her underwear, eat a whole pint of ice cream by herself if she craved it. But tonight she was aware of every creak in the wood, every sigh in the pipes, every sound that might

be an intruder but was probably just another adjustment in the settling of the old house on its foundation.

When the phone rang, she jumped. She hoped it was Lloyd,
though it was early for his call. She hoped he was coming over,
though he was due at the station.

But it was only her sister, Bonita, calling from her home in New
Jersey.

"I'm fine," Neet replied to her sister's usual queries. It was hard
to tell whether she was really okay or not. Neet had one of those
voices that sounded as if she were sobbing even if she had a smile
on her face. "So is Della. Her Girl Scouts went on a bus trip to D.C.
today. I wouldn't have let her take off from school to go, but she's
on the honor roll. Delores is—well, Delores. You know."

Beth knew. Their mother, as she aged, became more of what
she'd always been—rigid, demanding, hysterical when frustrated.
And social—intensely social, putting the agenda of her women's
club, the Links, ahead of everything and everyone else in her life.

"She's copped an attitude because I won't put Della in Jack and
Jill," Neet said.

"Good for you," said Beth. She hated the idea of elite social clubs,
especially for children.

"She wants her to meet 'our kind of people.' Now, I ask you, who
are they?"

"Damn if I know," Beth said, though she did know. The black upper middle class started to control the activities, friendships and futures of its young very early. Delores wanted her grandchild to
know, and someday date, the children of other Links, who were
mostly teachers, and their husbands, who were doctors, lawyers,
and successful businessmen. For the most part, there was nothing
wrong with these people, but Della, she felt, was far too fine to
have her horizons limited to them. Perhaps in her parents' day such
social restrictions were necessary, but today things were different,
and a child with Della's brains and potential should be open to all

the world's rainbow of possibilities. She was the light of Beth's life—and of course of Neet's; she was, so far, their only future. Beth wanted that future to be unlimited.

"Don't let Delores put our baby in a box, Neet." It was their mother who had encouraged them to call both parents by their first names, saying that *Mom* was low-class, and *Mother* made her feel old. As with most issues concerning his daughters, their father Curtis seemed to have no opinion about what they called their parents.

"You know I won't."

"You haven't said anything about Curtis." Nor, she did not add, had Bonita mentioned her husband, James. The couple had been separated many times and just as often reunited. She would wait discreetly to learn whether their marriage was on or off this week.

"He's why I called. Now, I don't want you to panic, Beth—"

"What is it?" Beth asked, too loud. She was holding the phone with a grip so tight her hand hurt. "I don't panic easily," she lied, forcing her voice to be lower and calmer.

"Yes, you do. You turn every spark into a five-alarm fire. Curtis is in the hospital. Now, before you start shrieking at me, let me explain. He had a tiny stroke."

"Oh, my God," Beth said. She felt her heart begin to pound so hard it shook her chest. She had just been thinking yesterday that she had not spent enough time with her father; that she had never really gotten to know him.

"I said, a *tiny* stroke. He's fine. There are no detectable effects. They just want to keep him a couple of days to check on him and run some tests. I don't think you should bother to come until the weekend."

"I'll be there tonight," Beth said.

"Don't you have classes tomorrow?" Neet inquired.

"I'll cancel them."

"I wouldn't do that, Beth. . . . Look, if something really serious happens, I mean, if Curtis or anybody ever gets really sick, you'll need to cancel your classes then. You should save that option for when you need it. Right now, Curtis is doing fine. He doesn't need you."

"Sure?"

"Sure. He even recited two new verses of 'The Pool-Shooting Monkey' for me tonight."

"Two whole verses?" "The Pool-Shooting Monkey" and its progenitor, "The Signifying Monkey," were predecessors of rap—long, funny rhymed narratives recited by men of their grandfather's day in pool halls and bars, and preserved by men like their father. The verses had also been preserved by one clever white folklorist who recognized them for what they were, great folk epics, and as a result was now head of his department at the University. In spite of his wife's disapproval, and to the delight of his daughters, Curtis Barnes recited the poems frequently—omitting, however, some of the raunchier language.

"I kid you not," Neet said. "They went, 'The big-eyed bullfrog put his two cents in / Said, "Bet fifty dollar Mister Baboon win." / The monkey said "Dag. Who pulled your chain? / Why, you wasn't even invited to this game." ' "

"I bet he didn't say 'Dag.' "

"Yes, he did. Della was there. He promised to give me the uncensored version tomorrow."

"I'm jealous," Beth said. But, in the end, she let her sister talk her into teaching her scheduled classes tomorrow and Thursday, and postponing her visit to their father until Friday.

Chapter Six

S ometime during the night, Lloyd let himself in and slipped into bed beside Beth. It had to be after 2 A.M., because he worked at the station until then. She awakened to his lips and hands moving over her and his knee rudely parting her legs.

"No fair," she complained. "You're supposed to wake me up first." But she protested only weakly. After the terrors of the earlier evening, she was so glad of his company that she welcomed his pushing and probing with open arms, and returned his eager kisses with long needy ones of her own. His eagerness and his eternal youthfulness were the things that turned her on most about him. Even at forty-five, even after an eight-hour shift at the post office and a four-hour shift at the radio station, he had as much energy as a boy. One long coupling atop her did not satisfy him; he had to turn her over and enter her again from behind (though she was wet and slippery as a seal by now), all the while sucking on her neck and licking her ear and moaning "Oh, baby, baby" against her ear.

"Greedy boy," she said, rubbing his thick, ruglike hair as he nuzzled her breast.

"God, Beth, it's been so long since we've been together. Do you realize how long?"

"Yes," she said, and continued to stroke him. "Five whole days."

"It seems longer. Are you sure?"

"You took me to brunch on Sunday."

"Oh, yeah, Sunday we had brunch at the Jambalaya Jam. Rudy Morris played. But afterward, you had work to do—"

"So I came home."

"And left me by myself." He groaned. "God, how I missed you."

Sunday didn't count because we didn't have sex, he means, she realized. Men were so simple. So terribly, gloriously simple. "I missed you, too," she whispered. "I wished you were here earlier tonight."

"Baby, you know if I could've been, I would have."

"I was having scary thoughts."

"That's not like you."

"Lloyd, what do you know about skinheads?" she asked abruptly.

"Now *that's* a scary thought," he said, and pulled her to him. "Nasty people. Gun nuts. Wear Nazi symbols and shave their heads. Want to get rid of everybody who isn't white and Christian, and get rid of the government, too. I think they're mostly out West, though. That makes us safe. Why? Why are you concerned about skinheads?"

He raised himself up on one elbow and turned on the bedside light. Beside it, her little clock radio was tuned to his station, Jazz 89.1. Its large red digits informed her that it was 3:30 A.M.

"I heard we had some of them on campus, that's all. Turn out the light." She figured she must look like a witch at this point.

Instead of killing the light, he stared at her. "You're beautiful, you know that? You're amazing." He rolled over on his back, his strong brown arms behind his head revealing armpits stippled with balls of black hair. "Did you catch the segment I did tonight on New Orleans jazz? Jelly Roll Morton, Buddy Bolden, J. C. Higginbotham?

Louis Armstrong? God, Satch was fantastic. And to think people used to disrespect the guy, call him a Tom."

"Yes, I heard it," she lied. "It was wonderful. Now turn out the light. I don't know about you, but I need some more shut-eye."

"First, for me, a shower," he said, and leaped up as energetically as if he had not just gone through a twelve-hour day and night ending with some strenuous lovemaking. He came back with a towel for her and stood there, silhouetted, nude and glorious in the moonlight. Long legs, tight butt, no gut, a perfect male animal, hungry and howling, unconscious of anyone's needs but his own. "What you got around here to eat?"

"Bananas, I think. Some cheese and some French bread." She heard him slamming cabinet and refrigerator doors, banging drawers. She wished he did not have so much energy all the time. Living with him would be like living with a young, exuberant animal that was always active, always hungry, always needing exercise. Still, after her earlier anxieties, she enjoyed the security of his noisy male presence, and she fell asleep soothed by the sounds he made slamming around her house.

His arm flung heavily across her chest woke her in the morning. That, and the sunlight streaming across their faces. He slept peacefully. He was not so young-looking in the daytime, she noticed with a pang. There was gray in his mustache, and plenty of it in his hair, too, and there was a sagging in his cheeks that dug furrows from his nose to his mouth. She traced her finger along the tan line where his hat shaded his forehead. He was really quite fair-skinned where the sun had not touched him; a couple of shades lighter than Beth. And, though he was not exactly handsome, he was quite presentable. Damn presentable.

His eyes opened at her touch. "Morning, beautiful."

"Morning, handsome."

He rolled his eyes and looked over his shoulder. "Who you

speaking to? Ain't supposed to be no nigger in here but me. Damn. That clock right?"

She saw the clock, and gasped. "Oh, my God." It was after nine-thirty.

"Whoops. You get dressed. I'll make coffee."

He had until two o'clock to be at work, but her class was at eleven, and she had done none of the reading. Well, she would just have to wing it.

While she showered, she combed her brain for what she could remember of *The Book of Daniel*. Not much; not enough. Maybe she could stall; go over last week's reading first, see what they remembered of Sinclair Lewis's *It Can't Happen Here*. Yes. She hated short-changing her students like this, but it would be necessary. Other teachers did it all the time.

"You're asking for it in that outfit, ma'am," Lloyd said when she came out of the bathroom fragrant with Joy and dressed in a purple satin bra and matching bikini panties. "If you brought charges, any judge would rule it justifiable rape."

"Please, Lloyd, not now," she said, and pushed past him to her closet. She was already in daytime mode, moving briskly and purposefully, a quarter of her mind choosing clothes, the rest of her head full of her lecture. Then she remembered. "Oh, my God. Got to call home."

"What's up?"

She took the mug of coffee he handed her, the gift mug from Sherri with SEX GODDESS inscribed on it in gold. He knew just how to make it for her—cream, two Equals—another point in his favor. Were *they*, perhaps, two equals? Whether they were or not, did it matter? She sometimes wondered about both questions.

"They took my father to the hospital last night. A slight stroke, Neet said." She dialed first one number and then another while stepping into her pumps.

"And you're going to *work*?" His forehead was deeply furrowed, as if he were troubled about something. "Baby, I don't mean to get all up in your business, but if one of my parents had a stroke, I wouldn't be thinking about no job. I'd be outta here and heading home on the first thing smoking."

That's why you're a mail clerk, she thought, *while I am a college professor.* She was immediately ashamed of herself for thinking it.

There was no answer at either Neet's or her mother's; they must already have left for the hospital. She would try to reach them there from school. Shrugging into the gold blazer she wore with a black-and-white striped blouse and black silk pants, she turned her back so he could fasten the gold chain around her neck, and said, "Neet persuaded me to wait till tomorrow night to come home. She said Curtis was doing fine."

"I don't know, baby," he said, shaking his head. "Your priorities are wrong, seems to me. I think family should come before work. *Way* before. Suppose it was me in the hospital. Would you go to work like nothing had happened?"

"I'd be at your side every minute," she said, and kissed his smooth cheek. He had managed to shave and dress in less than ten minutes. He smelled of Polo. He was amazing. "I'll call you from home tonight. Sorry to ruin our weekend."

They had planned to drive up to the Poconos, order meals from room service, watch movies, and take long walks in the woods. Now all that would have to be postponed.

"We'll have other weekends," he said, and grabbed her keys. "I'll start your car for you. I'll be praying for Curtis. Call me." He clattered down her stairs.

By the time she got down to the street, her Mustang was warm and roaring, and Lloyd was nowhere in sight.

Chapter Seven

For years to come, Beth would have the nightmare. She was running down hospital corridors with white tiled floors and white walls, hampered by high heels, racing against time, trying to find her father's room. At each white door she entered, a nurse would say, "The patient has been moved to room twenty-six." Each nurse had the same blank face, like an egg, until she reached a room where the young nurse was Dana Marshall. Dana beckoned her inside. Beyond Dana, she saw that the room's beds were empty. Sometimes the patient was Lloyd instead of her father, sometimes it was her mother, sometimes an unknown person—but it was always the same dream.

It was almost like that when she got to Reviva Hospital forty minutes before visiting hours ended. There had been sleet all afternoon, and driving the short distance, which usually took her only an hour, took three this time. The area's drivers simply could not cope with precipitation, and traffic had moved with the speed of a glacier when it moved at all.

Three years ago, when Delores had her biopsy, this place had been called, simply, South Jersey Hospital. The more they changed the names of things, the worse they got, she thought as the woman behind the desk fumbled to find her father's room assignment. It was the waking start of Beth's nightmare. "Room eight thirty-three, Window," the woman finally said, and gave her a visitor pass. Beth punched the UP button only to have to let two elevators go by because they were already overcrowded. Then, at the eighth floor, they told her Curtis had been moved to the fifth.

And on the fifth, they told her he was down in Intensive Care.

Beth did not wait for another elevator. She ran, her heels holding her back, all the way down two flights of stairs. There, on the third floor, her mother and sister sat with their heads together, whispering, on a bench outside. Just the two of them, terribly alone. They had never looked so small to her before, or so helpless and vulnerable. Beth, rushing up to them, felt big and rude and intrusive. "Mom, Neet, what's going on? They sent me down here."

"Your father had a second stroke," Delores said distinctly. "It happened this morning, before we got here. There are aftereffects. Where have you been, Bethesda?"

"Mom, it's my fault. I told her she could wait because he was doing fine yesterday," Neet said.

Bethesda examined her sister's worried face. Frown lines and all, she still looked like the skinny kid Beth had called the Twerp, the kid who was all motion, forever tripping over her skates and losing the hair ribbons that bound her pigtails. She didn't look that much different nowadays, even when she was dressed in uniform and weighed down by all her hardware—cuffs, truncheon, pistol, and radio. Bonita was seven years her junior, and why she had taken her kid sister's advice on a situation this grave was beyond explaining, unless it had given her permission to do what she felt like doing anyway. Work. Avoid unpleasantness.

Not that work had been very pleasant that day. The quiet, mysterious young man in the army camouflage clothes had finally spoken up in class. "I think Sinclair Lewis was right, Professor," he had said. "It can happen here."

"Tell me why," she said, looking down at her class list for his name. Ralph Witmayer. "Explain why you think so, Ralph."

"A lot of Jews are in power since Clinton took office, and people resent that," he said. "The Secretary of State, the Secretary of Defense, the head of the Federal Reserve—that's a lot of power for such a tiny group of people."

"What have you got against Jews, Witmayer?" someone yelled.

"Please wait until I call on you," Beth had interposed, holding back the tidal wave of angry chaos that she sensed was threatening to take over her class.

"Nothing," the boy said mildly. "I personally have nothing against Jews. I just know that some people think they have power out of all proportion to their numbers in the population."

As she passed his desk, returning papers, Beth saw his white scalp through his close-cut hair. His sleeve was rolled up, and she also saw that a swastika was tattooed on his skinny wrist.

She tuned back in to Neet. "Everybody was surprised that this happened, Beth," her little sister was saying apologetically. "They're doing all they can for Daddy. One of the doctors said, sometimes a big stroke does follow a little one. They don't know why it happens."

"Idiots!" Beth exclaimed, not sure who she meant. "Why is he in this place, anyway? The place where I work, fifteen miles from here, has the best hospital in the area. Just because you live in Jersey, do you have to put my father in this butcher shop!"

"He wanted to come here," Neet said. "He always comes here. Besides, his insurance—," she added with a helpless gesture.

"You were not here, Bethesda," her mother said coldly. "If you had been here to help us with the decision, things might have happened differently. If we could count on your presence—and why, when you work just across the river, your father and I don't see more of you—"

"It wouldn't have made any difference, Mother," said Neet, squelching the argument. It was good that she did, because all three of them had been screaming, and nurses were looking their way. Typical unruly black females, they were probably thinking. Acting up in the quietest zone of the hospital.

"I want to see him," Beth said, and headed toward the door of the unit.

"Sure, Beth, but wait." Her sister pulled her back. "I want you to be prepared. Dad's not moving much, and he isn't talking."

A sliver of ice cut through Beth's chest. "Will he know me?"

"I don't know," Neet said. There was a long silence. Then she pointed to the nurses' station opposite. "You have to go over there first for permission."

Beth spoke to the nurse on duty and got permission to go into the intensive care unit.

Curtis's eyes were open when she reached his bed, but they did not move, and they did not seem to be seeing. Looking down at her father's twisted, immobile face, Beth began to cry. She had begun to mourn her father already—the man she had known long ago, who was vital, wise, full of knowledge and stories and fun. She mourned all the times they had not talked, all the walks they had not taken, all the games of checkers and gin rummy they had not played because she was busy or away.

Her father had been fun before he became old and grumpy and pessimistic. She blamed Delores for the change in him, without knowing how her mother had turned her lively father into a sour old man who sat in his chair grousing about the evening news. Once Curtis had taught her to swing dance; taught her other dances, too: The Stroll, the Camel Walk, the Funky Chicken. He had taught her songs and their history: "Hut Sut Rawson on the Rilli-raw," which he explained was a corruption of a song about a black longshoreman called Hot Shot Ralston on the Delaware; and "The Yellow Rose of Texas," which was, he said, really a love song about a mulatto woman. She felt sure that they would never dance together again or take nature walks again, picking up leaves in the park, identifying trees and birds and insects. Her father mumbled a few broken syllables. She bent her ear to his lips, but could not understand him. His hand tapped on the covers. She took it.

"Beth," she thought he said. Maybe they would sing together again, she thought with a leap of hope. Maybe he would tell her more stories and recite more verses of "The Signifying Monkey."

But then his eyes closed, and a dribble of spittle ran down his chin. She wiped it away with a tissue. His limp hand dropped away from hers. His eyes did not open again. Frightened, she looked at the monitor beside her father's bed that tracked his vital signs. The green blips of his heartbeat made a reassuring pattern. Her own heart, which had plummeted to her stomach, moved back into place and slowly resumed its normal rhythm. He was alive, if you could call it alive, she thought.

But what kind of life was this? What kind of life could he be expected to have?

"Do the Hucklebuck," she sang softly against his ear. "Do the Hucklebuck / If you don't know how to do it, man, you're out of luck." She could not be sure, but she thought her father smiled, a lopsided turning up of only one side of his mouth, lifting only the right side of his face. She would sing to him every time she came.

The nurse was signaling that her visiting time was over. Only fifteen minutes was allowed per visit in Intensive Care.

"Where's Dad's doctor?" she demanded when she rejoined her small family. "What's his name? I want some answers."

"Hi, Aunt Beth," said a voice like a church bell. "How's Grandpa?"

It was Della, her niece. Neet's child—the glorious fruit of her troublesome marriage. Della's tawny golden eyes were full of light; her whole face shone with it. Beth stooped to hug her. She did not have to stoop so far, now; Della was almost eight, and came up to her breastbone. It was where she belonged; the child was her heart.

"He's sleeping, baby," Beth said, and stepped back to look at her niece. Della still wore her school uniform, and her sandy, nappy hair was plaited in two thick pigtails. In spite of that, in spite of the freckles that bridged her nose over a peanut-butter complexion, she was an extraordinarily beautiful child, so beautiful that Beth was often scared for her.

Her father, who had brought her to the hospital, loomed over the girl like a giant bronze Buddha. He was tall, golden brown, and handsome, with a flat, impassive face. Beth had always found James Bowen inscrutable and hard to know. "Hello, James," she said, and extended her hand. He took it, but did not say anything.

"Aren't you going to speak to Aunt Beth, Daddy?" Della reproved him.

His child's criticism seemed to bring James alive. His somber expression melted into tenderness. "Of course I am, baby. How you doin', sis? They treatin' you all right at that university?"

"Oh, I'm doing all right. You know how it is. Neet, who is Daddy's doctor?"

"He has a bunch of them. I don't know which one is in charge," her sister said.

"Dr. Macpherson, I believe," said Delores. She was drinking water from a cup and fanning herself with a magazine. "He's a tall man with red hair."

Not a brother, then. Beth was ashamed that she felt relieved. But all the black doctors she had known seemed to be jive, more concerned with their frats and their investments than with their patients.

"Is Grandpa awake?" Della asked.

"No, baby. He's sleeping," Beth told her.

"Are you sure he didn't die?" she asked with the terrible direct-ness of children. Bethesda, who had been lied to a lot, had sworn never to lie to her niece or to any other child. She returned the girl's gaze steadily. "No, Della, he's alive."

"That's good," Della said, and sat down beside her grandmother.

"Let's go down to the cafeteria, Beth," Neet said abruptly. "You must be starving. Mother and James can stay here with Della."

Beth was not hungry, at least not consciously, until her sister mentioned food. Whenever someone mentioned food or offered it she always became hungry. She had gained three more pounds, she had noticed that morning. Her hunger was not urgent yet, but in the telepathic way the sisters had developed over the years, she knew that Neet was suddenly uncomfortable and restless. She had just dismissed James, who stood shifting from foot to foot as if not knowing where he belonged. The marriage was off, then.

"Okay," Beth said, and followed her sister to the elevator, though she was reluctant to leave her father alone back there.

"They'll come get us if anything changes," Neet reassured her. "Mother will go in and sit with him while we're gone. Della will probably hang out at the nurses' station. She's become their mascot."

The crowds had mysteriously thinned. They entered an empty elevator. As its doors closed, Bonita asked, "You and Lloyd still tight?"

"Tight as a size twelve dress would be on me."

"That's good. Don't marry him. It ruins things." And Neet let out a long hissing sigh like a deflating balloon. "I thought James was the greatest thing I ever laid eyes on till we got married. Then he changed. Running around being a playboy, chasing floozies, pre-tending to have a business but never having any money. He turned out to be a great, big, handsome, empty phony."

"The ones that handsome usually do," Beth observed. "At least he takes an interest in his daughter."

"You kidding? This is the first time he's seen her since August. He just agreed to pick her up from school because I told him we had a family emergency. Tell me this, Beth. If he cares so much about Della, why has he accepted a job in Chicago?"

Beth had no answer to that one. James was a computer technician; she had heard they could find work anywhere.

"Visits at Christmas and presents on birthdays do not a father make. Della cries herself to sleep some nights because, she says, her daddy doesn't love her. I'm definitely divorcing him, and I want sole custody."

As they stepped off the elevator, Bonita took off her hat and flung her head back defiantly. Her many short braids whirled around her head.

"They must have relaxed the rules for the force," Beth observed.

"Why do you say that?"

"Your hairstyle."

"I had to fight for this, believe me." Neet's chin tilted toward the ceiling. Beth was amazed by her scrappy kid sister. Neet had always been a fighter, in spite of being what dress manufacturers called petite, or maybe because of it. At age seven, though she was so scrawny she looked as if a breeze could blow her away, she had beaten up older boys who were almost twice her size.

Neet hardly looked like her voluptuous big sister at all. If anything, she was her opposite—skinny where Beth had curves, pinched where Beth was generous, tight where she was loose, except for the wide purple mouth they shared. Studying her sister's dainty heart-shaped face—her tilted eyes, her pert nose, her high cheekbones, the mouth that was like her own—she realized who Neet looked like. Or, rather, who resembled her. Dana Marshall. Beth sometimes thought that people keep running into the same characters over and over in a lifetime. Dana was Neet at nineteen. Neet was Dana grown up.

She had not seen Dana at school today. The girl had missed class, which was unusual for her, and had also failed to show up for the appointment they had made to discuss the progress of the girls' complaint. Beth realized that underneath her great worry about her father as she drove to Jersey was another small, gnawing worry about Dana.

"I took my bosses to court and got permission to wear these braids," her sister said. "They have to be short, though, and kept under my hat."

It was not the first time Neet had taken her police department superiors to court. The last time, it had been to protest an assignment to the vice squad that required her to pose as a prostitute. Her refusal had sound reasons: objections to the stereotyping of black women as whores, the belief that no crime was committed by adults who bought and sold sex, and the wish to be of more serious use to society on her job. But going to court over a *hairstyle*? Beth thought hairstyles were trivial, and said as much.

"It's not about a style," Neet said, looking as disappointed, as hurt and angry, as Dana had when she told Beth she'd been called "water buffalo" and Beth had asked "Is that all?"

"It's about my right to be my black self. Next they'd be asking me to straighten my hair and put it in a ponytail. Jeez, Beth. Are they taking over your mind at that Ivy League place? Brainwashing you? *White*washing you? Don't let them do that."

Beth did not want to deal with these issues. She was thinking about how she had always wanted college, and how her parents had wanted it for them both, but how Neet, the rebel, had refused, and taken and passed the police exam right out of high school.

"Do you like your job?" Beth asked abruptly. Neet had been transferred to foot patrol after she had refused the undercover vice squad assignment. Recently, though, she had been assigned to a car with a male partner.

"Love it. I don't like this guy they've got me paired with, though. He's a bigot, I can tell, the kind who beats his wife. I make him respect me, though. He has to. I have too much mouth for him to do anything else.

"It can get pretty grim, Beth, but sometimes I really believe we're making a dent in the drug trade. It sure beats harassing the poor hookers. We locked up a couple of drug dealers last week. We must be getting to them. They shot at us."

"Then, if you like your job, don't get yourself labeled a trouble-maker. Don't stand out so much you become a target," Beth said, even as she wondered what could be more dangerous than being shot at by armed drug dealers. "You have to obey at least some of their rules some of the time, you know."

"Oh, Jeez, Beth. I don't know how to talk to you anymore. You've gotten so conservative, you sound like Delores."

"God, I hope not," Beth said, and laughed, and felt the tension ease between them.

But Neet sighed. "I swear, Sis, I really *don't* know who you are anymore. What happened to the big sister who told me to always speak my mind, always stand up and be counted when it came to my important beliefs?"

"I'm still that big sister. I just think you've overlooked one word. You quoted me, and I'll quote you, 'Stand up for your *important* beliefs.' I just don't happen to think the way you wear your hair is important."

"Then you're out of touch. Hair is important. That's why I fought for the right to wear my hair the way God made it. Just like I wear my skin the color God made it."

"With about a half-inch layer of Revlon makeup on top," Beth said.

"You should talk," her sister said. "What is that lipstick? Purple Passion by Maybelline? On your salary, you still wear that cheap shit?"

"It's Black Orchid by Max Factor," Beth said. "I don't believe in spending a fortune on cosmetics." She opened her compact to see if her lipstick was still on smooth. It was. God, what idiots women were. Still, maybe resorting to the trivial helped them deal with the terrible aspects of life. She snapped her compact shut so loudly it sounded like a pistol shot. "It doesn't look good for Curtis, does it?"

"I don't know," Neet replied. "I'm not a doctor. You should talk to one of them." She fiddled with her artificial-looking fruit cocktail for a few seconds, stirred it with her spoon, picked up an orange cube of something unreal, and brought it almost to her lips; then she put it back. She lifted her eyes to Beth's. "No," she admitted. "I mean, you saw for yourself."

"Yeah." With unspoken accord, the two women rose from the table as one, leaving behind their barely touched chicken platters. As they entered the elevator, they encountered a new father with several other people, probably relatives, who bore about two dozen blue and silver balloons proclaiming, IT'S A BOY! and WELCOME, ZACHARY.

"I have a boy. His name is Zachary," the young man said, laughing.

All the extremes of life experience seemed to occur in this sterile place. "Congratulations," Beth said. She wished she thought she would ever feel that much joy again. She knew, and half believed, the old notion that a new life arrived to carry on whenever an old life passed. But she was in her forties and single, and, in spite of all her speculations with Sherri about adoption and other extreme measures, she did not believe in unmarried motherhood. Neet's only child was a girl, and Neet was divorcing her husband. Who would carry on for Curtis? Who would express his humor, his knowledge, his special self?

Her gloom lifted. Maybe, someday, Della would have a son. After the graduate degree, and the tour of Europe, and the fulfilling job, and the deliriously happy marriage, all of which she wished for her niece, the boy who would be another Curtis would be born.

And maybe a tired chemist would mix the wrong two potions by accident tonight and come up with a concoction to reverse the effect of strokes. *Might as well let your imagination run wild, girl,* she thought. Maybe a UFO would land tomorrow and take them all to Brazil, where, in the rain forest, they would find a witch doctor who could cure Curtis.

Chapter Eight

Beth never scheduled classes on Mondays, in case she wanted to party hearty over the weekend, though lately her hearty partying seemed to consist mainly of watching videos with Lloyd or Sherri. This meant that she was free to spend three days at home with her family. Most of that time was spent at the hospital, but on Sunday evening, while Bonita was out, she had the privilege of putting her niece to bed. To read Della to sleep, she chose *Spin a Soft Black Song*, a book of poems by Nikki Giovanni that she had given the girl for Christmas. Just before she fell asleep, Della opened her incredibly incandescent eyes and looked straight up at Beth and into her soul.

"I love you, Aunt Beth," she said. Then she closed her eyes.

Beth felt herself melting with gratitude. She could die then and there and not feel that she had missed anything important. She tiptoed to the door, thinking her niece was asleep.

"You can't go yet," Della announced. "You have to hear me say my prayers."

"Okay," Beth said, and came back.

"God bless me and my family. Please help Grandpop get well. And please protect my mother from bad people. Amen.

"I worry about Mommy," Della confided, looking up with eyes like candle flames. "She goes looking for bad people and locks them up. Sometimes they shoot at her. If she gets killed, I won't have anybody."

"You'll have me," Beth said. "But that won't happen."

The child seemed to need this reassurance. "Okay," Della said, and let out a big sigh. "Promise you'll be careful in that big city, Aunt Beth. Don't talk to strangers. Whatever you do, don't bring strangers home."

"I promise," Beth said. Della closed her eyes again and began to snore softly. Beth was angry. Obviously, she thought, Delores had scared the child by talking about what she imagined Beth's lifestyle to be.

On Saturday, Curtis was moved from Intensive Care to a regular patient room. On Monday, he was discharged from the hospital, but he was not ready to come home. Instead, with Della safely back in school, Beth helped her mother and her sister move her father into the rehab facility that was supposed to restore his speech and motor skills. He was immobile and unresponsive, but they chattered with one another brightly as he was wheeled into the paratransit van, and Delores ended every remark with "Isn't that right, Curtis?"

At her mother's house afterwards, hanging up her father's pants, folding his underwear, she helped Delores and Bonita maintain the fiction that Curtis would soon be back home, as good as new. She did not think that would be the case, but she joined in the pretense, dusting his personal things—his pipe, his lighter, his eyeglass holder, his letter opener—and replacing them in their exact same places. This ritual, she came to realize as she folded his knit shirts and put them in their drawer, was more for their sakes than for his.

At one point, the strain of smiling and lying got so intense that she had to flee to her old room, fling herself on one of the girlish, ruffled pink beds that had been hers and Neet's, and cry into the pillows.

When she finally turned over and opened her eyes, they hurt from the pain of so much pink. Delores had indulged herself in an orgy of pink when decorating this room for her daughters. Beth had spent the last three nights here, but mostly in the dark. Now the merciless sunlight poured in, reminding her that the curtains, the bedspread, even the baseboards were a vivid pink. She wondered how she had managed to stand the room all those years. It was not a small room, but she felt smaller in it—confined by the walls of Delores's tastes and aspirations—and less than fully grown.

On the first Tuesday in Black History Month, Beth drove back to Philadelphia over the Ben Franklin Bridge above a gray river filled with ice floes, gripping her steering wheel with sweaty hands and feeling unsafe. This bridge was suspended by cables and often swayed in the wind. She had never told her parents, but the panic attacks she often had when crossing the bridge kept her from visiting them more often. She was ashamed of her phobia and had told few people. She had had therapy, and knew she was not supposed to rush over the bridge, she was supposed to breathe deeply and take her time, but she hurried anyway. Once she had crossed the middle of the bridge, passed the hump in its center, and could look down at the exit lanes, she felt safer. She was always in a hurry to get to this point. Once she reached it, her heart would stop thudding so hard, and she could breathe again.

Once she crossed the bridge, also, she felt as if a curtain had closed on one stage-set for the drama of her life and opened on another. The dreaded bridge served a function; it kept her life in compartments and prevented her emotions from becoming an overwhelming flood. As she passed the midpoint of the bridge, the part of her life that was back in New Jersey began to fade, and the part that was in the city claimed her attention.

She remembered belatedly that she was supposed to introduce a playwright at tonight's Black History Month program and to moderate a panel on black theater tomorrow morning. She was not prepared for either duty. Damn. There were so few black humanities faculty on campus that all of them were overworked, especially in February.

She swerved into her allotted parking spot and headed for her building, sneaking in the back way through a door she had discovered. Maybe, just this once, her students would leave her alone for a morning, and she could begin to catch up on her reading.

No such luck. It was 9 A.M. and her office hours did not begin till eleven, but three of the four Gamma Pi Gammas were waiting outside her office.

Some of her dismay at the girls' early arrival must have shown on her face, because Cynthia apologized. "Sorry to be here so early, Professor Barnes, but we needed to confer with you. We tried to reach you at home last night, but you weren't there."

Dana plunged in before Beth could explain that her father had been taken ill. "We've heard from the Judicial Inquiry office," she announced. "They've scheduled our hearing for Thursday and appointed a prosecutor for us. We want to meet with you before we talk to her."

"Come in, come in," Beth said, trying to keep the weariness out of her voice. "Rest your coats somewhere. Grab some chairs from that empty classroom next door."

They put the chairs in a round arrangement like the reading groups she remembered from first grade, making Beth no longer an authority figure, but one of a circle of equals. "Who's your prosecutor?" Beth asked.

"Professor Hinton at the Law School," Dana said.

Natalie Hinton was black and brilliant, with the soul and instincts of a shark. She was one of Beth's resource people, but not someone she could be comfortable around. She would have sent the girls to Lisa Smith, another law professor who was warm and accommodating.

Rhonda read her thoughts. "Professor Smith is on leave this semester," she explained.

These tenured people seemed to always be taking leaves. One of the drawbacks of Beth's appointment was that she never got to take one. She had a feeling she was going to need a leave this year.

The girls seemed to be suppressing an excitement, a gleeful anticipation of their hearing. Beth hoped they were right in expecting vindication.

"Now," said Dana, who was clearly in charge, "we have to be in complete agreement on what happened that night. If we're questioned, we can't afford to have our stories contradict each other. You start, Cynthia."

"At about midnight on the evening of January thirteenth we met on the Green and began rehearsing for our sorority's Founder's Day program."

"Wasn't it eleven-thirty when you met?" Beth put in.

"No, it was midnight," Cynthia said. "Big Ben had just chimed." Big Ben, like its London namesake, was a deep-voiced clock in the tower of Alumni Hall that bonged the "Westminster Chimes" every hour. "First we rehearsed one of our songs; then we began stepping."

"You mean," Beth inquired, "you were doing one of those numbers where you stamp out rhythms with your feet?"

"Yeah," said Rhonda. "Step shows are da bomb. We do them at every Greek function."

Inwardly, Beth groaned. She understood that rhythmic percussion was a deep part of every African-descended person's heritage. When the masters took away the drums on the plantations, the slaves simply clapped their hands, slapped their thighs, and stomped their feet. Stepping had started back then, probably. Certainly it provided a deep, inherent satisfaction. Now, she thought, technology had added a new and less creative source of noise: the car stereos that thumped beneath her windows all night, interrupting her sleep and her work with their insistent beats. But neither the drivers nor the Gammas had any business thumping and stomping after midnight. Imagining the racket they must have made, she almost felt sympathy toward their accusers.

One of her weaknesses, though, was a tendency to see all sides of every argument. She determined to listen to the Gammas attentively and sympathetically, and to try to help them build their case.

"And then what happened?" Dana prodded.

"Some white boys threw their windows up and yelled at us," Rhonda said.

"Did they yell words? If so, what words?" Dana asked. She was not one of the prelaw women, but her impressive interrogatory skills made Beth wonder why not.

Rhonda said in her most precise, almost British enunciation, which was, Beth had realized, a way of distancing herself from her utterances, " 'Shut up, you noisy cows! Moo, moo, moo! Stupid niggers! Dirty black behemahs!'—That means 'beasts,' or 'water buffalo.' 'If you want a party, there's a zoo two miles from here. Take your fat black asses to the zoo! That's where you belong—not at a civilized school!' "

"Did they use any profanity?"

"Yes," Rhonda said with ladylike precision. "They called us fat-ass bitches, fat black bitches, dirty cunts, noisy cows, and two-bit black whores."

"And they threw things, don't forget," Cynthia put in.

"What things?"

"The objects hurled at us," Rhonda intoned with great elegance, "were trash, garbage, soda pop bottles, and, I believe, a condom filled with urine."

"What happened next?" Dana asked relentlessly.

"Harriet led the charge," Cynthia replied. "We need her here to tell it."

"Just say what you saw from your point of view," Dana urged.

"Hold it just a minute." Beth held up her hand. "Where is Harriet?"

The girls avoided her eyes and looked at each other. It fell to their spokeswoman to explain, "She's in the hospital. I guess she cracked under the pressure."

"And you—you come in here and start planning strategy for some *hearing* before you even tell me that? Just sit here calmly discussing the events of last week while your friend—your *soror*—is going through God knows what hell by herself? *Soror* means 'sister,' you know. This is like turning your back on your family."

There was an uncomfortable silence. Then Dana volunteered, "I was the one who took her to the hospital, Dr. Barnes. I was with her until the doctor came. I was at the hospital again when I tried to call you."

"And I was away this past weekend because my father was suddenly taken ill. You never gave me a chance to explain. I had to help move him into a nursing home." There, she had said it—though until now she had not allowed herself to think it. The correct name of the facility where her father now resided—*"Nursing home."*

"Sorry, Professor," Rhonda and Cynthia mumbled with lowered heads.

"Sorry," Dana repeated. "But Harriet believes in our cause. She would want us to go on fighting, Dr. Barnes. I know she would."

"You don't know anything," Beth said coldly. "You didn't even know your leg had been cut until it got infected. What's the matter with you, Dana? Have you lost all your feelings? What's the matter with all of you? Have you no human feelings at all?"

Integration is what's the matter, she thought. *It's just like Lloyd says. We have become integrated with a group of people who cannot feel, and we have become just like them.* "Girls, your priorities are wrong, it seems to me. Harriet is your soror, your close friend, and people with whom you are close should come before any political concerns. *Way* before. When did Harriet become ill?"

"Saturday night," Dana volunteered. "She's my roommate, you know." Beth hadn't known. "She started talking all jumbled and out of her head, saying the skinheads were coming to get us, so I took her to the hospital. I was there again on Sunday."

Beth felt ashamed of herself for putting Dana on the defensive. *Hypocrite. It's because you should have gone to your father last week instead of teaching, that you're taking your guilt out on these children.* Also, she had been supposed to take Harriet shopping Saturday afternoon, but had completely forgotten their date. She could at least have called the child. Would it have made a difference? Probably not, but she would never know.

She glanced at her large, rhinestone-encrusted watch. "Well, I still have three hours before class, so I'm going to visit Harriet. We'll have to finish this planning session later."

The Gammas began getting to their feet with a loud scraping of chairs. "Don't return those chairs to the room next door—stack them in that corner. We'll need them next time. Anybody going with me?" She flung that last question over her shoulder as she was shrugging into her coat and moving purposefully to her door.

She strode across the campus self-righteously with the three young women straggling behind her and was almost at the hospital entrance before it dawned on her that she had berated Dana and the others almost in Lloyd's exact words.

Chapter Nine

Harriet looked like hell, Beth thought when her former student was brought in to see her in the visitors' lounge on the top floor of the hospital. She was not raving as Dana had described—sedation had probably put a stop to that— but she was still agitated, jerking her head to look over her shoulder and plucking invisible lint from her ugly sweater. Her matted, frizzy hair was flattened against one side of her head and stuck out like porcupine quills on the other.

"Hello, Harriet," Beth said. "How are you feeling?"

The girl did not respond. Instead, she lowered her head like a little girl who was ashamed of herself.

Without really thinking, Beth dug in her purse and came out with a large plastic comb. "Mind if I comb your hair?" she asked.

Harriet mumbled something that might have been "No" and might have meant "No, I don't mind" or "No, don't do it. Don't touch my hair."

Beth moved to a position behind Harriet and began gently teasing the mass of kinks on the girl's head, first detangling the top layer and then getting to the roots. As she worked, she heard an amazing sound. She bent her head to listen.

Harriet was humming.

Encouraged, Beth hummed along and combed a bit more vigorously, until Harriet said, "Ouch." Then she returned to the top layer, the part that was already free of knots, and simply moved the comb back and forth. Harriet really had nice hair. Thick, healthy, and springy. The girl gave a long sigh and stretched.

"You're a genius, Professor Barnes," said Dana, the first of the girls to arrive. The other two were behind her.

"So I've been told," Beth said. "But that was over thirty years ago, and, since we lose a few brain cells every year, by now I'm probably just average. Anybody got a mauve lipstick?"

Dana silently obliged. She and Harriet were about the same complexion, a few shades lighter than Beth, whose dark lipsticks would be too strong on Harriet. Carefully, Beth applied color to the girl's well-shaped mouth and dusted it with a fluff of powder.

Then she had another inspiration. She pulled the comb from the back of her own hair, detached the purple bow, and unraveled its stitches. This left her with about a twenty-inch length of wide ribbon, which she used to pull Harriet's hair back from her face and tie it.

Finally, she took the purple print scarf from around her own neck and tied it around Harriet's with a flourish. She opened her compact and held it up.

"Look at yourself," she said softly.

Harriet obeyed. Her eyes enlarged and filled with wonder. She wet a fingertip and used it to smooth her brows and her lipstick to her satisfaction. Then she pronounced with surprise, "I'm pretty!"

The other three Gammas applauded.

"Yes, you are," Beth said. "I'm sorry I couldn't go shopping with you on Saturday. How about this weekend?"

Harriet's face brightened. "For real?"

"For real," Beth said. "If you can come, I'll meet you for lunch at noon, at the Japanese place in the food court. Excuse us for a minute."

She beckoned Harriet's sorors to a far corner. "I've got to go," she told them. "Can you stay with her a little while longer?" They nodded. "Please keep the talk light. I suggest no political discussions or strategic planning. Just light topics like clothes, movies, and music. Let's try to get Harriet out of here, girls." She really had no idea of when they would be able to do that. She was no mental health expert, but she feared it might be a long time. "And, oh—" She rummaged in her purse and found five dollars. "Will somebody please get her some lotion? She's so ashy she looks like a ghost." Rhonda took the money and nodded.

"Thanks, Rhonda. Dana, Cynthia, I'll see you in class."

They promised solemnly to keep their conversation frivolous.

On the way back to her building, Beth was crowded off the sidewalk by a rude group of young men who came striding toward her, three abreast. They wore brush haircuts, camouflage uniforms, and high brown work boots. Their staring blue eyes did not seem to see her. If she had not stepped aside, they would have walked right into her.

"Hey! Didn't anybody ever teach you manners?" she yelled at them.

They did not seem to hear her, either. For them, she realized, she simply did not exist. The feeble sun went behind a cloud just then. She was wearing a silly fake-leopard swing coat without buttons, and the cold went right through her chest. She clutched her coat around her and hurried into her building.

She managed to read her notes for this afternoon's seminar and skim over the text. Fortunately, she had practically memorized this Flannery O'Connor novel, *Wise Blood*.

But either her students were being deliberately obtuse today, or they were blind to its meanings. "As a Christian," said one boy, "I find this book offensive."

"What, precisely, do you find offensive about it, Ralph?" She had thought that Hurston's novel about Moses, which they had discussed two weeks ago, would be far more disturbing to holders of orthodox Christian beliefs. But the class had slid over it as easily as toboggans over ice.

Now this intensely Christian work was bothering someone on religious grounds. Students were totally unpredictable.

"Well," he said, "I don't like this mummified thing that Enoch calls 'the new jesus.' I guess it's some kind of take-off on death and resurrection, but O'Connor doesn't even capitalize the Lord's name there. I find that blasphemous."

"But—," she began, and then searched around the room for responses. This was, after all, a seminar; she was not supposed to be lecturing. A small hand fluttered on the front row. "Dana?"

"That's the whole point O'Connor is making," the girl said. Dependable Dana, always prepared, always insightful. "Substituting man-made objects and human works for God *is* blasphemous. That's why she doesn't capitalize 'the new jesus.' It's just a man-made thing."

"Thank you, Dana." *And thank God for you.* She could always depend on Dana to come up with bright, well-reasoned answers. "Would you say this is a religious novel, and, specifically, a Christian novel?"

"Totally. She is promoting Christianity and putting down secular humanism on every page. She just does it in a weird way, with grotesque symbols. My favorite scene is where the Devil tempts Hazel by offering him all the junk on his used-car lot."

"What is the author saying there, do you think?"

"She's saying that all the worldly goods the Devil is offering him for his soul amount to no more than a bunch of junk."

Beth turned to the complainant. "I think you ought to read this novel again, Mr. Witmayer, and read more carefully this time, before you make up your mind that it is blasphemous. Some people in the class see it as a profoundly religious book. So do I, and so have many critics before me."

The boy in commando clothes had a smug smile even though redness was spreading around his ears and up into his exposed scalp.

He isn't offended by this novel, Beth intuited suddenly. He was offended by that story we read last week, but he doesn't dare say so. They had begun their discussion of O'Connor with her fiercely comical, antiracist story, "Everything That Rises Must Converge." *He hated that story, but he doesn't dare come out with his racism to me,* she realized. *So he's finding fault with this text. He isn't too stupid to understand it, or he wouldn't be here. He just wants to raise some objections, any objections.*

After class, the boy was joined in the hall by a couple of his associates in army fatigues and high boots. They were blocking the exit door. *They might as well have on swastika armbands,* she thought as she tried to pass them and was forced to say, "Excuse me." Two of them, staring past her with eyes like dirty chips of ice, refused to move. Finally, reluctantly, the one who was in her class stepped aside. She saw the silver swastika pendant he wore as he let her pass.

Beth, her heart thudding as if she were in a high place and having a panic attack, gathered her things into her briefcase helter-skelter and left the building. It took all her self-restraint to refrain from running. Outside, the other campus buildings loomed in toward her like unfriendly giants, their shadows already melting together into large, menacing black pools on the green.

This school had gone through a building boom in the eighties, adding dormitories, classroom buildings, and research facilities at a dizzying clip. Its enormous investment in edifices was probably the only thing that kept it from moving to the suburbs. It was spreading out to the western portion of the city, too, like some sinister oil slick, buying up beautiful old houses and tearing them down or rehabbing them. She had seen a story in which a university spokesman actually said they were doing good things for the neighborhood. The people who were being put out of their homes were not convinced.

As Beth crossed the campus, she noticed that all the old moss-covered eighteenth-century buildings looked cold and haunted, like mausoleums. The new dorm towers and office and classroom complexes, all of the boxlike bare-bones school, just looked cold, with black windows like the staring eyes of idiots.

Beth badly needed to work the soreness out of her muscles, but she decided to skip her swim. She wanted to get to her car before dark. She had almost forgotten that she had to pick up the visiting playwright, take her to dinner, and then take her to the panel discussion on black theater at Evers House.

February seemed to be heating up with activities, but not much else. Privately, Beth called it Black Misery Month. It was nasty, brutish, and short, like Thomas Hobbes's cynical description of life. Short days, horrible weather, ice on the streets, and the need to be everywhere at once watching grim reminders of distant history in far-off places—slavery and lynchings in the South, fires and genocide in Tulsa, beatings in Selma, bombings in Birmingham. Tomorrow was the mass-choir concert of dreary spirituals and the lecture by the black congresswoman from Florida. After the congresswoman left, there would be a performance of a new play about the Underground Railroad. Her attendance at all these events was compulsory. Maybe she could skip the play, which was sure to be depressing. Over the weekend, please God, she would have time to grade papers and prepare for the coming week's classes.

After the panel discussion ended in a burst of screaming disagreement over some issue that no one would remember, Beth drove the playwright to her train and then raced back to her house to get ready for class. Black History Month was just beginning, and she was already dangerously close to burnout. With events scheduled almost every day and a total of only six black humanities faculty to cover them, plus regular classes, office hours, grading, and preparation, they all needed roller skates and B$_{12}$ shots.

Plus, one or more of the Gamma Pi Gammas visited her almost daily, even when there were no new developments in their racial harassment case. They were beginning to suspect that someone was running games on them. Beth was inclined to agree. Their hearing had been scheduled and rescheduled twice, only to be postponed again. They had been ordered by the judicial officer to keep quiet about their case, and they obeyed him, but the other side was doing the precise opposite.

The white boy, Otto Jurgen, had selected an advisor, an intense, partisan professor in the history department named Ted Corrigan. "Wrong Way" Corrigan, intent on protecting white rights, had been feeding tidbits to the press, putting a slant on them that made his client seem like a victim and the black girls like fools. What, he asked, was so terrible about the phrase "water buffalo"? In the boy's country of origin it meant, simply, "idiot," which was appropriate for people who made rude noises at midnight. Who but a bunch of selfish, pampered, oversensitive opportunists would interpret it as a racial slur?

"And that's all Otto Jurgen will admit to saying, Dr. Barnes," Dana complained on the morning after the panel discussion. "The other boys won't admit to yelling anything at all at us. We know they said all those other things, but we can't prove it."

"Of course they won't admit it. Would you?" Cynthia asked. She seemed very impatient today. "You've got to stop expecting anything from those guys."

"What about your leg wound, Dana?" Beth asked.

"Professor Hinton says we can't bring that into the case unless I can prove how I got it. They'll just say I fell somewhere and hurt myself, she says. They've already been nosing around, asking other people in the dorm how much I drink."

"*Do* you drink?" Beth asked.

"No!" Dana exclaimed. "Not at all. Oh, maybe a little bit, on week-ends, but not much. I don't want to drown my intelligence."

"Good for you. Do you have any character witnesses who can support you in that?"

"We've been asking around, but we haven't got any yet. People will offer us support in secret, but they're afraid to stand with us in public."

Cynthia, meanwhile, was tapping her foot impatiently. "I don't know about you, Dana, but I can't stay around here yakking all day. I'm getting tired of spending all my time in these meetings. I have other things to do. Right now I have a class."

"Go to your class, then," Dana said, rolling her eyes as if to say this was what she expected of Cynthia, who switched out in her gorgeous tweed wrap jacket and matching pants.

"I think Cynthia's copping out," Dana said. "She's decided that we're wasting our time pursuing this case. I talked to Dr. Vernon, by the way. She doesn't think we have a strong argument, either."

Carolyn Vernon was a counselor in Psychology. Beth had heard of her, but didn't know her very well. She was rumored to be hard to approach—very private and standoffish.

"How did you get to talk to her?" Beth wondered.

"Oh, she was counseling Harriet, and she offered to help us, too. But she wouldn't meet with us in a public place. She met us in the dark, in an alley between the hospital and her office building."

This seemed strange to Beth, but she let it pass.

Dana seemed deeply depressed this morning. "It doesn't look good, Dr. Barnes. I think our case is falling apart."

"Don't give up," Beth told the girl.

"I got this in the mail today," Dana said, waving a piece of paper. She passed it to Beth. "The president of our sorority doesn't sup-port us, either."

Beth scanned the letter, which was from the sorority's national headquarters in Washington, D.C. "We expect behavior consistent with our high ideals . . . conduct reflecting credit, not embarrass-ment, on our sorority," et cetera, et cetera. It was signed by the so-rority's national president.

Translation: "Be good, grateful little colored girls, and don't make trouble."

Beth became angry. "But this is unfair," she said. "She's way down there in D.C. How can she know what you went through up here?"

"She doesn't have to," Dana said. "She's ancient. She dates back to the time when we were happy just to be at a white school."

"Oh? How old is she?"

"Forty-five or fifty," Dana said and then looked at her. "Oh. Sorry, Dr. Barnes. Actually, she's closer to sixty."

"Oh, sixty. *That* old. No wonder," Beth said wryly. She had often wondered how old she seemed to her students. Well, today she had her answer: ancient.

"Make me a copy of that, please, Dana," she said. "Have you seen Harriet today?"

"No. I'm in no shape to visit her. I couldn't cheer anybody up right now. But Rhonda and Cynthia went over, and they say she's being discharged on Friday." She added, "I can't concentrate, Dr. Barnes. I tried to do the assigned reading in Faulkner last night, and I kept reading the same page over and over."

Beth tried to make a joke. "With Faulkner, that's understandable. Sometimes his pages all seem alike to me."

This time, she couldn't get a smile out of Dana. "That isn't nor-mal for me, Dr. Barnes. I usually zip through the reading assign-ments and retain everything. I think I may need some help. I'm going to make an appointment with Dr. Vernon for myself."

"Do you like her?" Beth asked.

"I don't know. I only met her once. Why?"

Beth was cautious. She'd already heard that Carolyn Vernon was strange and difficult, and her stipulations about meeting secretly with the girls supported that, but she didn't want to sabotage Dana's decision. "Well, if I were going for counseling, I'd want a person I liked. Someone I found sympathetic. Even if they were white."

Dana seemed clearly shocked. "God, no, I couldn't do that, Dr. Barnes. I don't know how you can even suggest that. How could you confide in . . . I mean, I wouldn't even consider going to a white counselor. Especially with the problems I'm having right now."

"I guess I wasn't thinking," Beth admitted.

"I guess not." Dana still seemed indignant. She gathered up her things and left.

After her talk with Dana, Beth had trouble concentrating on her own reading.

Chapter Ten

Education integration undermining de Nation," Beth's best friend Sherri chanted, rapping her knuckles rhythmically on the scarred tabletop. "Niggahs getting blinded, becoming white-minded. They think the white man is a friend to us, when he wants to put an end to us."

"Whose dreadful rap is that?" Beth asked.

"NWA, I think," Sherri said. "Or maybe it was Tupac's. It doesn't matter. It's not dreadful; it's related to our conversation. You haven't answered my question."

It was Saturday morning. They were sitting in one of the high-backed, dark mahogany booths like church pews that the University had installed in its food court to differentiate it from the open tables in malls, and make it appear that the main business of the place was something high-minded and noble like religion or education, not just crass profits. Or so Beth thought. They had met early to catch up on each other's recent doings before Harriet joined them. "Sorry. My mind must have wandered. What was the question?"

"I asked you what you were teaching, and you said Faulkner and

Flannery O'Connor in one course, and Sinclair Lewis and E. L. Doctorow in the other. Then I asked you why you thought those Gamma girls seek you out and want to hang out with you."

"Oh. They want a friend, I suppose. A friend they can trust."

"A *black woman* friend," Sherri emphasized. "When you speak of trust, your race and sex are automatically implied."

Beth opened her mouth to argue and then closed it again, remembering Dana's amazement that she would consider a white psychologist. The girl's reaction still bothered Beth, because it suggested that something was wrong with her own outlook. "Also, they may see me as some sort of role model."

"Of course they do," Sherri said. "They most certainly and absolutely see you as a role model. No credit to you, because there are no other African-American females teaching in your department—but they also keep hoping for you to teach something with which they can identify. That is why I want to know, why are you stretching your asshole over a doorknob, teaching white writers?"

"I cover black writers, too," Beth said in self-defense.

"Oh, of course you do. You include them as an afterthought, as a footnote to your grand designs—if you have time to get around to them. I'll bet the semester flies by so fast you'll never even get to mention Richard Wright and Margaret Walker."

Beth was silent for a moment, because she had been looking at the calendar the other night and thinking the same thing.

"I guess," she said, "I just don't want to be categorized. I don't want to be limited." She said this even though she knew that she was not permitted to teach white writers from the canon, except for women's topics, which didn't count. After a few attempts, she knew better than to try, just as she knew it was wisest to stay off the tenure track, where so many had touched the third rail and perished. As for polemical writers like Sinclair Lewis, they had never been part of the canon and never would be.

"Girlfriend, girlfriend," Sherri said, shaking her head. "When will you learn? You are already categorized by your beautiful Hershey-chocolate complexion. As well as by your daddy, your mama, your sister, and your niece, all of whom were, the last time I looked, definitely people of color."

"Don't be talking about my family," Beth said. She was only half kidding. "It's bad enough that white folks want to lock you up in a ghetto. When your friends try to do the same thing, it's terrible."

"Well, sorry. But as far as being locked up and limited is concerned, do you remember those sonnets you wrote, back in our dear old school days?"

Beth nodded. She had dug some of them out and read them not long ago. They weren't bad. A couple of them had held up really well.

Sherri went on relentlessly, "You were limited to fourteen lines, five beats per line, and a definite rhyme scheme. Yet, within those limits, you managed to express yourself most eloquently. You made of limitation a free and glorious thing. I want you to do the same with your teaching, and so do your students and everybody else. You do remember how I helped you out with your dissertation, don't you?"

Beth remembered. She had proposed a Melville topic. Her committee had kept finding fault with it, and she was ready to tear out her hair in frustration when she told Sherri about her problem.

Her friend had responded, "Of course they keep finding something wrong with your proposal. You are on their turf. That's a dangerous place to be. They won't come right out and say it, but they don't want you there. You're not supposed to be an authority on dead white male writers. You're not supposed to know anything at all about white folks. Pick a black topic."

She had doubted Sherri's logic but, being desperate, took her advice. Her dissertation on Chester Himes, which later became the kernel of her book on Ohio writers, breezed through without any problems. For one thing, she suspected, no one on the committee had read Himes; they just approved her work because it put her back in the ghetto where she belonged.

"The rules haven't changed, girlfriend," Sherri said. "It looked as if they had for a while, but that was just an illusion. We were in a beautiful bubble, and it was full of rainbows while it lasted, but it burst some time ago. This water buffalo mess is just another indication that it's gone. So let the dead white men teach the dead white men. You, teach some live blacks."

"Doctorow's not dead, and Faulkner is forever," Beth said. "I mean, we will always be saddled with him and others who think like him. Let's talk about you for a change. How are things at work? Miss Anne still menacing your security?"

"Miss Anne is gone," Sherri said with a wicked grin. "Kaput. Vanquished and vanished."

"Wonderful. How'd you manage that?" She was really glad to hear this news. It would be a shame if, after all that hard work creating and developing her program, a stranger walked in and displaced Sherri.

A glint of mischief brightened her friend's eyes. "I owe it all to you. Your suggestions inspired me to get creative with the computer. Technology is amazing these days. The things you can do with photographs."

"Tell me."

"Well, say you have old pictures of somebody lying around the office, or you have someone take new pictures and tell her it's for employee ID cards. Then you superimpose her face on a picture of a couple coming out of a motel. Do it again on a picture of the same couple, nude, in bed. Throw in a solo porno pose for extra titillation, then mail your creations off to the appropriate party—in this case, the head of the foundation that pays most of your bills."

"Don't they put people in jail for stuff like that?" Beth wondered.

"The tabloids do it all the time," her friend said airily. "Besides, no one can prove I did it. I erased my files."

"Wow," Beth said in admiration. "What a fiendish use of talent. It was in self-defense, though. I guess it was justified."

"Damn right. If somebody thought I was going to just lie down and roll over and let some upstart steal my program, they had another think coming. Just cause Sears robbed Roebuck, Elvis robbed Big Mama Thornton and Willie Nelson is still stealing from Charles Brown doesn't mean it has to happen to us every single time."

Beth applauded. "Well, bravo. I do get tired of you reducing everything to the issue of race, though."

"When will you learn, Beth? As far as we're concerned, it's the only issue that matters."

"It's Black History Month. I hear this stuff day and night. Give me a break," Beth said, and changed the subject. "How are you and your new man getting along?"

Sherri played with her teriyaki. "He's still keeping me at arms' length. I've been trying to convince him that unconventional positions don't count, but I haven't succeeded."

"Is he still talking about getting married?"

"Yes."

"And are you still thinking about it?"

"I don't know," Sherri said, stirring her tea. "Depends."

"Depends on what?"

Sherri managed to evade the question. She half rose from her seat and looked over Beth's head. "Hey, isn't that your charge? She looks lost."

Harriet did indeed look lost. She also looked like a forlorn waif, in an outfit that only a man could have selected, and even then he would have had to be a blind man—a blue denim vest with an attached red plaid skirt, a pink turtleneck and a woolly brown sweater. Beth stood up in the booth and beckoned to her.

"Retail therapy is definitely indicated," Sherri mumbled. "Dress Barn to the rescue. Hurry."

But other therapy seemed indicated first. Harriet kept her head down, chin wedged into her chest. Offered Japanese food, she mumbled, "Do you think it would be all right if—? Do you think maybe I could—? Would it be possible to—?"

Shocked at the uncertainty that afflicted this once assertive girl, Beth wedged Harriet into the booth beside Sherri and got her the burger and the chocolate milkshake she finally admitted she wanted instead of sushi. Both women pretended to ignore Harriet's tremors and her confusion, which seemed to clear up after she ate.

"I need a suit for job interviews," she stated clearly after draining her milkshake. "And some stuff for weekends." Questioned, she admitted that her weekends consisted mainly of sports events, sorority meetings, and an occasional movie—nothing like dating or dancing.

Then the three of them, as rapt as teenagers, got into a passionate discussion of stores.

"Not the Gap, that's for girls who want to be boys," Beth said. "And not Eddie Bauer, it's for boring WASP wannabes."

"Definitely not the Gap or Eddie Bauer, and not Lerner, either."

"Why not Lerner? You get more for your money there."

"Why don't we ask Harriet how much she has to spend?"

After seeing the small roll of bills Harriet pulled from her pocket, they considered the One Price Clothing Store and then settled on JayMart, a somewhat better discount store where you could find almost anything, including cheap knockoffs of designer styles.

But first, Beth decided, something had to be done about Harriet's hair.

"My treat," she said firmly as they marched her into her salon, Classique Afrique. She said one of her numerous thank-yous to God when she saw that Claude was there. He was the best stylist in town, and a genius at haircuts. "Do something about this head, please," Beth said, pushing Harriet toward his chair.

"I don't want it straightened," Harriet announced. Her abrasive personality seemed to be coming back. "I am proud of the hair I was born with. I don't want any greasy, stringy mess hanging around my face. I don't know how you stand it, Dr. Barnes."

"I don't," Beth said calmly. Learning how she appeared to young people was becoming a second education. "These greasy strings are all mine, dear. I was born with them. Feel." She bent her head so Harriet could touch her hair.

"Sorry," Harriet said after feeling the crown of Beth's head. "I didn't know, Dr. Barnes. I thought you had a process."

"I wouldn't speak to her if she did," said Sherri, who wore her hair in an artistically braided crown.

"Of course you are proud of your natural hair, dear," Claude said to Harriet, "but you could show your pride a little bit more by combing it." Only Claude could get away with saying things like this to his customers. His voice was so sweet and soothing they usually overlooked the sarcasm. "I'm going to cut it, okay? Then I'll give you some moisturizer so you can take care of it more easily."

Forty-five minutes later, Harriet emerged from his booth crowned with a cute, curly natural and clutching a pink bottle of goo to help her keep it in order.

At the next stop, JayMart, they searched for a suit. "I want one like yours, Miss Davis," Harriet said, "but with a skirt, not pants." Petite, tan Sherri, always sharp as a Sabatier paring knife, was wearing a winter white cotton-knit pantsuit today, with a black ribbed turtleneck underneath.

It turned out that what Harriet wanted was a suit not the same style as Sherri's, but the same color—white, or anything other than black, navy, or gray. She was right, Beth thought; the drab local winters cried out for bright colors. That was the idea behind the rainbow in her closet.

The store did not have anything in white, but they found a fabulous dark red suit that put a glow in Harriet's complexion and came with both skirt and pants, all for sixty-nine dollars.

"It may fall apart in a year, but so what? By then you'll have a great job and can buy a dozen more. Here, try this under it." Sherri waved a cream-colored blouse with a lovely crush neck.

While Harriet changed in the dressing room, Sherri said to Beth, "She seems pretty fragile to me. Actually, I can't imagine her holding down a job."

"I can't even imagine her finishing the semester," said Beth. "I don't know what they were thinking of, letting her out of the hospital so soon."

"They were probably thinking of her insurance coverage, which was about to run out," Sherri said. "This is a cold, cruel world our children are growing up into. Brrr." Sherri shivered. "Where is she living?"

"In a dorm with one of her sorors,"

"The black dorm, I hope," Beth said.

"Where else, as political as she is? You know, they're trying to abolish it. The black dorm, I mean."

"They're trying to take back everything we have, Beth. Face it, we're at war, and that child is a casualty. Lloyd wouldn't like it, but you might have to move her in with you for a while."

"After what she just said about my hair? No way." The child had no mother to teach her manners, just as no one had taught her how to dress, and it showed just as obviously. "Besides, what would I do if she freaked out again? I'm not qualified to handle a psychotic."

"Hush. Here she comes."

Poor Harriet, Beth thought. Unloved, unlovable, and alone in a hostile world. But at least today she was happy, made so by her new hairdo and all of her new outfits, especially the bright red fleece pant set for attending basketball games and the colorful little striped knit cap they had picked up from a clearance table for a song. They were about to exit the store when Harriet asked, "Who has a watch? Is it four o'clock yet?"

"Yes," Beth said, glancing at her gold and fake-ruby Citizen. "It's four o'clock exactly. Why? Do you have a date?"

"Nope. It's time for my medicine. I hate it, but it keeps me from going off."

A helpful saleswoman pointed out the fountain, and Harriet trudged toward it. Behind her back, the two old friends exchanged a hasty high five.

Chapter Eleven

A unt Beth, is the mummy still alive?"

"No, baby. He's been dead for thousands of years."

"Then why do they keep him standing up in here? Why don't they bury him?" Della wanted to know.

"Good question," Beth said. She herself had always been more concerned, as she remembered, with how small the mummies were and how much larger people seemed to have gotten since. "I guess they want us to see how the Egyptians took care of their dead people. It's amazing how long he's lasted."

"Well, he doesn't look very good," Della said. She wrinkled her exquisitely freckled nose. "I bet he doesn't smell very good, either."

"Probably not," Beth agreed, repelled by the stained, tattered strips of blackened cloth that encased the mummy. Della had a point. Maybe someone should give the poor dead thing a decent burial instead of this improper public exposure. "His sarcophagus is pretty, though. Look how his picture is painted on top."

"I like that. I think they should do that for all dead people. Paint their picture on the casket, instead of making us look at the actual person."

Della continually amazed her aunt with insights and experiences far beyond her years. What, for instance, could she know about viewings and funerals?

Her niece answered without being asked. "You know that Holiness church up the street? My friend Jamila and I went inside a couple of times when they had funerals. We got in line and walked past the body along with everybody else, and then just walked outside again. It was gross. Ewww.

"On Sundays," the child continued, "we like to stand outside that church and listen to them sing. We used to dance to their music, too, until some of the church people stopped us and said it was wrong. Why was it wrong, Aunt Beth?"

"I guess they thought you weren't showing God enough respect."

"But that music was good, Aunt Beth! It rocked! They had drums and a bass and everything. Does God get mad when we dance and have a good time?"

"Some people think so," Beth told her niece, and added carefully, "but I don't."

"You don't?"

Careful, Beth, she admonished herself. *You don't know what kind of religious instruction James and Bonita are giving her. None at all, probably,* she decided, *if she's dancing on the sidewalk outside a church during Sunday services.*

"No, I don't," she said decisively. "I think God wants us to have fun."

"Good," Beth said. "Popsicles are fun, I think. So is this jewelry the ladies and men wore in Egypt."

Beth's father had brought her to the museum when she was small, and she took her students there, too, as often as she could, because it was crammed full of African artifacts and history. *Their* history. The last time she had brought a class there to hear a lecture, Sherri had been with her. A guard had attempted to turn her and Beth and the motley group of young people away. He demanded IDs. Beth had obediently produced hers. But Sherri had stopped in the middle of the Great Hall and told Beth's class, "This place and all the stuff in it belongs to you, and you belong here. I want you to come here as often as you want, and act like you own it. Because you do." The guard, by now red-faced, gave them no more trouble.

After Beth and Della tired of looking at the ornate gold and amber and jade necklaces, and wishing they owned this one or that one, they bought Dove Bars from a cart outside the museum and ate them sitting in a bus stop shelter.

"Did somebody steal those ancient treasures from Egypt, Aunt Beth?"

"I've heard people say so."

"Then why don't the Egyptians make them give them back?"

"I don't know," Beth said, not wanting to get into a discussion of balances of powers and international finance, topics about which she knew shamefully little. "This is a big country we live in, with a big army and stuff. Maybe the Egyptians are afraid of Americans."

"That's a shame."

"Yes, it is," her aunt agreed.

"What are we going to do now?" The eternal children's question. Beth sighed; she had run out of ideas for the moment. But without waiting for an answer, Della ran over to the reflecting pool in front of the museum and began exclaiming over the fish.

Maybe that was one secret of raising children, she thought, knowing that all their questions did not require answers. And that if you ran out of things for them to do, they would find things for themselves.

"Look at these gigantic fish, Aunt Beth! How old do you think they are?" Beth went over to her niece's side and looked down at the huge golden carp.

"Oh, a couple of thousand years old, maybe, like the mummies."

"For real?"

"No. I was just kidding. I don't know how old they are. They're pretty tough; they've lived here a long time."

"Like Grandpa?"

"Yes, exactly."

"But Grandpa isn't getting any better. Maybe he's not so tough."

"Maybe not. Let's get to the car." Beth held out her hand and led her niece to the parking lot.

First, she took her downtown to Love Park so they could watch the inline skaters perform their graceful tricks on the sidewalk beneath the kooky "Love" statue, with its *O* leaning right and all four letters painted bright red. Miraculously, she found a parking spot on Twelfth Street and took Della to Delilah's for a soul food supper. They had fried chicken, macaroni, greens, and candied yams. Della's favorite was the corn bread, so Beth gave her piece to her niece.

"That proves I love you," Beth said. "I wouldn't give my corn bread to anyone else."

"You should give me all your food, Aunt Beth, so you won't get any fatter."

"That's rude, young lady, and besides, it's unkind."

"It's true, though."

"Give me back my corn bread," Beth ordered.

Della bit a huge chunk out of the yellow square and then held it out to her.

"I don't want it now. You've been eating off of it. Where are your manners?"

Her niece, knowing she had done something wrong, lifted her chin and burst into a wild peal of laughter that showed all her pretty teeth.

"I'm taking you home. You can get away with bad manners with some people, but not with me." Did Neet let Della get away with this sort of rudeness? Or, with the crazy shifts she worked, did she simply not have time for the child? She was working thirty-two hours this weekend; that was why Beth was keeping Della.

"Home to your house, or home to New Jersey?"

"Home to New Jersey."

"Oh, no, Aunt Beth, please, I'll be good. I won't be rude anymore. There's nothing to do in New Jersey. I'd rather be with you. We have fun."

Beth let the girl think she was being driven home to her mother in New Jersey while she told her that manners were more important than brains and would carry her further in life than money, looks, or education and that she, Beth Barnes, would personally see to it that her niece's bad manners improved. Then, practically at the foot of the bridge, she turned onto a westbound street and headed to her apartment with a silent, chastised niece beside her.

The rest of the evening, Della quietly watched a video Beth had rented, *My Girl*, and read *The Soul Brothers and Sister Lou* to herself while her aunt graded half of the twenty-eight papers in her briefcase.

The poets and playwrights and politicians had all given their speeches and left. With students preparing for their midterms, the campus was mercifully quiet. Beth could get some work done at last, but she was tired. Her eyeballs felt dry and dusty. She might have to pull an all-nighter soon to get caught up.

She read another paper, a dull one that made her sleepy; then she stretched, yawned, and looked around for Della. She had made up the living room sofa bed for her niece, but she was not in it. Instead, she found the child in her own queen-size bed, arms flung wide, snoring softly.

Beth tiptoed back to her living room. When the phone rang, she snatched it up immediately, not so much because she was eager to talk to Lloyd as because she didn't want to wake Della.

"Hey, sweet mama," he said.

"Hey, sugar," she said.

"My love is 'bout ready to come down. Yours?"

"Can't have thoughts like that right now. Wish I could, but I'm baby-sitting my niece. She's asleep."

The disappointment in his voice was palpable. "Seems like your family is taking up more and more of your time."

"You're the one who told me they should be the most important thing in my life."

"I didn't mean to exclude myself. Why don't I come over anyway?"

She was alarmed. "Lloyd, no."

"Why not? You said she's asleep."

"She might wake up."

"Kids never wake up. Trust me."

"She might. It would be different if—" She almost said, *"if we were married."* "Besides, she's in my bed."

"Ain't she a little old for that? How old is she?"

"Seven and a half, but she hasn't been here often enough. She needs to get comfortable with new surroundings."

"Uh-uh, baby, *you* need a bigger place, so you can close some doors. I'm all for bonding with our little kinfolk and all that, but I miss you."

"Miss you, too." Beth made a kissing sound.

"Rrrrr," he roared softly. "Ooh, it's good you can't get inside my head and find out what I'm planning to do to you when we finally do get together."

After they said good-bye, Beth undressed quietly and slipped into the unoccupied side of her bed. Della stirred briefly and then went back to her peaceful snoring. Watching her sleep, marveling at her innocent trust, Beth held her breath to keep from waking the child and thought she had never known such bliss, not even with the best of her lovers—who was, she decided, Lloyd.

In the morning they had Mahalia Jackson and The Five Blind Boys on tape, and pancakes with pure maple syrup, and the funnies, which they read together. Beth was disappointed that Della's favorite strip was "Hagar the Horrible," not "The Boondocks," which she always read first. All too soon it was time to take her niece home.

She found Neet drinking coffee and reading the paper in the kitchen of her garden apartment, though the strong odor of lye indicated that she was also cleaning her oven. In another woman's house Beth might suspect the woman of processing her hair, but not here.

"Well, I see you survived the weekend, Sis," Neet said. Her head was tied up in a bandanna. "Did she behave herself?"

"Mostly," Beth said. She might bring up Della's rudeness later.

Della danced around the room. "We had fun, Mom. We went to see the mummies and the fish and the Rollerbladers."

"Write me a note and tell me how much fun you had," Beth said. She was a firm believer in the importance of thank-you notes, and in training children to write them.

"Can I sleep over at your house again next weekend, Aunt Beth? Can I, Mommy?"

"If your aunt can stand you again," Neet said without looking up from her page.

Beth hesitated for a fraction of a second, thinking of Lloyd, and then said, "Sure."

"Would you get me a goldfish like the ones we saw?"

"Maybe, if your mother says you can have a goldfish. I'll think about it after I see how you behave next weekend."

"I won't touch your corn bread, Aunt Beth, I promise."

Neet was instantly attentive. "What's this about corn bread?"

"I'll let Della tell you," Beth said, and kissed the child good-bye. As she bent to hug her sister, too, the scarf fell away, revealing Neet's newly lank, dead-straight hair.

"I got tired of fighting," Neet said, and tied her hair up again. "These sixteen-hour shifts are for punishment, to put me back in my place. Well, I can't take anymore." Her face looked weary and streaked, as if with tears.

"I understand," Beth said.

The sisters exchanged a long, deep look that conveyed *"These folks can really be rough sometimes"* and *"Sometimes you gotta do what you gotta do"* and *"Girl, you know I understand."*

Then Beth headed for her mother's house, a suburban ranch less than a mile away. She disliked the small, stuffy all-black town where she had grown up because it was as cold and unfriendly as white suburbs. It was also conservative in the extreme.

The conservative people of all-black Refuge, New Jersey, had refused to allow the Nation of Islam to open a factory there, because Muslims were not Christians, though they allowed white chain stores to buy up and occupy half the town.

The town's citizens did not discuss the fates of Martin, Malcolm, and Medgar or of the Black Panthers, except, shockingly, to call them troublemakers. Instead, like all other Americans, they immersed themselves in material concerns. They were constantly comparing the sizes of one another's houses and cars and refrigerators, and so deeply into imitating white folks that they kept each other at a distance.

When the ambulance had come for Curtis, all their neighbors had watched curiously from behind their curtains—but no one had asked about him or come over to offer help. No one, as far as she knew, had inquired yet. Yet she was sure everyone in town knew every detail of his condition. She would bet on it.

Her mother's picture window contained a large lamp, identical in shape and size to all the others on the street, but distinguished by gold fringes on its red shade. Delores was inordinately proud of that lamp and of the red velvet furniture in her rarely used living room. Over the sofa hung her other prized possession, a painting of a red-and-black-clad toreador provoking a black bull that was decorated with tiny sparkling Christmas-tree lights.

Delores greeted her in that tone of voice that always seemed to blame Beth for whatever was wrong. "I just came from the rehab."

Nursing home, Mother, Beth thought, but did not say.

"There's been no change."

"I'm going over there, anyway," Beth said. "I might stay tonight, but don't bother to change the bed or anything."

"I wasn't planning to," her mother said with irritating serenity. "You know how to do those things. After all, I taught you."

"Yes, Mother," Beth said, already changing her mind and thinking she would go back to town tonight, even though it was late and she had stuffed a pair of clean panties and some thigh-highs in her briefcase.

They knew her at the nursing home, and waved her without any questions into the private room where her father slept in the faint light that crept in around his door, his breathing harsh and noisy. "Hi, Daddy," she said, and wiped away the drool that was trailing down his chin. "They treating you all right in here?"

He did not respond, but, during her visits, she always acted as if he might. You were supposed to question stroke victims and other comatose people, according to the articles she'd read. Stimulation was the best thing for them. "I know Mother was here today. Did Neet come, too? Sometimes they make her work extra-long shifts, Daddy. She can't come when that happens."

His breathing quickened. His next snore was louder and seemed almost like a groan.

Encouraged, she sang to him, one of the old songs he'd once amused her with:

"Hot Shot Ralston on the Delaware/and the brawla brawla suet . . ."

There was, as her mother had seemed almost pleased to tell her, no change. He had shown no response to her singing since the first time. But she kept on trying. Kept asking questions.

"What do those last three words mean, Daddy? You told me about the first part, but I never did get around to asking you about the rest. Are they just nonsense, or did they mean something once, too?"

There was no reaction, of course. No change. She thought she would turn on the light. Might as well use this time, read some of those midterm papers, she thought.

But she didn't. Instead, for an hour, she sat by her father in the dark, holding his cool, unresponsive hand, just being there with him, just breathing. Then, realizing she was getting sleepy and had to drive back, she got up to go. The bridge loomed up ahead of her, as always a terrible barrier. Someday she would figure out why it was worse when she was leaving New Jersey, not driving to it.

Her family would never know what it cost her to come home, she thought, her hands gripping the wheel with knuckles that would have been white were she pale enough. Heart thudding with terror, chest tightening, she ascended the first part of the bridge. Because she wanted to get this part of her trip over with, she pulled into the center lane to pass a pickup truck that seemed stalled in front of her, only to realize too late that she did not have enough room. A black van without lights was right on her tail and speeding. On her right, a red sports car zipped past. Horns blew. Her head tightened till it hurt.

She did not make the split-second decision to swerve sharply and get back into her own lane, where a bus was bearing down but had time to apply its brakes. The wheel seemed to turn by itself under her hands, a hard right. Her speeding car regained its proper direction just in time to keep from going off the bridge, one of her major fears, then dropped to a sedate forty-five miles per hour. The van passed her on the left, its driver yelling soundlessly and raising his middle finger. Once she would have opened her window and yelled, "Up yours, motherfucker! Put some lights on!" but not tonight. Tonight she was feeling too much awe and amazement. Her heart slowed to its normal rate. She breathed easier as she finished crossing the bridge and the cabin of the car filled unaccountably with the odor of fragrant burning pipe tobacco. Rum and Maple. Curtis's brand.

"Thank you, Daddy," she said softly. For all their faults, her family had given her two precious gifts in one twenty-four-hour span. First Della's trust, and now the miracle of being rescued by her father.

Filled with an unfamiliar peace, she went to bed and fell asleep knowing what had happened long before her phone rang at 6 A.M.

Chapter Twelve

If there was one hymn Bethesda hated, it was "Amazing Grace"—a dismal dirge written by a guilty slave trader. What did it have to do with black people, why were they calling themselves wretches who needed saving, and why, for God's sake, was the choir of Mt. Zion ME singing it at her father's funeral?

One thing she did like about her family's church was its frequent hospitality to female ministers. This year, the pastor was one Rev. Paula Taliaferro. Reverend Paula, a woman younger than Beth, did not know the subject of her eulogy, who, like his daughters, was rarely in church, but she was soothing and kind—a person Beth felt she would like to get to know. She made a note to ask if the minister was related to Harriet.

But why had all those extra ministers appeared in a grim procession like ghouls coming up from a crypt in the cellar, with long skirts swishing around their ankles and large crosses swinging on clanking chains about their necks? What was their function?

None, she decided, except to be noticed and admired. She looked at her program, most of which she had stayed up half of one night

to write. Each of the chain-rattlers was from a different church. Her
father had been a more important man in the community than she
had realized, to call all of these ghouls out of their lairs.

After the choir sang a lovely rendition of "Swing Low, Sweet
Chariot," the Masons suddenly took over the service. They descended like blackbirds, a large flock of them, about thirty in all,
formally dressed in tuxedos and Masonic aprons. All of the ministers, including Reverend Paula, disappeared into the vestry and let
the Masons hold sway. The men in tuxes and aprons spread out
around the walls of the church and took up vigilant poses six feet
apart, like the menacing Senegalese guards she had seen once at a
reading by that country's late president, the poet Léopold Sédar
Senghor.

The lead figure in the Masonic ceremony, with his top hat and
white gloves, was familiar. With a shock, she suddenly realized that
he was identical to Baron Samedi, Lord Saturday—the Devil in Hai-
tian voodoo rites. The Devil was in charge of this funeral, then. He
had come to claim her father's soul. Is this how Curtis had paid for
her toys, her clothes, her tuition, her life? Had his soul been swapped
for her comfort and freedom? Probably. No Christian minister was
seen or heard from the time the scary interlocutor began his remarks, gesturing with gloved hands, until they left the church.

Oh, this was evil. She would have no part in it. She would not be
lectured by this sinister Mr. Bones. She started to rise, to exit the
church, and felt the firm pressure of a hand on her shoulder.

"Easy, baby," Lloyd said from behind her. "Hang in there."

The moment passed. She had not known he was sitting back
there. *If we were married, he'd be sitting beside me,* she thought
with a stab of resentment. But knowing he was there helped her to
endure the terrible ceremony, the colorless singing of a black choir
using a white hymn book, the overwhelming Masonic presence, and
the awful passage of that closed box up the aisle. Beside her, Delores was stony-faced, but Neet and Della were both weeping. She

was glad to see that James was with them. Shorn of their father, her little family was pathetically short of men.

The night before, Della had been busy with her crayons—making, she said, a portrait of her grandfather to decorate his closed casket, like the sarcophagi of the Egyptians. Beth wished her mother and the funeral director had allowed it. It was a decent likeness, copied carefully from a photograph, and would have been so much better than the sad shadow in that box.

But what did this Masonic mess mean? All she knew about Curtis and Masonry was that he went to weekly meetings. Everything else he had kept secret. He had been sworn to secrecy, he said when he was asked about the organization.

For one thing, it meant that they were barred from the burial service. Once the Masons took over a funeral, even the family was excluded.

They could come back tomorrow, the funeral director said, and inspect the grave they had paid for, and decorate it with their flowers and their tears and a stone. For now, though, they were free to go home. Probably a Mason himself, he was pleasant but firm.

But what were his gangsters up to? "What are they doing with my Dad?" she asked Lloyd, who simply tightened his arm around her shoulders. "What are they doing to him?" she asked Delores, whose face was clamped so tight it seemed likely to break. Her mother shook her head. She did not know.

Later, after the few relatives, Aunt Kate and her daughter, Leslie; Uncle Terence and his wife, Aunt Gerry; and most of the friends had come and gone, the Masons arrived at the house, large confident men in expensive suits, gripping their well-dressed wives by their elbows, their aprons and tuxes put away again in some dark, secret vestry. After politely greeting the widow and her daughters with murmured condolences, they went to the kitchen, lit smokes, poured themselves drinks, and laughed softly and confidently among themselves. Beth carefully made a mental list of their names and committed it to memory. She would remember. They were men she had known as her father's friends, but she would never trust any of them again.

"Lloyd, are you a Mason?" she asked the comforting presence beside her.

He laughed. "Of course not," he said. "You know I don't have time for all that gobbledygook."

She was relieved. "Is that what it is? Gobbledygook? What's it all about? What do they do?"

"I don't know, hon. Probably like the Mystic Knights of the Sea. 'Conscience, somebody's askin' for it,' " he rumbled in imitation of Andy of *Amos 'n' Andy*. "I know they help each other out in times of need. The white ones even help the black ones."

"That may be, but I'm glad you're not one of them," she said. "I don't like them."

"Oh, I know a few of the lodge brothers," he said. "They're all right. They certainly seem to be more successful than the rest of us."

"I'll bet," she said as the lead devil, the interlocutor figure, strolled past her with an unlit cigar. "Jesus saves, but Satan pays." Spotting her, the leader came back and bowed. She nodded, acknowledging his condolences, but refused to take his offered hand. After a moment he shrugged and moved on.

"Why'd you dis him like that?" Lloyd wondered.

"I told you, I don't like the Masons." The room was crowded, and the level of talk was rising. "Come on outside with me a minute. I need some air."

The sun had set, leaving a serious chill in the early evening atmosphere. But Beth was comfortable in her new black suit with its substantial lining. She had seen it at JayMart when she took Harriet shopping, and went back and bought it yesterday, along with a crystal-pleated white blouse, after realizing that she had nothing black in her colorful closet. No wonder Cornelia, the undergraduate chair, had looked bemused when she told her the news and asked her to cancel her classes. She had been wearing her bright orange blazer with her yellow flannel pants.

Beth and Lloyd leaned against the balcony of the front porch her mother never used because it was too public. Across the street, a shade snapped down.

"Come on over. There's still plenty of chicken left!" Beth yelled to the blank window. Lloyd laughed.

"They won't come, though." She turned her back on the nosy neighbors. "They might as well be living on the moon, for all the good it does us to have them across the street. Lloyd, remember that day I first heard that Daddy was sick? Remember you told me I should go to see him right away, instead of going to work?"

"Uh-huh." He squeezed her hand.

"You were right, I should have gone. I was never able to have another conversation with him."

"That's too bad. But don't be guilt-trippin' about it, baby. Guilt is stupid. It hangs you up. Just learn a lesson from it and move on."

"I have learned my lesson," she said.

"Which is?"

"From now on, I'm going to pay attention to everything you say."

"Let's go inside, before you inspire me to some disgraceful behavior in public."

"I didn't say I'm going to do everything you say, now. I said I'm going to pay attention."

"I noticed," Lloyd said, and held the door for her.

Feeling suddenly sorry for her mother, who would be left all alone in this house now, she went to her. She found Delores in the kitchen. She could always tell how upset her mother was by the speed at which she worked. Tonight she was a dynamo—packing up salads, wrapping the ham and the turkey, washing, wiping, and counting her sterling silver forks and spoons.

"Mother, come and sit down. Let your friends do that."

"Beth, I've told you before, the only way to get something done right is to do it yourself. Sometimes it's the only way to get anything done at all. If you can't help, leave me alone. Oh, darn. Was that thirteen spoons or fourteen? Now look what you've done, interrupting my count. I have to start over."

Beth shrugged and sat down. While her mother recounted the spoons, she started counting knives.

But it was only Beth, it seemed, who had the power to distract Delores. With one half of her attention, her mother continued to count tableware without missing a beat, while with the other she shook hands and greeted folks. "Laura, thanks for coming. Take some of that potato salad, will you? We'll never eat it all. Oh, Jessie, how nice of you to come. Please take home some ham."

And when they were all gone, friends, club members, Masons, even a couple of neighbors, Delores kicked off her shoes, stretched out her short legs, and said, "Whew! Thank you, Jesus, for giving us the strength to live through this day."

"Amen," said Beth, and brought her slippers. Della, who had been watching television in the den, came in and started to brush her grandmother's hair. "Your gray hair is pretty, Gramma," she said. "Why don't you let it show?"

"I don't have gray hair, baby," Delores said, and reached up to take her hand.

"Yes, you do, Gramma."

"Shut up, Della," Neet said, and added to Beth, "Out of the mouths of babes come all the things people would rather not hear." To Delores, she said, "I'll run a tub for you."

"Bless you," her mother said.

And when their mother, who was once not very modest, had gone into the bathroom and shut the door so that no one would see her scars or her mouth without its partial plate, Neet said, "She'll make it."

"We'll all make it," said Beth, "whatever that means."

They tucked Della into the sofa bed in Curtis's den and then retired to their old room with its pink frills. Each of them stretched out on her twin bed and contemplated the pink ceiling.

"I used to call this room the Pussy," Neet said suddenly.

"Neet! Watch your mouth!" Beth said. She was thinking of Della in the room on one side of them and Delores in the other.

"Well, look at it! Pussy pink everywhere you look. Walls, curtains, bedspreads, everything pussy pink. I used to lie here and think that she regretted our being born, that maybe she wanted to shove us back up there and keep us inside. Warm and safe and confined."

"Maybe you had something there," Beth admitted. As a result of growing up in this room, she never wore pink, though she told herself it was because society had relegated the color to girls and she disliked being stereotyped.

"Sure I did. She wanted to wrap us up in pink satin and white lace. That's why I busted out into the roughest, toughest occupation I could find. A navy blue uniform, a black nightstick, and a gray .357 Magnum. It took all that to beat the dreadful Pinks."

Beth laughed and looked fondly at her kid sister. "Twerp," she said. "Pinkie's daughter, the Twerp."

"Breast-heada," Bonita responded, using the name she had coined for her sister long ago. "Bust-heada. My friends think I ought to be jealous of you, you know."

"Why?"

"You got the good hair and the good education. I got neither."

"Hair is hair," Beth said, "and you chose not to go to college."

"Not quite," Neet said. "Daddy and Mother spent all the college money on you. Daddy even had to borrow on his insurance to pay some of your school expenses. Mother had to get a loan on this house to pay for his funeral. We're supposed to help her pay it back."

Beth was shocked. Her father was an unpretentious man. He

would not have wanted his widow to borrow money on her house to pay for a grand funeral. She had probably done it to impress her club members, who were into lavish displays. "We will pay it back," Beth said. "I will." After a pause, she asked, *"Are* you jealous?"

"No," Bonita said. "You were smarter than me, so I figured there was no point in trying to be as good as you in school. They were so proud of you. So sure you were going to become a doctor."

"I didn't, though." The plan, she knew, had been for her to teach grade school and marry a doctor. Second best would have been for her to *be* a doctor. A Ph.D. in English, unmarried status, and a college-level teaching job were not what her mother had in mind for her at all. But Beth was not interested in medicine or its practitioners. Instead she had gotten dizzy over Donne, mad for Melville, besotted with Baldwin. Delores never said so, but Beth knew her mother was disappointed in her.

She rolled on her back and stared at the ceiling. This small pink room, which had been her world for almost half her life, seemed tight and confining now. She wanted to open it up, to crack its ceiling like an eggshell, and let in air.

"No, you didn't become a doctor, and no, I'm not jealous," Neet said. "I got to do everything I wanted to do, maybe because they were guilty about not sending me to college. I got to stay out late and hang out with the boys and get pregnant by the one I wanted most and marry him. Even though my marriage broke up, I love my rough-and-tumble job and my beautiful child and my nappy-headed self, and I'm not jealous of my big sis, I look up to her. Though it *would* be nice not to have to put chemicals on my hair."

Everything always came down to hair, Beth thought sadly. The one with the best hair wins. She watched Neet lie on her belly and kick her shapely tan legs while her hair never moved. "Maybe you could settle for a nice, neat Afro," she said. "Your superiors wouldn't object to that, would they?"

"Nah."

Beth was not sure whether her sister meant no, they wouldn't object, or no, she didn't want to wear a teeny-weeny Afro. She decided not to push it.

"Delores hates my hair," Neet said. "When I was little, I heard her tell one of her friends on the phone that when I was born and she saw it curled up so tight on my head, she cried. She said if we'd both had her color and her hair, she could have accomplished wonders with us, probably married us off to millionaires. She went on to say she wished she had gone ahead and taken advantage of her own opportunities, instead of having to bring up daughters who would never rise in the world."

Curtis's complexion was like maple, a rich reddish brown. Beth had always been proud, even vain, at having inherited it. She was horrified and deeply pained by her mother's remarks, but not surprised. "Delores will always be Delores," was all she said.

"Yeah, I know."

"You were an absolutely beautiful baby, you know."

"Not as beautiful as Della," Neet said.

"No baby was ever as beautiful as Della," Beth conceded.

Her kid sister rolled over in seeming contentment. She reached under her bed and pulled out a plastic bag. "They gave us this at the nursing home last week." She dumped the bag's contents on the bed.

Wallet, card case, comb, class ring, watch, change. She looked up, eyes suddenly streaming. "Is this all that's left of a person, Beth? A plastic bag with some junk in it?"

"No, Neet," Beth said confidently. She went over and hugged her sister. "No. That isn't all."

"Then where is our father?" Neet's eyes were wild. "Where is he?"

"Well, for one thing, he's in us. In you and me, and in Della."

"Yeah, I know. Sometimes she cocks her head and looks up at me in a way that reminds me so much of him, I can't believe it. I—" A sob interrupted her. "Oh, Beth, I'm going to miss him so."

"Me, too," Beth said. "He's with us, though. I know it. I'm going to tell you how I know. Turn out your light." Neet did so, shutting out the stifling pink, opening up the room to the moonlit sky.

"Now, this is just for your ears . . . just between you and me," she started, giving her narrative the familiar, formal beginning she and Neet had always used with each other. It implied that the tale to follow was a secret never to be told. Neither of them had ever betrayed the other.

Lying there in the dark, the way they had as teenagers, Beth shared her most intimate experiences, just as she had back then when she told about her adventures with boys. She described her drive across the bridge, her near-accident, her terror, her rescue, and the peace that followed. And the unmistakable aroma of their father's pipe tobacco in the car.

"Wow," Neet said when she had finished. "Promise me something, Beth."

"Sure."

"When Della's a little older, say about thirteen, promise me you'll tell her that story."

"You can tell her yourself."

"No. It happened to you. I want her to hear it from you. You will tell it just right."

"Okay, I promise."

"Good. G'night," Neet said, yawning like a sleepy little girl who had just been told a reassuring bedtime story.

Chapter Thirteen

Beth felt like a mole that had lived underground for a season and was just coming out of its tunnel as she emerged from the secure cave of home and family onto the brilliance and bustle of the campus. The crowds rushing around in bright sunshine dazzled and energized her. It was a treacherously warm day for March, and many students had taken advantage of the mild weather to come out in shorts and T-shirts. She read a few of the legible shirts. MY PARENTS WENT TO BELIZE AND ALL I GOT WAS THIS LOUSY T-SHIRT. SPERM DONORS, INC.—CALL 838-4220 FOR FREE DELIVERY. Picture of a condom: DON'T LEAVE HOME WITHOUT IT. Pictures of a Confederate flag and a fist: WHITE POWER.

Clenching her jaw, Beth grabbed a student newspaper from the stack in the hall and went into the department office to get her mail.

Eloise spoke to her. "Dr. Barnes?"

"Yes?"

"I see you picked up the *Daily Collegian*. If you ain't feeling strong this morning, you better sit down before you read page three."

Of course she dropped her briefcase and her mail on the counter and opened the paper and read it then and there. A student columnist named Owen Garwood had taken on the Gammas' charges as his personal crusade. His take on the issue was that in reacting to what he called a harmless slur, the Gamma Pi Gamma women were interfering with his personal freedom of expression. An editorial next to his column supported him, citing the sacred First Amendment.

Beth read both pieces again. What she despised about them was their underlying racism and their refusal to admit to it. Some people, the columnist stated, did not understand the United States Constitution and did not belong in places, such as academic environments, where its lofty principles were practiced.

"Bullshit," she said aloud, and looked up. The chairman was standing there with his reptilian smile. "Oh, pardon me, Dr. LaRosa," she said.

He said nothing, just continued to smile like a snake who had just eaten a large, juicy mongoose. The way he looked at her, she felt like she might be on his menu for dessert.

"The *Daily Tabloid* is worse," Eloise said, and handed it to her. In this paper, which called itself the "People Paper," and which Beth called the "Poopy Paper" because she felt its best use was cleaning up after dogs, the girls appeared in a photograph that made them look fatter, darker, and surlier than they did in person.

"Thanks," she told Eloise. "May I keep this?" Sometimes she wished she were suited for a job like Eloise's, an anonymous, low-level job that would let her disappear into the crowd rather than be noticed and made to take the heat. She suddenly felt quite conspicuous in her bright purple suit, and wished she were still wearing the black one.

"Sorry to hear about your dad," Eloise said as she brushed past her desk.

"Thanks, Eloise. I appreciate your saying that." She did. She knew better than to expect any condolences from her colleagues on the faculty.

"Student Buffaloed," the headline said. The lead paragraph began

Otto Jurgen, a freshman from Germany, found himself bewildered and hurt when some upperclass African-American girls hauled him up last month on charges of harassment. They were making noise under his window and interfering with his studying, he said Friday. He was only trying to get them to be quiet when he called them an innocent name that has no racial connotations in his native language.

The women, Dana Marshall, Cynthia Forrest, Harriet Taliaferro, and Rhonda Harris, assert that the word was a racial slur and that Jurgen violated the University's racial harassment code by using it.

"Nonsense," said Jurgen's advisor, Dr. Theodore Corrigan, professor of history. "If my advisee is found guilty of harassment, it will be a violation of his First Amendment right to freedom of speech."

The *Daily Tabloid* agrees.

"*Damn* them," Beth said, not caring who heard her curse this time. These writers were deliberately, willfully distorting the truth, turning a clear case of insult and intimidation into an issue of freedom of speech, turning the victims into the villains.

"What really makes me mad is, he's a foreigner, and they are defending his right to intimidate *Americans*," she said to no one in particular as she marched down the hall. Anatoly Kazurinsky, a visiting professor of literary criticism from Rumania, looked at her strangely as he passed. "Yes, I said that," she called after him. "You can quote me." She unlocked her office door and let the patiently waiting Dana in.

"I see you've got the papers, Professor. Have you read them?" Dana asked.

"Yes, unfortunately."

"That guy in the *Collegian*, Garwood, has been on our case all week, saying who do we think we are, we're just affirmative action admissions, we aren't even qualified to be here."

Beth seldom read the *Daily Collegian* and had not realized it was such a racist rag. "Well," she said, "he's only broadcasting his own ignorance."

"Maybe," said Rhonda, who had been just behind Dana, "but he's got a column and we don't." She was wearing a long, flowing gray jacket with a hood over matching pants. She looked like an abbess.

"It gets worse," said Dana. She mutely handed over a postcard that had been addressed to her. It was signed merely, "A Proud WASP Male," and said, "I saw your pictures in the paper yesterday. No wonder you Gamma Pi Gammas were called water buffaloes. Where is your sorority house? In a zoo?"

Beth started to ball it up and trash it, but Dana snatched the card back from her. "No, Dr. Barnes! I have to save this in case we have to back up our statement about the hostility of this environment.

"There will be more," Dana added. "Corrigan has been churning out press releases like a publicity machine. He has press conferences every morning, even though Bartlett has asked everybody involved not to speak to the press." Ross Bartlett was the Judicial Inquiry Officer, the judge who heard campus cases. "Then he goes and postpones our hearing again."

"Bartlett and Backus are afraid of demonstrations," Rhonda said. Dr. Starkey Backus was the president of the university and the author of the speech code. Beth's impression of him was that he was liberal, but too weak and wavering to back up his beliefs. "They're afraid they might turn into riots. Not that they care, it's just the negative publicity that bothers them."

"We're a national joke. They're laughing at us from coast to coast," Dana said. "They were chanting 'moo, moo' at us all the way across campus."

"They were throwing garbage at us last night. I caught some

eggshells on my sleeve," said Rhonda, making a face and looking down at her wide poet sleeves.

"People are afraid to be seen with us," Dana added. "But C. T. walked us over here, anyway." C. T. Jones, her boyfriend, was short, stocky, and self-contained. And courageous. Leaning nonchalantly against her door, he blessed Beth with one of his rare smiles.

"Hooray for C. T.," Beth said. She was glad Dana had the good sense to latch on to this smart, manly fellow. He was premed and a good catch for someone. Last year several rude Northern women had laughed at his Southern accent, and he had clammed up in class. Now he was talking again.

In his easy South Carolina drawl, C.T. said, "These people, they're just a bunch of ignorant rednecks. They don't scare me. I've dealt with rednecks all my life. If you don't back down, they will leave you alone. I paid my money, and I got a right to go anywhere they go." It was the most she'd heard him say all year.

"Good for you, C.T. Are there any more like you?"

"I know a couple, I reckon."

"Round them up, will you? We can't let these girls struggle through this all by themselves. And thanks for walking them over here today."

He smiled again, a slice of sunlight. "Pleasure."

Looking around her little office, she counted only three students—C.T. and the two regulars, Dana and Rhonda. The three musketeers. *Mouseketeers* was more like it. They were brown and young and small, even tall Rhonda—and terribly vulnerable. And there had been four of them once, not counting C.T. Where were D'Artagnan and Porthos?

"Where are Harriet and Cynthia?" she asked.

"Harriet took medical leave and went home for a little rest, Professor. She should be back next week. Cynthia dropped out of our case," Dana said.

"When did that happen?" Beth wanted to know.

"Well," Dana explained, "she's been in a mood to quit ever since she saw that letter I got from the national president. Then she got a letter from home that clinched it. Her parents told her to get off the case or get a job."

"I'm sorry," Beth said, but she was not surprised. The last time she saw Cynthia, she had been whining and complaining about having to attend so many meetings. It had amazed her that Cynthia had hung in with them for so long.

Dana shrugged. "It's no great loss, Professor. She's a spoiled baby. She can't stand the heat, and I have a feeling it's going to get pretty hot around here soon."

"Well," Beth said, "I can see I've got a lot of catching up to do. I seem to have missed a great deal while I was away."

Rhonda drew herself up to her full height of five feet ten inches. "Professor, I know I speak for all of us when I say I was very sorry to hear about your father."

It was late, but still welcome. Beth ducked her head. "Thank you. Now, if you don't mind, I have tons of work."

"Our new hearing date is next Thursday," Dana said. "We need to meet with you and prepare for it."

"Let's meet back here after class. Five o'clock, okay?"

They filed out obediently, C. T. bringing up the rear. After they left, Beth wondered what work really could be as important as advising and supporting the Gammas.

She burrowed into her books, anyway, finding Faulkner's web of words distinctly inferior to Flannery O'Connor's bluntness, a judgment any intelligent, unbiased reader would make. She felt he was afraid to speak the truth plainly in his story "The Bear," probably because he was ambivalent about slavery. Beth read rapidly, underlined, made notes. She was at least prepared for today's class, if not for the days and weeks ahead. She had just enough time to run over to the library and get a copy of the *Life* interview in which Faulkner had said he would go into the streets armed to defend the Southern way of life.

The girls' only crime, she thought as she trotted along the path to the library, was taking the university at its word and believing they would get justice. In so doing, they had taken on more than an institution; they had taken on the country's entire white establishment, it seemed, and were in danger of being crushed by its weight. She had to find a way of steering them, if not to victory, then at least to safety.

Chapter Fourteen

After reading the *Daily Tabloid*, Beth thought she had seen everything the enemy could throw at them. But the other local daily, the *Spectator*, was worse. Its editorials throbbed with sympathy for the poor persecuted white freshman. Its opinion columnists had nothing but scorn for the black girls—especially one woman who was notoriously anti-black and didn't bother to hide it.

A conservative Washington newspaper said,

> Some event like this was bound to come along that would sum up, with blazing clarity, the malignancy now residing in our universities under the banner of "multiculturalism" and speech and harassment codes, sensitivity training and the rest.

Translation: "Stop accommodating those blacks."

A *New York Times* editorial said, in part,

> The disciplinary furies of the speech police have descended on freshman Otto Jurgen . . . The racial harassment case against him reads like something from the theater of the absurd. . . .

She balled up the paper, lobbed it into her trash can, and then dug into her purse for a match with which to set the offensive paper on fire. She could not find one; she no longer carried matches since she'd stopped smoking five years ago. The way she felt today, she might start again.

All the newspaper articles and editorials mentioned the First Amendment with fierce protectiveness and a reverence usually reserved for holy writ. No wonder the published opposition to the harassment code and the Gammas was so massive. The First Amendment was the media's license to say or publish whatever they pleased.

Next, she opened the copy of the university alumni magazine that had arrived in her campus mail. The chorus of indignation at the potential curtailment of free speech on campus was so shrill and unanimous, it was almost audible. The girls were dismissed as immature or hysterical, and held up to ridicule by every correspondent. *Why so much virulent opposition?* she wondered. She put it down to white resistance to change. And also, as she had already surmised, media opposition to anything that seemed to weaken the First Amendment. Combined, these attitudes had produced a monolithic wall of resistance to the Gammas and their cause.

Beth realized that she could not go on looking up and reading everything that was written about the case. It would take up too much of her time and make her ineffective by keeping her emotions churning. Even the *Wall Street Journal* seemed to be on the white boys' side, covering its rationale, of course, in a cloak of concern for the First Amendment.

She stopped by the Black Studies office, which was always a ready source of help, to see if they had an available work-study student. She was in luck. One was sitting right in their reception area, leafing through magazines while waiting for an assignment. He was a small, skinny, intensely serious African named Patrick Mukamba and called Paget for short.

As soon as she explained the job to Paget and gave him ten dollars, he ran out to buy newspapers and magazines and to look up the back issues she had missed.

Beth went to her classroom and tried to lead a balanced discussion of the relative merits and defects of Flannery O'Connor and William Faulkner. She did not succeed. Faulkner, and that student columnist Garwood, and those other newspaper writers had combined to make her too damn mad.

The boy with the shaved head tried a stupid gambit to trip her up in her argument. "If Faulkner is such a dishonest writer, Dr. Barnes, why did he win a Nobel Prize?" He was wearing a leather jacket embossed with a Confederate flag.

"I don't know," she snapped. "I wasn't on the committee." It wasn't a good enough answer, but it would have to do. She was tired.

On second thought, she decided as she unlocked her office door, closed it behind her, and fell into her swivel chair, it was an excellent answer, if anyone took the time to think about it. Her feet hurt. She might have to trade her high heels in for some sensible shoes for everyday, she decided, rubbing her sore toes, and added "Shoes?" to the scrawled list in her purse that included "Ambi Body Wash, L'Oreal Hair Mousse, Robe for Mother, Call Rev. Paula Taliaferro (thanks for Daddy; related to Harriet?), Cartridge for Epson 740, and Look Up Wright's Poems." Fearing she did not have enough time to cover their novels, she had been thinking about comparing the poems of Richard Wright and Margaret Walker. A poet would have screamed at her shortcut strategy, but it would require less reading.

Dana was tired, too, when she showed up at a quarter past five without her sorors. "Dr. Barnes, Rhonda and I would like to postpone our meeting. We have papers to write."

Not so long ago, Beth would have approved of giving papers priority over politics. Why did it seem unacceptable now?

"You also have a battle to fight," she said.

"Can't we meet after the weekend, just the three of us?" Dana asked. "They'll probably just postpone the hearing again anyway."

Beth simply stared at her. Echoes of old, stern injunctions whispered in her ear like ghosts. Always be prepared. You've got to be prepared for *them*. *They* expect you to be prepared.

Dana said, after an uncertain pause, "Well, if they schedule a meeting on Monday, we'll just have to wing it, I guess. We're being thrown off balance by all these postponements. I guess that's their strategy. We keep trying to get ready for a hearing, and they keep changing the date. Meanwhile, we're stressed and on the verge of flunking out."

"You can't let that happen," she said to Dana. "Your enemies would like it too much."

"I know. That's why I want to ask you, Professor Barnes, will you penalize me if I'm late turning in my paper?"

Beth was silent, considering. Her policy was to take a point off for every day a paper was late. Sometimes that made a difference in a student's grade. But it got the work turned in on time, and the due date for her students' midterm papers, which she had assigned in lieu of giving an exam, had already been moved up a week because of the days she had taken off.

"I can't concentrate, Dr. Barnes. I'm in therapy with Dr. Vernon for burnout."

Beth thought for another moment. She also saw it as part of her job to discourage sloppy habits.

"Dana, I simply can't make an exception in your case and be firm with the others. You will be penalized for lateness, unless you request an Incomplete. Are you graduating?"

Dana's expression became closed off and neutral. "I hope so."

"You might have to wait till January to graduate, and make up your Incompletes over the summer."

"That's what all my other professors said, Dr. Barnes. I was hoping for a little more flexibility from you."

"Why?" Beth said, and looked at the girl over her reading glasses.

"Because—because we're on the same side." Dana looked as if she were about to cry.

Translation: "We are on the same side of the racial line. We are in this mess together, and we ought to help one another." Beth had always resisted such appeals. She did so now.

After the girl left, her shoulders shaking as if she were about to give way to a flood of tears, Beth realized that her own shoulder muscles were screaming for a healing immersion in water.

As usual, Edwina was at her counter in the chicken-wire cage in the old, nearly abandoned women's gym. She handed Beth two towels, but she did not greet her beyond a gruff, formal "Good evening," or ask her any personal questions. Beth was disappointed. She had been looking forward to sharing her concerns, or even just some banter, with the wise older woman. But Edwina stood like a statue, her rigid back and impassive face somehow making it impossible for Beth to approach her. She sensed disapproval in the older woman's posture, but could not imagine why.

Edwina's companion, Lincoln, was at his post, guarding the entrance of the gym and taking no notice of her whatsoever. What had she done to make them mad?

The water was as cold as a slap in the face, like one of Delores's angry slaps! Beth yelled at the shock when she jumped into it. It brought goose bumps to the surface of her flesh in less than a minute. She tried to adjust to it, flailing and kicking to get warm, but it remained icy.

Grumpy and defeated, she stepped out of the pool and began to rub herself vigorously with the towel. "Why didn't you tell me the water wasn't heated tonight?"

"Nobody swims in February unless they have to, except fools," was Edwina's calm, infuriating reply.

"It's March," Beth said.

"Same difference," Edwina said. "Too cold for foolishness."

Beth dried off hurriedly. She had been swimming in winter for years, and Edwina had never said anything about it before. She would probably catch cold this time, though. The water had been icy, and she had not taken her vitamins all last week.

Edwina and Lincoln both looked at her as if they thought it would serve her right.

Chapter Fifteen

Paget met her in the morning with two folders—one thick with clippings, the other one almost empty. He handed her the thick one first. "These all support the other side."

She sighed and took it from him.

"In favor of your young ladies, there is only one letter." He smiled. "But it is a good one."

"Thank you, Paget." She found it hard to intrude on his reserve and dignity, but she asked a rare personal question. "How do you stand it here in this country? You must think it is a terrible place."

The little fellow shrugged. "I think about my goals, getting an education, saving myself and my family from starvation, bringing health care to my village." He was, she had learned, from a rural section of Zaire where AIDS and hunger were rampant. Several of his relatives had died from these plagues. He bore these sorrows and others with sweetness, good manners, and grace. He added, "I don't let myself expect too much."

In this country, perhaps we do expect too much, she thought.

That means we're bound to be disappointed. "You must be lonely."

"Of course. The black American students, they look down on me. The white ones look down on all of us, Africans and black Americans alike. I keep mostly to myself. I stay in my room, reading and writing." He pointed to the thick folder. "You want me to sort those for you? Pull out any special ones?"

"The national newspapers, I think, Paget, the important ones like the *Washington Post* and the *New York Times*."

He took the folder to the corner and dropped gracefully to the floor, folding his legs under him. In his most comfortable posture, he looked like a beetle in reading glasses.

"The *Village Voice*, is that an important paper?" Paget asked.

She thought for a moment. Once the *Voice* had spoken for all artists and intellectuals, but she had the impression that it had narrowed its focus lately to an odd combination of gay news and virulent conservatism. "No," she said.

"*Rolling Stone?*"

"*Rolling Stone* is against us, too? *Rolling Stone?* My God. Yes."

"What about the *Charlotte Observer?*"

"Not so important. Let's confine ourselves right now to cities of a million or more people. I think I really need to see that favorable letter."

The angry writer addressed his letter to Otto Jurgen and "all the racist journalists at the University."

Otto Jurgen, you owe the ladies of Gamma Pi Gamma and all the rest of us civilized people an apology. Suppose you were one of the ladies whom you rudely dubbed "water buffalo," how would you feel? You have unleashed a tide of hideous retaliation against the sorority sisters, who are being portrayed as a bunch of racists because they had the audacity to be angry when someone shouted obscenities at them from the safety of a large building. Meanwhile, you are being hailed as a champion of free speech and an avenger against political correctness. Stopping noise by making more noise is a dim-witted response in the first place.

Because this is a racist environment, the ladies you insulted are being chided, slandered, and belittled, while you are hailed as a hero. Well, you are not a hero. You are a person who picks on people weaker than himself. There are many names for someone like that, and *hero* is not one of them.

"Bravo!" cried Beth, already half in love with the writer. The letter was signed, "V. Addison, Faculty." Of course. Unlike Joe Morgan and some of the others who slithered around this place, Vincent Addison was not a worm, but a man.

"Paget," she said, "go read some more publications and see if you can find me any more letters like that one."

"I will try, Miss Professor, but it will not be easy." As Paget was leaving, Beth thought she recognized a familiar back receding down the hall. There was something about the small figure's stooped shoulders, and its lingering limp, that she recognized. Besides, no one else had a burgundy puff coat quite as big as that.

"Dana!" she called. "Come here a minute, please."

The girl turned and approached her, but with dragging feet that moved more slowly than what was left of her limp could justify.

"Yes, Professor?"

"Please come in and close the door."

After Dana did as she asked, Beth said, "I've been thinking about your request, and I've decided to give you an extension on your paper." She held up a warning hand to stem the girl's effusive flow of gratitude. She had wrestled with the issue all last night. Which was more important, consistent standards or group loyalty? Loyalty had won out, with plenty of help from her guilt.

"Dana, this exception I'm making has to be strictly confidential. If I hear about it from anybody, my rule goes back into effect. Even if you end up with a grade of minus 20 on an A-plus paper."

"Thanks, Dr. Barnes," Dana said. She had come in looking depressed, but now her heart-shaped face was glowing. "If they need it, will you cut Rhonda and Harriet some slack, too? Harriet especially has a lot of work to make up."

Oh, boy, she thought. Give these children an inch, and they'll try to take a mile every time. "Let them ask me themselves," she said. "And if I catch a hint that you spoke to them about our arrangement—"

"I won't, Dr. Barnes, believe me. I'm too grateful. If you hadn't granted me an extension, I think I'd have given up. See, I don't mind the stories in the papers. I expect that from those media people. I don't even mind so much being taunted and made fun of on campus. But yesterday, the worst thing I could have imagined happened to me.

"A black man old enough to be my father came up to me on the street, a perfect stranger who'd seen my picture in the paper, and stuck his finger in my face and shook it, and said, 'You ought to be ashamed of yourself, causing all that trouble up there at that school. You're just making it bad for everybody else.'

"It made me want to cry," Dana said. "We thought we were trying to make things better." And then she did cry.

"Most people know that," Beth said, hoping it was true. "You're bound to run into a few old-timey, conservative folks who don't see it that way."

"He was a nice-looking old guy, too, Dr. Barnes, not a bum. Well dressed, the kind of man I would want for a father. Except he wasn't." The girl's tears became a torrent. With difficulty, Beth restrained herself from comforting her with a hug.

Dana always reminded Beth of her sister Neet. She was about

the same size and had the same butterscotch complexion, a face with the same heart shape, even a similar catch in her voice when she got excited. After her student had dried her eyes and left, Beth thought how Neet, all by herself, was going through much the same thing on the force, with a different emphasis, that the Gamma girls were suffering on campus.

Beth didn't know why, but men had always been drawn to her sister like bees to a flower. Maybe it was the sob in her voice, or her seeming fragility. More likely it was her high, generous butt and the way it twitched when she walked. Whatever the reason, her fellow officers wanted her. They did not, however, want a black woman as their equal on the force, especially one as sassy and demanding as Neet.

Love, if you could call it that, was very close to hate, Beth had observed. At least, lust was. Some of the cops Neet worked with had left obscene messages on her voice mail, while others who were bolder propositioned her almost daily. Rebuffed, they put up porn photos in the common room of the precinct headquarters, put nails in the tires of Neet's bright red Chevy Blazer and wrote "Good Pussy" in white paint on its rear. Neet was charging six of them with sexual harassment—all by her feisty little self.

At least there were three Gammas still fighting this particular war. Beth made four.

Beth wondered, given Dana's disturbing encounter with the older man, whether people of Dana's age viewed *all* people of Beth's generation, not just teachers, in loco parentis and expected them to act like good parents. She thought the answer, if all the parties were African Americans, might be yes. Perhaps all blacks really were members of one large extended family.

Only two students of the twelve who were enrolled showed up for her class on Political Fiction—Dana and a quiet white boy, not the skinhead. It must be the nice, unseasonably warm weather. Beth was feeling a bit of spring fever herself. She assigned some reading, dismissed them, and caught a bus downtown, having decided to spend the bonus of a free afternoon on a few important personal errands.

At the beauty supply house that carried Ambi products, the shelf where they were kept was empty. Beth was disappointed. She liked that brand of body wash not just because it was made by a black company, but because it was the only one she had found that did not smell like groceries. All of the other bath products on the market seemed to come in flavors—melon, strawberry, apple, peach, vanilla, even pomegranate. Beth did not care to go around smelling like food.

The young girl at the counter, a shorter version of Rhonda, confided that all the bottles of the product were in the back, " 'Cause we supposed to mark them up fifty cents before we put them out. But wait." She looked around for her boss. "She just went out. She probly won't be back for a couple minutes. How many can you use, ma'am?"

Beth was afraid the girl would fall as she ran to the stockroom and back on high-heeled sandals with flapping straps. Heels, straps, and all, she broke the record for the hundred-yard dash and accomplished her mission before her boss returned. She came back to the front of the store with six bottles and rang them all up at the lower price. "You might as well get them now. Next time, you'll only get five for the same money."

Beth thanked the young girl and left. There was a gourmet butcher shop around the corner, and she had a taste for rare calves' liver. Lloyd liked it, too, and he had said he might be coming by tonight.

At the butcher shop, she was waited on by a woman her age, who asked her, "You got any other shopping to do?"

"Yes," Beth told her.

The woman's voice dropped to a whisper. "I got to mark it all down fifty percent at five o'clock. You come back then. It's a sin the way these people overcharge."

"You're right about that," Beth agreed. She always felt guilty about buying meat here because it was so expensive.

"We got to help each other all we can. I'll wrap yours up and have it ready for you. You come back at five. Yes?"

Beth had not noticed the expensively dressed blonde ease into place behind her. The butcher, whose name was Margaret, addressed her brightly. "Yes ma'am, we got nice fresh calves' liver, just brought in today. How much you want?"

Margaret gave Beth a wink. Beth wanted badly to return it, but she had never been able to do tricks with her eyes, so she smiled instead.

At the department store across the street, Beth found some warm pants and sweaters she liked for 75 percent off. She had every color of blazer in her closet but basic red. Finding a red all-wool one at the same price reduction, she grabbed it and a pink velour robe for Delores; then she headed for the checkout counter. Last in line, she noticed that all the customers in front of her had newspaper coupons clutched tightly in their hands. Beth, far from taking the time to clip coupons, seldom even read the section of the paper that carried them.

It didn't matter. The sales clerk, a golden butterball of a girl, calmly removed the previous customer's coupon from her drawer and scanned it with Beth's purchases, giving her another 20 percent off.

"Thank you," Beth said. The girl smiled as she folded and wrapped Beth's things, and whispered as she handed them to her, "Reparations."

Stunned and delighted, Beth picked up her half-price meat on her way out. It felt hefty, like two pounds instead of one. She tried to approximate a wink for Margaret, but was unsuccessful. The other woman laughed at the way she screwed up her face.

At her father's funeral, her pathetically small family had made

Beth sad. Suddenly she felt warm and beloved, as if she had been received into a large one.

When she arrived at school the next day, Paget was waiting for her in the department office.

"I had one less newspaper to go through this morning, Miss Professor Barnes," he told her. "I heard that young man Garwood had an especially vicious column today, but I couldn't save it for you. Your young women and their friends stole the entire bundle of papers."

"They *what?*"

"Stole all of the daily student papers, the *Daily Collegian*s. All fourteen thousand of them. In his column, Garwood called them reverse racists and said they were uppity."

"Uppity? Oh, my God."

"Is that a bad thing to call someone, Miss Doctor?"

"Yes. It assumes that people have a place and criticizes their refusal to stay in it."

"Uppity," he repeated. "Uppity. Another American idiom to learn. I will remember it. I will try to find you a copy of that column. Also, I must go now and finish this morning's reading."

He was so earnest behind his thick glasses. Beth both felt sorry for Paget and envied him. He was lonely, but he knew his purpose in life and worked on it without distractions.

There was a knock on the door shortly after Paget left. Six students more or less fell into her office—the three Gammas, C.T., and two other young men. Behind them were another boy and a girl she did not know, adding up to a total of eight young adults who pushed in and squatted on the floor of her eight-by-ten office, filling it until there was no room to move and hardly any to breathe. Beth decided to accept this invasion calmly, though no one had asked her permission.

"Did you have fun stealing the papers?" she asked the students.

Rhonda was flushed and radiant. "It felt so good to get rid of those horrible things. They weren't fit to line the bottoms of the rat cages in the bio lab."

"That's where Garwood lives, I hear," said one of their escorts. "He's the biggest white rat they've got."

"Bigger than Bartlett or Corrigan?" Harriet asked.

"Well, maybe not," C.T. conceded.

The mood of the group was elated and self-congratulatory for at least five minutes. They were kids who had just pulled off a big stunt in defiance of their elders, and they were in a mood to celebrate.

Beth, however, felt a twinge of apprehension. "I thought you were going to talk it over with me before you undertook any direct action," she said.

"We tried to call you last night, Dr. Barnes," Dana said, "but you weren't home."

"I have the right to go out sometimes," she said. "Listen, you kids. I think, when you stole those newspapers, you broke the law."

"That's what the campus cops said," Dana said calmly. "That was no excuse to manhandle us. They roughed us up. Look." She showed the bruise on her lovely round arm.

"They cuffed us, too," Rhonda said.

"Dragged us off to their police station," Dana contributed.

"Treated us like dogs. We're going to complain about the way they roughed us up," Harriet said. Rest had brightened her eyes and put a becoming glow in her cheeks.

"We're going to do more than that," Dana said. "We're going to charge them with assault."

Soon the media would be saying that these uppity young women were bringing complaints and charges against everybody, she thought. There was no satisfying or appeasing these angry black females, they would write.

"Are you sure you want to do that?" Beth asked.

"Why not? These crackers are going to kill us all anyway." Beth looked around sharply to see who had said that. It was not Harriet, but Dana who had spoken—usually thoughtful, sensible Dana. She seemed to have picked up Harriet's angry paranoia.

"That didn't sound like you, Dana."

"Well, I said it," Dana told her. "I've just figured out what's going on. These white folks have declared war on us."

"Word," said one of the boys in agreement.

"I think that's a bit extreme," Beth said. "Stealing those papers wasn't so smart, either. What did you do with them?"

"Bagged 'em up and threw 'em in the trash," Rhonda said. "We timed it so the compactor truck would get them right away and they wouldn't be recovered."

"Did anybody see you?"

"Only one person that we know of. An old janitor named Roosevelt Walker. He says he didn't see anything." Rhonda demonstrated that, unlike Beth, she could wink.

Ah, Beth thought, another member of the extended black family who was in on the conspiracy. "Good. Nevertheless, you will probably be charged with theft as well as with First Amendment violations," Beth said. "I hope your prosecutor is also willing to be your defense attorney."

One of the boys said, "The hell with their laws. They don't respect them themselves. Ma'am, excuse me for saying that, you may be up on your book knowledge of history and all, and down with dispensing it, but, no disrespect intended, you may not be aware of what's happening here and now."

"She teaches English, not history," Rhonda corrected.

The boy shrugged as if it didn't matter.

"Well, tell me what's happening here and now. Bring me up to date," Beth said to him. "And tell me your name while you're at it."

"She means it," Dana said.

"Yeah, she's down," said Harriet.

"Darrell Minus, ma'am. I'm with Rhonda," the boy said. "This morning at two o'clock," he went on in the flat, even tone of a newscaster, "a bomb threat was received by the housemaster at Evers House. We were evacuated while a bomb squad searched the place. At four A.M. they let us back inside. Then, at six, another bomb threat came in over the phone."

"What was said?"

"The usual," Dana said. "Something about how we didn't really belong here in the first place, we belonged back in Africa or in a zoo somewhere, and how, if we were going to stir up trouble, they'd help us leave."

"How can they possibly expect us to study and turn in our work on time when our peace is disrupted every two hours?" Rhonda asked.

"I want to know how Corrigan can go on denying that this is a hostile fucking environment," Harriet said.

"Word," said one of the boys solemnly.

"That's why we got mad at the paper. They gave a whole page to Bartlett and Garwood, but they didn't even mention our bomb scare," said Dana. "Ignoring it means they approve of it."

"Did they know?"

"Oh, yes. Dr. Morgan is our housemaster. He phoned it in to their night desk right after he called Security."

This was serious. If the official campus organ condoned threats on the lives of students, the racial climate here was even worse than she'd thought. "Do all of you live in the black dorm?" she asked.

They gave assent with a chorus of yeahs.

Now she understood why so many of them had crowded into her little office. These poor, frightened children, was all Beth could think. Underneath all their bravado and their pretense at celebration, they were scared. Here, for a little while at least, was safety.

Looking at the group huddled around her feet, she thought that here was the answer to the whites' complaints about their sitting at segregated tables in the dining halls. Once, she had actually thought those complaints had merit. She had thought the complainers meant what they said about students needing multicultural experiences, instead of hiding a veiled threat: *Love us or leave.*

"It's pretty crowded in here," she said, "but you can stay for a while. Or I can call downstairs and see if there's a larger room available."

"We'll stay here," said the boy who had told her she was out of touch.

"Yeah," said one of the others. "Right here is where it's at."

One of the girls laughed nervously.

"Okay. It's not much, but it's home," Beth cracked. "Maybe campus security will increase their presence at your dorm tonight."

"That's a good one," said Harriet. "We're charging Security with assault, remember?"

"Oh," Beth said, chastised. "Well, I'm sure you all have work to do. I know I do. If you don't, I think there's a deck of cards in my bottom drawer."

The strange boy and girl actually dug out the deck and dealt hands for blackjack. The others took out books and tablets and pencils and tried to work with cramped legs folded under them and elbows jamming into each other. Beth found it hard to breathe, let alone concentrate on Doctorow's fictionalized Julius and Ethel Rosenberg story. She was about to slam the book down and cry aloud, "Why am I teaching this stuff, anyway?" when she decided it was all connected, all part of the same thing.

Dana tapped her shoulder lightly and whispered. "Can we have our meeting at your house tonight, Dr. Barnes?"

Beth hesitated.

"Of course, if you're afraid to have us there, we'll meet anywhere you say."

"Don't be silly. I was only trying to remember whether my place was clean enough for visitors. What time?"

"Seven o'clock?"

"Make it eight," Beth said. She scribbled her address in a note-book and tore the page out for Dana. The extra hour would give her enough time to straighten up the front room and put things away, though not enough to do a thorough cleaning.

Chapter Sixteen

Beth was happy to see Vincent Addison coming toward her on a campus path. It was a pleasure just to look at him. Her hip, handsome colleague walked with a jaunty stroll, and his expensive clothes hung on him just right. *Go 'head, you fine thing, you,* she thought. Step it till the sun goes down, as Sterling A. Brown once said.

"Vincent, I want to thank you for writing that lovely letter," she told him when they met.

He invited her to sit down beside him on a bench with a courtly bow and a sweeping wave of his hand. "I thought *somebody* ought to take those young ladies' side," he said. "Everybody else has been against them."

"Yes, they have," she said. "The opposition has been massive. It's like an atom bomb dropped on a street-corner fistfight."

"A sure sign that the establishment feels seriously threatened," he observed. He was brave to have written that letter, she thought, in spite of his plans to leave this place. A late April breeze lifted a few strands of his crinkled hair, which was only about half gray. Vincent was probably no more than fifty, though she had always thought of him as older, probably because of his formal manners and his double degrees in English and history.

"How are your young ladies doing?" Vincent asked.

"Those poor kids. I think they're going to lose."

She could not forget the worried faces of the girls when it came time for them to leave her house the other night. Though their boyfriends had called for them, they were obviously afraid to go back to their dorm. They were going, they said, to the library, and would probably spend the night there.

The next time the Gammas came to her house, she might let them bring sleeping bags. Better yet, she would buy some and keep them ready in her closet. It was too bad, but she would just have to put Lloyd on hold when the Gammas came.

That night their lawyer, Natalie Hinton, had not even tried to pretend optimism. With a face as grim as Plymouth Rock carved out of basalt, she had pointed out that their case, weak to begin with, had been further weakened by their escapade with the campus newspapers. She was one of those old-fashioned folk who believed in exemplary conduct for blacks who were breaking barriers—and she felt that black students, despite their increased numbers, were tearing down barriers by attending this institution.

Actually, the number of black students in the freshman class was down 50 percent compared to twenty years ago, Beth had noted from her new habit of reading *Letters*. Things were not as good as they had once been for black faculty, either. She had been blind to think that they were better off now than in the eighties. Their numbers were down by about the same percentage as black student enrollment in the current freshman class.

The girls, at first jubilant at being served sodas and store cookies in their teacher's house, had grown downcast. They kept picking at the details, trying to find hope in their remembered humiliation or in the latest letter from Judge Bartlett. Natalie did her best to make them see reality and then calmly laid out strategies to be used in the event they ever really did have a hearing.

Vincent pulled a thick corned beef sandwich out of his briefcase. "Have some?" After Beth shook her head, he bit into it and demolished it quickly. "Pardon me, but I don't have time for a restaurant," he said. "Those young ladies probably are going to lose. There's no point in kidding ourselves. The case is just being dragged out because the University is looking for a way of saving face. They have no intention of standing behind their liberal speech code. They just want to *seem* to stand by it." He washed down his sandwich with a container of chocolate milk.

"That doesn't make sense to me," Beth said. "Please explain."

Why create a policy if you don't mean to enforce it? was her question. She had always been dogged about wanting to understand things. Once she had made her poor tax accountant explain the formula for medical and dental deductions four times. She had really wanted to grasp the principle, and it had eluded her.

Vincent waved his hand irritably. Unlike her CPA, he had a low tolerance for stupidity, which, compared to his own formidable intellect, he probably found in everyone.

"Everything is public relations these days, Beth. Everybody's fronting. I used to think it was only black people who chose to live in their Cadillacs because they couldn't afford both the car and the rent. But everybody's living in the Cadillac these days, so to speak. Do you and the Gammas have a public relations person working for you?"

"No," Beth admitted.

"Well, this is only my opinion, but I think you ought to get one, or else do it yourselves. I've shown you the way. Write letters to the papers. Pass out flyers. Go on radio and television. Complain. Scream. You need to stir people up, gain sympathy for the victims."

"Why?"

Again, he seemed irritated by her obtuseness. "I told you, everything is PR these days. You may hate that fact, as do I, but it's the truth. I don't know how this thing is going to evolve, but if you win some of the public over to your side, there will be something in it for those girls. Free computers. Recommendations. Jobs. Student loans forgiven, maybe. If they make enough noise, they can probably get almost anything they want."

"Except punishment for that white boy."

"Exactly. Please don't ask me why again, Beth. You know why. This is a white institution. It is funded by rich, conservative white alumni. The school has to keep those alumni happy. Money talks, and the rest walks. How much have black alumni contributed to this school's endowment?"

She knew the answer. Precious little, if anything. There were few black alumni of the University, and fewer still with cash to spare. Of those few, most would give to African American causes out of loyalty and awareness of their people's desperation.

"I don't know, but I'd guess not much. Our folks have other priorities," she replied.

"Yes, but if blacks were big givers, I'd have a chair, and you'd have tenure, and Black Studies would have its own full-time positions." He had a point. As it was, the Black Studies program consisted only of courses taught by African American professors based in other departments.

"We can't complain to the press, Vincent. The young women have been ordered to keep quiet about the case. So far, they haven't violated that order."

"Has anybody put a gag order on you, Beth?"

"Well, I suppose, as their advisor, I am bound by it, too," she said and then gave it more thought. "Hell, no. Why should I keep quiet? That white boy's advisor calls a press conference every time his kid coughs."

"Start yelling and screaming, then. You really need to get some media attention for your side."

She admired Vincent's profile. No wonder the students called him Doctor Cool. She could go for him if it weren't for his intellectual snobbery and the stiff, old-fashioned demeanor that made him seem about two hundred years old.

"What about President Backus's speech harassment code?" she asked. "Was that just public relations, too?"

"It's beginning to look that way." Vincent wiped his well-shaped mouth with a paper napkin. "He may have intended to enforce it at the beginning, but Starkey Backus is a weak man, easily swayed. He's also a crafty politician. If his own future is at stake, he'll switch sides in a minute."

"These smug, hypocritical bastards," she said. "What gets to me is, they really believe they're right. They think they're fair-minded and reasonable. Reasonable monsters, that's what they are."

Vincent said, "Why do you think I'm leaving?"

"You? They've been messing with you, too?" Vincent was such a model of correctness, it was impossible to believe anyone could find fault with him. That impeccable accent in English and several other languages. That dark pin-striped suit. That crisp blue shirt and paisley tie. Impossible.

"You think I'm immune?" he said. "Oh, they like the package, the credentials and so forth, but they don't like the wrapper it comes in. They'll never get used to people like us, Beth. Black people who are as smart as they are, maybe smarter, challenge all of their cherished beliefs and make them uncomfortable."

What a fabulous man, she thought for the third or fourth time. If only he weren't so perfect. He made her want to put a grease spot on his collar or a wrinkle in his knife-edged trousers. Like Beth herself, he was probably a product of the "Make them perfect" school of black child-rearing. Only, in his case, no rebellion showed, there was no crack in the mold. Sometimes, while polishing their children to perfection, black middle-class parents rubbed away their souls. She turned away from contemplating Vincent's good looks. He was fine, all right, but he had no appeal for her.

Then he startled her by asking suddenly, "Did you hear the one about what they said to the black nuclear physicist at a scientific conference?"

"No, what did they say to him?"

"Now that you've given your paper on 'Thermonuclear Dynamics in Self-Contained Reactors,' Dr. Brown, would you sing us a spiritual?"

Beth was slow to catch on today. She stared at Vincent for a second and then laughed. She had not known he had a sense of humor.

"The point of that story, my dear, is that they all think like that. Always bear that in mind. Now, go crank up the PR machine. Although," he added, tamping and lighting the large pipe that went so beautifully with his profile. "I think I should be the one to get the word out, not you. I'm less vulnerable, and I'm out of here soon. Why don't you let me take over as advisor to the Gammas for the little bit of this semester that remains?"

She shook her head. "No, Vincent. It's sweet of you, and probably foolish of me, but when I make a commitment to something or someone, I like to see it through."

"You're right," he said, puffing. "It is foolish of you. Why don't you at least let me share the responsibility?"

She thought for a few minutes. She saw nothing wrong with his offer. It was kind of him, and might relieve some of the pressure on her. "I'd be glad to," she said, "as long as I'm kept informed."

"I wouldn't dream of doing anything without informing you, my dear," he said.

"I want to say again how much I appreciate that letter, Vincent," she said. "It's good to have somebody else on our side."

"But you need a more powerful ally, Beth. My time here is running out, and so is my little bit of influence," he said. "Have you got any support from standing faculty or department heads? Any high-ranking administrators who might be in your corner? How about alumni? What about the trustees?"

She shook her head. "I don't know any of those people, and I have no idea how to get to them."

"Neither do I," he admitted. Suddenly he looked lost and bewildered. Perfection had failed him, as it seemed about to fail her.

"It's okay, Vincent," she said, and patted his hand; then she squeezed it and walked away.

Chapter Seventeen

Vincent had suggested that she and the Gammas meet with the president of the University and alert the media in advance to their meeting. Beth thought it was a good idea. The press, he said, should be asked to stay for a briefing afterward.

In the week since their encounter, she had also taken his helpful advice and written three letters to the newspapers. To her surprise, two had been published—one last week in the local daily, the *Spectator*, and one in the *Daily Tabloid* just this morning. In it, she explained the difference between freedom of speech and harmful verbal abuse and attributed scurrilous motives to people who confused the two. She had tucked the clipping into her purse, ready to be copied and posted on her office door and anywhere else she could think of.

Luckily, President Backus had suggested a day when Beth did not have classes and could devote her entire time to getting ready for the meeting. She went over the points in her mind: the events of the night the girls were harassed, and then the Gammas' demands.

A swift hearing for Jurgen resulting in strict punishment—if not ex-
pulsion, probation. Enforcement of the speech code in all future
cases of harassment. Investigation of the bomb threats, apprehension of the culprits, and turning them over to the municipal police.
Since the University was not successful in policing itself, they reasoned, it needed to call in outside help.

Natalie Hinton had advised the girls to dress conservatively, and
Beth did her best to do the same, pulling on her standby navy blue
dress and adding a silver scarf at the last minute. Fortunately her nails
were without polish, because she had not had time for her usual
manicure. She even removed a couple of her largest silver rings.

Her outfit did not match the campus fashion statement of the
day, but there was no way she could have avoided clashing with it.
A sweatshirt with a picture of several robed Klan members and the
legend, BOYS IN THE HOOD, was worn by at least three young men.
Perhaps it was meant to be funny. Beth did not get the joke. She
tried not to look at it whenever she saw it coming toward her on a
campus path.

Unfortunately she could not avoid the administration building,
where about six dozen white students, half of them with their
mouths covered with masking tape, were picketing the president.
The untaped ones were chanting "Hey, hey, ho, ho, the speech code
has got to go, Starkey Backus is a water buffalo."

As she climbed the steps, she tried not to see the demonstrators.
Instead she focused her eyes on the group at the top that included
law professor Natalie Hinton, the Gammas, and their gentlemen escorts. She admired the fellows in their neat sweaters and khakis.
They looked good. From somewhere in the backs of their closets
the young women had managed to find skirts. Dana, she saw, wore
a garnet one that she appeared to have borrowed from Harriet,
who wore her old gray one. Rhonda wore a flowing navy vest and
matching skirt. Cynthia was missing.

Beth was mentally going over the points they hoped to make at the meeting when from somewhere just behind her, very close, came a hoarse male whisper.

"We know where you live."

Beth whirled. There was no one behind her or anywhere near her. The blue eyes in the young faces walking by seemed innocent. If she told anyone what she had heard, they would say she must have imagined it.

Beth felt a stab of fear. From now on, she vowed, she would make an effort to notice everything around her, whether it was pleasant or not, and she would also try to get witnesses. That way, she decided, lay her only hope of survival.

The president's secretary ushered them into a large office with yellow silk curtains that matched a golden Afghan rug of vast proportions. Beth had the impression of many rich, dark mahogany surfaces, walls of books, and at least a dozen comfortably upholstered chairs. Thousands and thousands of alumni dollars had been spent lavishly on this room. The secretary seated them around a large, dark coffee table and took their orders for coffee or tea. Another young woman brought their beverages. Then she vanished, and the president appeared, expensively casual in a soft gray tweed sports coat and navy blue flannel trousers.

President Starkey Backus was a courteous Southern gentleman with fine features, thick gray hair, and only a hint of honey in his soft speech. He was also a formidable scholar of Civil War history and, Vincent had said, a wily politician.

"I've just noticed that it's after five," he said, glancing at his watch. "Forgive me, please, for my lapse in hospitality. Will anyone join me in a cocktail?"

Beth glanced at Natalie, who shook her head very slightly. It was a trap. The school was coming down hard on student drinking lately, after two alcohol-related fraternity deaths, and faculty were supposed to set a sober example. Implied was a code of conduct: *No drinking around students, or even on campus.*

Beth could have used a drink or two just then, but she declined. Aside from the stiff new campus policy she had absorbed from reading *Letters*, she had to consider her tendency to say the wrong things when she was under the influence.

"—so I'd like to ask Dr. Barnes what she thinks about my suggestion."

It was a nightmare moment. She had let her attention wander and had missed a crucial statement by the president. She had to think quickly.

"I don't have legal training, Dr. Backus, so I'd like to refer that question to Dr. Hinton, if you don't mind." She felt cold sweat running down her sides from her armpits.

Natalie gave her a look as sharp as the razor she was rumored to carry in her bra. "I feel that nothing would be served by further delay. I think that the hearing should be held in a timely fashion, so that these issues can be resolved once and for all."

Beth jumped in. "These students have been threatened, Dr. Backus. They feel that their lives are in danger. The longer you drag this out, the more the bad feelings will escalate. On both sides."

"I'm not dragging things out. I'm on your side," the president said with a reassuring smile, the smile of a reptile. Who else smiled like that? Oh, yes. George Bush Sr., Geraldo Rivera, and her chairman, Dr. LaRosa, when he blamed the department's troubles on the administration and disclaimed his own responsibility.

"Dr. Backus," she said, "is the University investigating the bomb threats at the black residence, or not? Has anyone considered that they might be connected to the growing numbers of skinheads on campus?"

"This is the first I have heard of skinheads on campus," the president said. "Sometimes students adopt hair styles and fashions that have no particular meaning, you know. They are young and apolitical. They just want to express themselves."

Beth was almost speechless when she heard him say that. Almost, but not quite. "I can't believe you are dismissing the skinhead move- ment as a harmless fad, President Backus. It is serious and dangerous. What is being done about those bomb threats?"

"I can assure you that Security is doing everything it can to in- vestigate the threats, Dr. Barnes. Now let me move on to another issue that concerns me." He brought the tips of his fingers together for a moment and then cleared his throat.

"I can understand why you stole the campus papers last week," he said to the students. "That columnist gave you plenty of reasons for outrage. Still, it was an action that raises serious questions. Legal questions. So this is what I propose."

His visitors leaned forward with a single movement.

"I have had long talks this week with the advisors and staff of *The Daily Collegian.* They were hard to convince, but I am pleased to report that I have finally won them over. They will not charge anyone with theft or First Amendment violations if you young ladies will drop your charges against young Jurgen."

Young Jurgen, indeed. *Just a case of a boyish prank,* Beth thought. *Boys will be boys. White boys, especially, will be boys. Black boys and girls are required from birth to be men and women.*

Beth didn't even know where these angry thoughts were com- ing from. She had never had such thoughts before.

"Otto Jurgen is very young," the president went on, "and he is also very, very sorry to have offended you. He is willing to make a public apology."

"Well, that would be *something,*" said Rhonda.

"It would be nothing," Dana said decisively, rising. "What I want to know is, when are you people going to apologize for slavery? Your family did own slaves down in Georgia, didn't they, Dr. Backus?"

Her words were loud and defiant. When she stood to make the accusation, she swayed slightly. Natalie Hinton put out a hand to steady her.

You had to hand it to the president. He was cool. "I will overlook the tenor of your questions, Miss Marshall," he said. "I believe you are not entirely yourself this afternoon. While I appreciate the pressure you and your peers have been under, I hope that you can find a way of calming your nerves, though I do not recommend stealing private property as a release from tension. I am glad to know that you are in counseling with Dr. Vernon at Student Health."

Natalie rose to her feet swiftly, and the rest of them followed suit. "Thank you for your time, President Backus. Our main hope for this meeting was that a new, timely hearing date would be set and that a hearing would actually take place on that date. We are still hoping for that outcome. We will wait to hear from you or Dr. Bartlett."

"Good day," said the uncommitted president. "Thank you for coming."

"Damn you, Dana," Natalie Hinton said as soon as they were outside. Natalie was visibly upset for the first time in Beth's experience. She hadn't believed until now that the woman attorney, whose nickname was Black Ice, could feel emotion, let alone show it. "Why'd you have to jump all up in the man's face like that?"

"I'm sorry." Dana was sobbing. "I'm sorry. I was so angry, I couldn't help it. This mess has gotten on my nerves. It just seems so hopeless."

"Well, pull yourself together. It may be hopeless, but your life has to go on anyway." In a softer tone, she added, "It probably doesn't matter what you said. You heard him. He has no intention of giving us a hearing unless he's forced to."

Beth said, "I was shocked to hear him mention that she's seeing Carolyn Vernon. I thought counseling relationships were confidential."

"Nothing is confidential around here," Natalie said. "Don't you know that by now?"

Beth shook her head. She felt numb, rather than shocked by this revelation. Publicity might force the administration's hand, she thought, remembering her talk with Vincent.

"The press was supposed to be here. Where are they?" Beth asked.

Natalie pointed to the foot of the steps. "The press is down there, interviewing the demonstrators who came out in favor of free speech. Look, they're getting their pictures taken in those ridiculous gags."

As she walked to her building, Beth could feel the campus atmosphere thickening with menace. Ahead of her, four boys in boots and camouflage pants swung onto the path. All they needed was the Horst Wessel song or *"Deutschland über Alles"* to dramatize their marching.

It was a luxury to have a day on campus all to herself, without appointments or classes. She was hoping to relax, read, and take care of some minor chores in her office. Beth stopped in the outer department office to pick up her mail, and went upstairs to go through it at her leisure. There was a letter from Dr. LaRosa asking her to see him at her earliest opportunity. She decided to wait till tomorrow to make the appointment, since she was not supposed to be in today. Otherwise, her mail was fairly uninteresting. It included the usual offerings of texts and announcements of lectures, an invitation to a faculty meeting later today, and three announcements of job openings, one in California and two at black southern colleges. There were also a couple of very late midterm papers, and a piece of red paper on which were a crudely drawn Iron Cross and three swastikas.

"We know where you live" was printed beneath them in large block letters.

Terror raced through her, chilling her blood. She no longer wanted to be alone in her office. Even though she was not a voting faculty member, Beth decided to go to the meeting, which began in ten minutes. She would feel safer there. But first, trembling, she ran downstairs to ask Eloise if she had noticed anyone strange putting mail in her box.

Eloise shook her head. "Just your students. I pretty much know all of them by now."

Beth ran back to her office to get the overdue term papers she had forgotten. She planned to read and grade them tonight. She had also decided to retrieve the job announcements from the trash and keep them, just in case.

In case of what? she asked herself.

You never know, was the answer.

Inside her locked office, her telephone was ringing.

"Damn!" she said aloud. No one was supposed to know she was here today. She unlocked her door, grabbed the phone, and said, "Beth Barnes."

"We know where you live," a muffled masculine voice said.

Chapter Eighteen

Beth slipped quietly into the back row of the large library-classroom that was used for faculty meetings and found a seat beside her friend Irene Levinson. A few years back, before Beth was hired, Irene had fought and won a lonely battle to become the first woman tenured in the department. It had gone into court and taken two years, at the end of which Irene found herself assigned to a lonely post in charge of Independent Studies, which was really no responsibility at all—tenured and teaching, but virtually shunned. The chairman at the time, a dinosaur named Zimmer, had sworn to resign if she won. He had said, "We already had two tenured women. One was an alcoholic, and the other died," as if that justified his position. He resigned, and everyone breathed easier and went back to their routines as if all their problems had been solved.

Irene squeezed her hand by way of greeting. "Nice to see you," she said. LaRosa was droning on at the front of the room, saying something about the department's having too many Americanists and not enough people to teach medieval literature or the eighteenth century.

"I hope you're paying attention," Irene whispered. "He's gunning for Americanists." Today Irene was wearing a black velvet tunic with a purple velvet collar over a black wool skirt. She was known for affecting a Gothic look, complete with hoods, capes, heavy eye makeup, and dark nail polish, and enjoyed her reputation as a witch. At home, though, Beth knew, she wore flowered cotton housedresses and enjoyed cooking soups and stews for her husband and their two children. Their second daughter had been born while Irene was at home awaiting the verdict of the court. Irene credited little Thalia with saving her sanity during that time.

After the meeting, about half the faculty lingered and mingled, the junior ones sucking up to the chairman, the rest buttering up each other. Beth greeted the one or two colleagues she knew. Charles O'Donnell walked past her briskly without pausing. Cornelia, the undergraduate chair, wore a smug, hateful little smile as she focused her eyes somewhere off to the right, beyond Beth. It was as if a wall of one-way glass suddenly surrounded Beth. She could look out and see her colleagues, but they could not or would not look in and see her.

Cornelia's avoidance did not surprise Beth. That was what she expected from her. But Beth had once had a mild flirtation with Charles O'Donnell, a handsome Irishman with black hair, ocean-blue eyes, and a wild sense of humor. Their association started when she wrote him a note complimenting him on his book about class in America. It had not advanced beyond flirtation and innuendoes, but he had invited her to lunch, and she had met him more than once after that for cappuccino and conversation.

Irene, beside her, remarked as he passed, "An Americanist has to go. Guess who doesn't want it to be him."

"I can't believe it," Beth said. "He used to be so friendly."

"Believe it," Irene said. "Politics rules around here. That and money. Why should academia be any purer than a soap factory? I wish I had followed my first impulse years ago and told you how the game is played. But I thought it would harm you to be seen with me. I'm a pariah."

"So am I, I think," said Beth.

"Well," Irene said, "championing unpopular causes doesn't help. I saw your letter in the *Spectator*."

"Really? I thought no one on this faculty read anything but the *New York Times*."

"That's what they'd like you to think," her friend said. "But a lot of them carry the *Tabloid* and even the *National Enquirer* rolled up inside their *New York Review of Books*. They've read your letters, you can count on it. They've probably discussed them at a meeting of the inner circle. I'm not invited to those meetings, of course."

She took Beth's arm. "Come on up to my office. We can talk there. I think I can even give you something to drink."

In her office, which smelled of stale smoke, Irene lit a cigarette, reached into a drawer, and pulled out a bottle of Courvoisier. "Oh, goody. I forgot I had this. Yes?" Beth nodded. Irene held the bottle over a paper cup and poured, stopping when Beth nodded. "Water?" Irene indicated a bottle of Evian on her desk.

"Thanks," Beth said, and helped herself. She took a large sip of her brandy and water, and continued to drink too fast.

"I know I risk raising the ghost of the tenured woman alcoholic, but what the hell? Actually, I'd like to toast her, as well as the shade of the one who died." Irene poured a generous amount of brandy into her own cup. "There. To my predecessors, on whose shoulders I stand." The older woman leaned back and crossed her surprisingly shapely legs. "Now," she said in her husky smoker's voice, "I wish I had talked to you long ago, before you got into this mess."

Beth, surprised to hear that she was in a mess, listened closely.

"I read your letter in the *Spectator*, as I said," Irene continued. "I understand where you are coming from, and, privately, I agree, as would most of the thinking people around here. Those girls have been through hell, and they didn't deserve it, and you were right to befriend them. But it isn't smart to stick your head out when you have no protection. You haven't cultivated the right people, you're not known as a team player, and you don't have tenure, not that it helps if they really want to get rid of you."

Did they want to get rid of her? That was news to Beth. "Why would they want to get rid of me, Irene?" Beth asked.

"Because this water buffalo case upsets the alumni, who are overwhelmingly white and conservative, and they in turn upset the trustees. For every angry letter you've seen in the papers and the alumni magazine, there are a hundred more grumbling alumni out there. They are the source of our money, darling. The people who pay your salary and mine."

"I've been puzzled about something," Beth said. "The speech code was President Backus's idea, wasn't it? Why did he create it if he didn't mean it?"

"He meant it at the time, dear. Starkey always means what he says—until it is no longer advantageous to mean it. Then he changes his mind. You don't know these people like I do. They're a bunch of shits. Shits and sharks. Mixed metaphor, but you know what I mean. They didn't even want a white woman on the faculty, so how do you think they feel about you? The bunch who are in charge now are good at pretense, but they're no better than Zimmer. After my tenure fight, I learned not to trust any of them. But we were talking about you. Tell me, what have you published lately?"

"My book on Ohio writers—," Beth began.

"That was about ten years ago, wasn't it? What have you published since?"

"Nothing," Beth admitted. "I've been too busy."

"Busy at the wrong things—wrong, I mean, from the angle of your personal advancement. I've heard about your wonderful courses, male and female American writers, music and literature, political fiction, and the rest. Each of them should have been a book, or at least an article. You're not supposed to waste your new ideas on students. Get them into print. Then teach them later, if you want."

"I see," said Beth, dumbfounded.

"You know what you're known as around here? The Maid of All Work. Please believe me, dear, I didn't say that to hurt you. People really do call you that. It's because nobody else works as hard as you do, making up brilliant courses and teaching them. The others use ten-year-old lectures and get their new ideas into print before they teach them. As someone once said, students are niggers. Please forgive me for using that terrible word. It's not my phrase."

"You shouldn't repeat it, though."

"You're right. Probably I shouldn't." Irene lit another cigarette. "Forgive me. Put another way, students have no power, they are only passing through here on their way to acquiring some. When the chips are down, they can't help you. But you give them a great deal. You give too much, perhaps. I should have told you all this sooner. But I didn't want to hurt you by being seen with you. Image is everything."

Irene Levinson paused, her face showing kindly concern. "It was good for you to be seen with Charlie O'Donnell, for instance, in spite of the gossip—he's delicious, isn't he?—but not so good to spend so much time with your students. Better you had spent it in the library. As I said, image is everything. Take this getup I wear around here. It's odd, but it's comfortable. It's also vaguely literary.

The Gothic look is associated with Mary Shelley, Bram Stoker, and Edgar Allan Poe, as well as with witches and the Catholic Church. So, even though I'm not a Goth, a witch, or a Catholic, I have found it fun and profitable to affect this look. It scares people. After Zimmer keeled over with that heart attack, and people said it was because I had put a curse on him, I thought I might as well take credit for it.

"Your clothes, however, have no literary references. They suit you marvelously, and make you the envy of every female in the department, including faculty wives, which is probably not a good thing. They suggest a movie star, a pop singer, or some other entertainment celebrity, but they have no connection to literature or the academy. In other words, my dear, you are stunning, but you don't fit in."

"I never have."

"Well, if you insist on being a peacock among drab hens, don't expect the hens to like you. Sometimes I think you enjoy being defiant and standing out."

"I do, a little," Beth admitted. She wondered sometimes if her flamboyance was a way of making up for her diffidence with her colleagues. She would have to think about it. Perhaps, instead of reaching out to people, she used her appearance to get their attention.

"I hope I haven't made you unhappy."

"Not at all. I'm preoccupied with something much more upsetting."

"And that is?" Irene tipped the brandy bottle in Beth's direction.

Beth nodded, hoping the police would not pull her over tonight. She dug into her briefcase and pulled out the crude flyer. "This was in my mailbox today."

Irene read, shaking her head. Suddenly, lines and wrinkles appeared in her flawlessly made-up face, and she looked old.

"Oh, my God. This is awful. I'd heard there were some of those

Nazis around here, but this is the first evidence I've seen of it. Who have you told?"

"No one. I got it just before the meeting. Then I got an anonymous phone call saying the same thing."

"We know where you live."

"Yes."

"But you must tell someone, Beth. These are threats. I mean, the authors are probably just punk kids, but you have to take them seriously."

Beth grew impatient. "Just whom do you suggest I tell, Irene? Campus security? The Gamma women have brought charges against Security for roughing them up after they took the papers. I'm known to support the Gammas. Our chairman? He doesn't like me, I can feel it. He hated me at first sight, probably because he's from Texas. I imagine he'd like to see me strung up from the largest tree on the Green. As for the administration—Starkey Backus tried to buy the Gammas off today with a bribe."

Irene appeared to be thinking. "Do you live alone?"

"Yes."

"Then you mustn't go home. Come home with me. I have plenty of room. Thalia's away at college, you know. She's a freshman at Brown."

"That's amazing," Beth said. "I remember when she was wandering around here with a lollipop in her mouth."

Irene looked pleased that she remembered her daughter. "Well, she's in college now, so her room at home is empty. I'm told it's very comfortable."

"That's okay. Thanks, but I'll be all right."

"They have a new black woman president at Brown."

"Why bring that up, Irene?" In the past, when white folks dragged race into the conversation, as they usually did, Beth would let it slide. But today she was in no mood to take any shit, not even from a good friend. *Especially* not from a good friend.

Irene shrugged. "Just that it helped us with Thalia's decision. She could have chosen Harvard. Do you have a boyfriend?"

"Yes."

"Promise you'll call him, at least."

"I will."

Beth did not mention that she expected Lloyd to be working until 2 A.M. After she left Irene and went downstairs, she began to wonder what, really, she could do to be safe tonight. In spite of her confident assertion, she was afraid to go home. It was already quite dark. She wanted to sprint for her car, but restrained herself and walked to it with dignity, then got in and drove like hell.

Her first choice of a destination was Lloyd's house. Knowing his schedule, she expected him to be at work, but she hoped against hope that he would be home.

Lloyd was at home, as it turned out. But he was not alone. As she was gathering her things to get out of her car, he came out of his house with a blond woman who resembled Sherri's former rival at work, Anne Lawrence. She might even be the same person. Beth watched, burning with rage, as Lloyd put his arm around this woman with her golden helmet of hair and walked her to her car. As he came around to the driver's side and helped the white woman in, Beth noticed that he was wearing the red-and-blue plaid scarf she had given him for Christmas. She felt like jumping out and snatching it off his neck, but she restrained herself. Lloyd got in the blonde's car, and they drove away.

"Mother—!" she screamed inside the car, and added two more syllables and a string of other four-letter words. At the foot of the bridge to New Jersey, she pulled over. Fear of crossing the bridge, she told herself, had nothing to do with her hesitation. She didn't want to upset her newly widowed mother. Delores might ask too many questions about why she had come back so soon after her father's funeral. Then, too, her mother's house was home, but she was not really comfortable there. She and her mother had too many conflicts in values. She thought for a moment, then grabbed her cell phone, and dialed frantically. "Please be there," she prayed. "Lord, please let her be there."

Her prayer worked. Her prayers always did. Sherri answered, and when Beth said, "Fox One, this is Fox Two. I need a place to crash," she did not ask for explanations. She just said, "Come on."

Chapter Nineteen

Welcome to The Foxhole," Sherri said, opening the door of her apartment. Sherri's place was large and warm and inviting, illuminated by bright textiles and her paintings, which appeared to be landscapes but were wide swaths of abstract color.

Made up and opened, a sofa bed invited Beth with a stack of pillows and a colorful Navajo blanket. Above it stretched the yellow and orange painting that Beth always called *Sunrise*, though Sherri called it merely *Number 7*. Beside the painting was a mirror in which Beth caught a glimpse of her wild hair and rumpled clothing.

"Hi," her friend said, taking in her appearance with matter-of-fact calm. "Looks like you've had quite a day."

"I have," Beth said, and flopped onto the bed, and sighed with immense relief.

"I was just about to make tea," Sherri said. "Oh, excuse me. This is Solomon."

A long, lanky man unfolded himself from a chair in the corner and came over to shake her hand. At least six feet four inches tall, he wore plaster-stained jeans, a yellow dashiki, and a black kufi.

"Delighted," Beth said. "Sherri didn't tell me her new friend was Kareem Abdul-Jabbar."

"I have more hair than he does," Solomon said, laughing pleasantly. He removed his leather kufi to show a thick mass of mixed gray hair and then replaced it.

Beth was shocked at her own rudeness. It had been unforgivable to make a crack about his height, especially on first meeting. Her stress and fatigue were probably responsible, but still—

"I apologize," she said. "I should never have said that."

He shrugged. "I wasn't bothered by it. It takes a lot to offend me."

Sherri brought three mugs, a jar of honey, and a fragrant pot of apple-cinnamon tea, Beth's favorite. "Have you eaten?" she asked, passing out cinnamon sticks to use as stirrers.

"No." Beth suddenly realized how ravenous she was.

"I'll do the honors," said Solomon. He disappeared and came back with a plate of beans and red rice with a large piece of corn bread and red-peppered greens heaped on the side. Then he disappeared again, this time into the room that Sherri called her office, saying, "I have some reading to catch up on."

"Hope I didn't interrupt something," Beth said, nodding in his direction.

"Not at all," said Sherri. "And if you had, so what? You're my best friend. You needed a place. I have one."

Beth dived voraciously into the food on her plate, thinking that she had forgotten what a good cook Lloyd was. She grew hungry for Lloyd and his cooking even while scarfing down her friend's well-seasoned collard greens. *What a pig you are, Beth Barnes,* she told herself, and then commented, "What a nice man."

"Isn't he?" said Sherri, obviously pleased by her friend's evaluation, not that she usually considered Beth's opinions when it came to men.

"Have you overcome the problem with . . . you know?"

"We're working it out," Sherri said enigmatically. "What's been going on with you? Some sort of crisis, obviously."

"I think we've traded places, girlfriend. Now I'm the one with problems at work."

"You've been supporting the Gammas, and now you find yourself standing alone—right?"

"Right. You know, it's strange the way you and I have swapped situations. You solved your job crisis, now I have one."

"What about you and Lloyd? Is everything all right with you two? You know you're welcome here, but why aren't you at his house? Is something wrong?"

"Not exactly." Beth hesitated. "Well, there was something."

"Tell me."

"I went by his house before I came here, and saw him come out with some string-hair and get in her car. She looked like your nemesis, Miss Anne. Of course, there's probably a good explanation. I've been so busy, I haven't had time to see him in almost a month."

"Oh, no, girlfriend. We must do something about that right away." Sherri was rolling her eyes, but she was serious. "We must not let a man that good get away from us. Not when you and he are so right together. So what if you saw him with a white girl? You probably shouldn't have left him by himself so much." She plucked her phone from the end table and held it out to Beth. "Call him right now."

Beth shook her head. "I don't want to."

"Why not?"

Beth thought for so long that Sherri replaced the phone in its cradle.

"I have too many problems, Sherri," Beth said finally. "There's too

much going wrong in my life. I don't want to be a burden to him."
Lord, she thought, *what a cliché. I sound like Delores.*

"You're out of your mind. Lloyd's a good, solid man. He *wants*
you to be a burden when you have problems, so he can pick you
up and carry you. He wants to be your rescuer, your black knight in
shining armor. He also wants to marry you."

"How do you know? He hasn't asked me."

"He will. Now, tell me why you can't go home. Does someone
dangerous have a key to your place?"

Beth shuddered. "Oh, God, no. I'm not that crazy. That's the sort
of thing *you* used to do." She had been dragged into more than one
unpleasant adventure in the past by Sherri's preference for dangerous men. Once Beth had helped Sherri return some stolen jewelry
a thieving new man had stuffed into her handbag by using one of
Neet's colleagues on the force as a go-between. Another time, she
and Lloyd had rescued her best friend from the basement of a
house where one of her crazy drug-dealer boyfriends was holding
her prisoner. He had gotten high and paranoid and become convinced that his girlfriend was a DEA agent. Sherri had called an SOS
to Beth on her cell phone. She and Lloyd had to go to the coke-
head's house and pry open a basement window to get Sherri out.

Beth dug into her briefcase, rooted around, and came up with
the flyer she had found that morning. By now it was crumpled and
soiled. Sherri smoothed it out on her lap and read it.

"There's a skinhead group on campus. That Jurgen boy is one of
them," Beth explained.

Sherri looked at her soberly. All traces of amusement were gone.
"Poor Beth. I wanted you to understand about racism, how bad it
still is, how in some ways it's worse, but I didn't want you to find
out like this."

"I got an anonymous phone call, too. And a friend of mine on the
faculty hinted that my job may be in jeopardy."

"To hell with the job," her friend said. "There are plenty of jobs, but there's only one Beth. You're welcome to stay here as long as you want, you know, but if you want to move back to your mother's, I'll help you."

"I don't want to, but I may have to."

"None of us likes to move back with our parents, but sometimes that's the best choice. I think I'd like the protection of a river between me and those crazy bastards. Of course, there's also something to be said for having the protection of a man. You have several options, girlfriend. Isn't that nice? I'm sure Lloyd would be happy to put you up."

Beth shook her head. "That's too complicated right now."

"No, it isn't. *You're* too complicated. Let me get you some pillows." Sherri brought them from a hall closet, along with an extra blanket. "You need something to sleep in, too. Let me see." She disappeared into her office and engaged in a low, mumbled conversation. When she returned, she carried a V-necked cotton shirt, some towels, and a toothbrush.

Beth held up the shirt. It was extremely long. "Is this Solomon's?" she asked.

Sherri smiled and dimpled. "He doesn't need it tonight."

"I'll bet he doesn't. Good night, Fox One."

"Good night, Fox Two. Is there anything else you need?"

"Nope," Beth said. "Thanks for everything." She lay awake for a short time, smiling, thinking how much she and Sherri sounded like the young men of the present who called one another *Dog*; how, just when you thought the culture was wiped out, it proved itself to be indestructible and universal. Then she fell into an exhausted, troubled sleep.

When Beth awoke, stiff and sore from the night's tension, she saw by Sherri's wall clock that it was 5 A.M. She'd had only half of her usual sleep quotient, but she doubted she could get back to sleep that morning. Tiptoeing, she showered, put on yester-

day's funky, wrinkled clothes, made coffee, and then scribbled
a note:

> *Fox One, your hospitality was superb. Thanks for being
> here for me. Thank Solomon for me, too. Will let you
> know where I land next.*
>
>

Love,

Fox Two
>

Chapter Twenty

March was stingy with its sun, but even its thin, early gray daylight was enough to make Beth's fears evaporate. She doubted somehow that the skinheads were out marauding at dawn. She had to go home for some clean clothes, anyway. She would probably stay at her apartment from now on, no matter how many weird phone calls she got. Her health and psyche simply could not take the stress of bouncing from place to place.

After last night's anxiety and uncertainty, her familiar apartment was reassuring. Beth explored her closet, running her hands over wool and silk, enjoying the luxury of her choices. Finally she settled on a royal blue two-piece dress with black trim. That should be conservative enough, in case Dr. LaRosa wanted to see her later today. She took off the clothes she had worn last night, stuffed them into the hamper, and took a second shower. After that, she was hungry.

I don't take enough time for me, she thought as she chopped vegetables for an omelette and made toast. She resolved for the hundredth time to improve her eating habits, stop snacking on junk, buy fruit and vegetables. Also, she knew, she badly needed exercise. She would resume her swimming routine today, after class. What would they be discussing? Oh, yes, it would be a continuation of last week's examination of Faulkner's "The Bear." She dug out her notes and went over them while eating. The omelette was just right, firm on the outside, runny inside.

Licking her fingers, Beth went in her underwear to check her phone messages. The first message was from Lloyd. "Miss you, lovely," he said. There was a slight crack in his voice that caught at her heart. "Have I done something wrong? Please call. If you're not avoiding me, I'd like to take you to brunch at the Clef Club on Sunday. I'd also like to see you the night before. RSVP."

She was a lucky woman, she thought. She let the second and third messages wait while she sat down and savored the first one. Lloyd missed her. He cared. Her absence caused him pain. She had known some of these things all along, but they had never been so obvious. She would find out who that white girl was someday, if she still cared to know.

The second message was from her mother, who usually disliked talking on the phone. In her usual unemotional way, Delores said that she wished her daughter would call or visit her more often. Did Beth even care whether she was alive? She was just wondering.

Her mother's attempts to produce guilt always made Beth fractious. She played the third message.

It seemed to come from far away and to be spoken through a wad of cotton. "You have to come home sometime," the muffled voice said. "We know where you live."

Beth sucked in her breath. She put on her dress, stockings, and shoes, whirled to the closet, grabbed her bright red trench coat, flung it over her shoulders, and ran.

She was in such a hurry to get out of the building that she almost missed the dead mockingbird on the steps outside.

When had it been put there? she wondered. She would surely have noticed it if it had been there on the way in. It must have been left while she was in her apartment. She searched the street for possible culprits, but it was empty and innocent-looking in the bright March sun.

Then she saw a black car with dark-tinted windows make a U-turn and speed off in the direction of downtown. Beth was no good at recognizing makes or models of cars, but she knew this was an expensive one, the sort preferred by drug dealers. She was almost certain that the culprits were inside, hidden by those tinted windows Lloyd had told her were illegal.

Beth did not allow herself to think about the dead bird again until she was in her car with the doors locked. It was a death threat, she knew, one equally popular with the Mafia and the Klan.

On campus, Beth found a vacant parking spot and took it instead of going to her regular assigned place on the university lot, for which she paid $350 a year. She sat on a bench in the sun and prepared for class, rereading "The Bear" and her notes on it. Faulkner clearly disliked the men in "formalized regalia of hooded sheets and passwords and fiery Christian symbols" yet he thought that a card game in which a boy called Tomie's Terrell went to the winner was hilarious. She shut the book impatiently. His writing was foggy, hiding the sin of the slaveowner McCaslin, who sired a child by his own mulatto daughter. Flannery O'Connor's was direct, staring all sin, especially hypocrisy, unblinkingly in the face.

After her nearly sleepless night, the sunlight on campus was so brilliant that its glare hurt Beth's eyes. Her head hurt, too. She put on sunglasses, but they did not help. People passing her had haloes and auras. She had never seen so many twins on campus before, she thought. Then she realized that she was seeing double. Lack of sleep was the probable cause, she decided, not a stroke or anything else serious. She was oversensitive to sounds, too. Though she usually ignored the sounds of the city, horns made her jump today, and ambulance sirens seemed to pierce to the marrow of her bones.

It was still too chilly to sit outdoors. Though she was reluctant to go to her office, she rose and went to her building.

"Dr. LaRosa wants to see you, Beth," Eloise said as soon as she walked into the department office.

"When's his next available appointment?"

"He's free right now, I think. Let me ask Laverne."

Eloise talked into the phone with her hand cupped around it, as if her conversation required great secrecy, and then hung up and said, "Laverne said to send you right in."

Dr. Richard Columbus LaRosa, full professor of Victorian literature and chairman of the English department for the next five years, stood up to his full height of five feet three when she entered his large office. He was a small, balding man with little gray eyes that glittered behind his bifocals. He shook her hand and motioned her to a chair at his polished mahogany conference table. His hand felt like a moist lump of dough.

"Thank you for coming in so quickly, my dear. I felt that the sooner we had this talk, the better. How are your classes coming along? Are you enjoying them?"

"They're fine, thank you. One course is filled, and the other is overfilled." He knew that, of course. This was just the small talk, the preamble before he moved in for the kill.

"And, the young women you are, um, advising on their, er, harassment case, are they any nearer to their goal?" There was barely a hint of that tricky Faulknerian Southern syrup in his speech, but it was there, seductive as a snake, and just as dangerous.

"No," she said. She had an idea now of where this conversation was going, but she was going to make him spell it out for her.

"I see that you are also academic advisor to, let me see—Dana

Marshall and Rhonda Harris, two of our majors. Did you know that their grades have been slipping lately?"

"No, I didn't." Early on, she had tried to warn the girls about keeping up their grade point averages, but lately it had somehow seemed less important.

"As their advisor, you are supposed to know, Dr. Barnes," he chided her. "Didn't you get a note from Cornelia about them? Miss Harris is now on academic probation, with an F and an Incomplete, and Miss Marshall failed to turn in two midterm papers, jeopardizing her own academic standing. So I feel that I must ask you—" He took off his glasses, put on a brisk show of rubbing them, then looked at her with penetrating coldness. "—Dr. Barnes, do you really feel that your efforts have been in these students' best interests?"

Beth returned his stare. "Yes, I do."

"Even if, as a result of their bringing charges against another student, they face academic failure?"

"If they face academic failure, it is the result of their feeling the pressure of a hostile environment. They are seeking a remedy to reduce at least the overt expression of that hostility. A remedy, Dr. LaRosa, which was made available to them by an official policy of the University."

"Surely *you* don't believe that the University is hostile to members of minorities." Implied in that presumptuous remark was the fact that they had magnanimously allowed her, first, to attend undergraduate classes here and graduate, and then to teach. "Surely your experience here has proved otherwise."

"No, it hasn't," she said. "Let me show you something. She went into her briefcase and took out the much-folded and wrinkled piece of paper. "I received this in my campus mail. I have also received threatening phone calls here and at home."

"What did the callers say?"

" 'We know where you live,' among other things."

His eyebrows rose as if he found the message less than threatening, but he said, "This is very distressing, Dr. Barnes. I can offer you the services of our security people, if you think that might help. Of course, were you to give up pressing the young ladies' cause, these annoyances would probably stop, don't you think?"

"They are more than mere annoyances." She had been almost certain that this was where he was going.

"Perhaps." He inclined his bald head. "But things seem to be going from bad to worse where the involved students are concerned, wouldn't you say? Remember, these students are special admissions. They need to focus all their attention on their work in order to succeed. They have lost academic standing and may lose their stipends in consequence, all while waiting for a hearing that may never take place. They may even fail to graduate if they don't stop this extracurricular effort which seems to be absorbing too much of their time and energy, and probably a great deal of yours, too. Perhaps you can persuade them to drop their charges."

The bastard. Everyone was lining up against the Gammas and putting the screws on her to stop their complaints. He had called them "special admissions" students, meaning affirmative action kids who were expected to fail. "You must have access to information that isn't available to me, Dr. LaRosa. How do you know their hearing won't take place?"

"It hasn't happened yet, has it?" This little creep was smooth, almost as smooth as his landsman Backus when it came to evading issues. Now he turned on her with lethal swiftness. "I have also received word that your teaching has begun to slip from its usual high level."

She had not expected this. Not really. Stunned, she had no response.

The pompous little gnome prattled on. "Each of us has his or her own approach, of course, but when I teach, I do not dismiss classes when attendance is low. It is my habit to proceed to carry out my responsibility of teaching, whether others fulfill theirs of attending or not. I have been known to lecture to a group of one or two when only that many show up out of an enrollment of twenty. If the rest miss some important points, they will know it at exam time."

She answered, "Dr. LaRosa, I chose to dismiss my class last week because I am not comfortable teaching only two people. I may have been wrong, but in my judgment, they were better off doing extra reading."

The chairman's smile was genial but false. "Well, as I said, each of us has our own standards. I am proud to say that I have never canceled a class in my entire career."

Fuck you, you cold bastard, she thought. "Dr. LaRosa, I lost my father. Didn't Cornelia tell you?"

"Yes, well, that was regrettable, of course." What was regrettable to him? That her father had died, or that his death had obliged her to cancel a week of classes?

Those glasses should be sparkling like diamonds by now, he was polishing them so hard. "Another area in which our approaches to teaching may differ is that I encourage free discussions in my classes on matters of opinion, though, of course, I insist on the acceptance of matters of fact. For instance, whether or not William Faulkner was a bigot is a matter of opinion."

"I passed out an interview with him in which he said—"

LaRosa clamped down on her firmly. "His personal feelings had little to do with the quality and meaning of his work. Faulkner drank too much. He might have said things in an interview that he did not mean. Our job here is to study and interpret his *writing*."

A surge of anger rose in Beth. She had been told when she was hired that her classes would be unsupervised, and, simpleminded girl that she was, she had believed it.

The chairman picked up some papers and ruffled them, a sign of imminent dismissal. "Dr. Barnes, I urge you to consider abandoning your efforts to press on in a lost cause espoused by only a few students. It is taking a toll on your work. There were a few warning flags when your student evaluations came in at the end of last year, but I chose to ignore them in view of your overall high performance over the years. You have done brilliant teaching in the past, and at this moment you have my full support for retention on our faculty, but I do not know what I will recommend when the time comes to consider your reappointment."

Now, that's *a threat*, Beth thought.

"That time is soon. I called you in to explain that there are a few things you might do to help assure a positive outcome. You should prepare a long curriculum vitae that documents your credentials, your publications, and any awards you have won. Include detailed descriptions of all the courses you have taught, please. Make ten copies. The office staff will be happy to assist you. Also, you should solicit letters of recommendation from people at other institutions who are familiar with you and your work, and invite your colleagues at this one to write letters in your behalf. All letters should be addressed to me."

She rose to her feet, but remained in one spot, as if shell-shocked. He had asked her to produce full-scaled support for a tenure review, when all that was at issue was the renewal of a four-year contract. She was trying to think of people on the faculty here who would write good letters for her. There were none. Except for Irene, she had no friends. She was beginning to understand why Carolyn Vernon had insisted on meeting with the Gammas in secret.

LaRosa looked up and smiled pleasantly, like a well-fed anaconda. "Oh, should you decide to apply elsewhere, I will be happy to write you a strong letter of recommendation. Of course, we won't cross that bridge until we get to it. It goes without saying that I hope we never do get to it. Any questions?"

Just one, she thought. *Will I have time to write my will and make my funeral arrangements?* "No," she said in a barely audible whisper, and shook her head.

"Well, think about our conversation. Good luck. Be careful." He held out his hand, but she did not shake it.

The roomful of secretaries was so quiet when she came out, she wondered if they had all been listening. She decided that she didn't care.

There was trash in the hall upstairs. She kicked a box out of the way without bothering to inspect it before she opened her office door on a ringing phone.

"We know where you are," the familiar voice said. "We saw you park on the street. Why didn't you use your regular parking spot, the one you already paid for? We saw you sitting on the bench in your pretty red coat. You left your house in a hurry; did you have anything on under it? Wear the coat again tomorrow, will you? It helps us imagine what you look like without it. We definitely plan to get it off of you soon."

After being scared for days, Beth suddenly got mad. "Get a life!" she yelled into the phone, and hung up. That felt good, until she realized that she had just been threatened with rape. She called Security to report it and arranged for an escort to take her to her car after class.

It was only one o'clock. Lloyd was probably still at his house. She called him.

"Can you take off from work tonight?" she asked him after his delight subsided.

"Baby, I can take off anytime for you," he assured her. "The rest of my life, if you require it."

That made her smile. "Then meet me at the Bastille after class, please. Five o'clock. No, wait, I need some exercise. I'll have a swim at Weightman first, then swing over there by six. I really need to see you."

"Have you missed me?"

"Like coffee misses sugar, like pancakes miss syrup, like bread longs for butter."

"That sounds good, but really, you know, you didn't have to be away from me so long." He began to sing softly, " 'Corinna, Corinna, gal, where you been so long?' " He had a sweet, pleasant tenor. He was sweet and pleasant in every way, all over. Suddenly she couldn't wait to be with him.

"I've been going crazy," she said, and thought that she was telling the truth. She had to be out of her mind to have kept him at a distance for so long. She made kissing sounds into the receiver and then hung up. After class, which seemed to last forever because she could not get the usual lively discussion going, she returned to her office and saw the box she had kicked aside earlier perched squarely in front of her door. It bore a familiar design: a picture of a full-faced woman with a dark Hershey complexion, smiling invitingly above the legend, Aunt Jemima's Pancake Mix.

Above it, her published letters, which she had posted on her bulletin board, were torn and scorched brown around the edges. Someone had ripped them and set them on fire, probably with a lighter. Luckily the fire had burned out.

Waiting for Security to show up, Beth sat in her locked office and went through her mail. It included another crude flyer drawn, this time, on yellow paper and decorated, as usual, with an iron cross. Under the heading "Don't Mess With Bill," it said, "Faulkner is a god, you dumb black bitch. You will never be smart enough to appreciate him, so lay off of him."

The writer would be happy to know that her department's chairman agreed with him. She was treading on a minefield, she realized, when she dared to criticize a member of the white male literary canon at this conservative school. It was dangerous to do so, like railing against a saint while in a Roman Catholic church.

She dropped her head on her desk, suddenly tired of fighting and deeply weary of everything. It might be time to opt out of teaching and drop out of fighting for causes. The ultimate relief, of course, would be to opt out of her life.

It took a long time for her uniformed escort to finally arrive, take down her report, and drive her to her car. Beth got in, locked the doors, and drove to the old, deserted women's gym. Its entrance was dark, but she lacked even the energy to be afraid.

Edwina looked serious and troubled when she handed Beth the usual pair of towels. The water was warm tonight, warm and dark, silky, caressing. She slipped into it like a favorite gown and thought that she never wanted to leave.

She knew how to make herself heavy. She expelled all the air from her lungs. Gratefully, she pointed her hands downward and sank like a stone till they touched the bottom. Soon the water and everything else turned darker. She felt peaceful, able to rest down there, letting the weariness drain away. Then she heard Curtis say in a firm voice, "No, daughter," and she felt her father's strong hands grip her under the armpits and haul her upward. She was angry. It had been nice down there in the darkness.

Then, painfully, the world turned bright again, hurting her eyes. Her legs were still in the water, but she was lying on the cold tiles that rimmed the pool, and Lincoln was pressing rhythmically on her back, dropping down on her with all his weight, forcing her to expel great gushes of water and take in air. The old man was surprisingly strong and heavy. He must have hauled her out of the pool before he began working on her. She didn't want to breathe anymore, but he kept forcing her to take in air. Then, suddenly, she did want to breathe as she caught a glimpse of Lloyd standing behind him with a dear, tender, worried face and then moving in to take over. He knelt, straddling her, put his hands on her back beside Lincoln's, and began moving in rhythm with the old man in a strange parody of double intercourse. She giggled, then coughed up more buckets of water. Lincoln moved away, and Lloyd continued the rhythmic pressure. Then, suddenly, he got her to her feet, gasping and coughing, fluid still streaming from her nose and mouth. He threw a blanket around her and asked, "Aw, baby, what'd you want to do that for?"

Chapter Twenty-one

I went to that bar, the Bastille, and waited for you. You were late, so I got worried. I remember you said you were going to the pool at that old gym, so I walked over there. What a grungy, moldy old place," Lloyd said.

"To know it is to love it."

"Like me. The better you know me, the more you love me. Grunge and all."

"Exactly." She snuggled against his shoulder, enjoying the movement of his muscles as he drove. Lloyd had turned the heat up full blast in the car, making her sleepy. He let her sleep until they got to her house. Then he roused her. "Up! Up! No more sleep for half an hour at least, maybe longer. Then soup and brandy, then bed."

She paused at the foot of her steps. "I don't want to go up there."

"Why not?" He pulled back from her and inspected her face. "Who is this I have here? Not Bethesda the Brave, Bethesda the Ballsy. Surely not. What are you afraid of?"

"Call me Bethesda the Baby. I don't want to go up there." She threw back her shoulders, letting the blanket slip off her and reveal her wet red swimsuit. "But I will, if you promise to stay with me."

"Where'm I going?" he asked, with a flash of smile. "C'mon, let me help you upstairs."

"Those two old people must really care about me."

"Who?"

"Edwina and Lincoln, the pool attendants. The ones who dragged me out of the pool and worked on me."

"*I* dragged you out of the pool," he said, "and I worked on you till you came around. Talk about scary moments. I was praying the entire time. I didn't see anybody in there except you, on the bottom. You shouldn't go swimming in a place where you're all alone like that."

He was mistaken, she thought, but she was too tired to argue with him. She yawned.

Lloyd put her under the shower and got in with her. He soaped her back, rinsed her off, let the water run cold until she yelled, and then dried her off with her biggest towel. He made her put on a nightgown, and then a robe because she was still shivering. Then, wearing an old sweatsuit he kept in her closet, he walked and danced her around the apartment. " 'Corinna, Corinna, gal, where you been so long?' " he hummed against her ear.

"I've been running," she told him. "Bad people are after me. Can I go to sleep now?"

"Ten more minutes," he said, and turned on the radio and eased her into The Stroll. " 'Come on, baby, let's stroll around the floor. / Now come along, baby, let's stroll some more,' " he sang. "Who are these bad people?"

She told him about the Gammas and the meeting with Backus, about the bomb threats at the black dorm and the phone threats against her, about LaRosa's remarks threatening the loss of her job, about the Aunt Jemima box and the dead mockingbird and the anonymous notes and the rest of it, until he pushed her face into his shoulder gently and said, "That's enough. Let's dance."

Her father had taught her this dance: eight long, lazy steps forward to the left of your partner, then change to his right side and do eight more; then change again and stroll elegantly backward instead of forward. "Oh, my God!" she cried suddenly, and leaned back and looked up into his face.

"What's the matter?"

"I just realized how much you remind me of my father."

"That's good. Happily married women always pick men who remind them of their fathers."

"And do men always marry their mothers?"

"Usually."

"What's your mother like?"

"Stubborn. Smart. Independent. Beautiful. Hard to deal with. Like you." He spun her about and caught her in midspin. "Tell me about these bad people. Who are they?"

"They're campus skinheads. At least I think they are. Mad at me 'cause I've been helping the Gamma girls with their water buffalo case against one of them."

"Then you have to stop doing that."

"Lloyd, no! I can't stop now."

Lloyd laughed softly. "See what I mean? Stubborn. Drink this, and then you can go to sleep."

He handed her some brandy in a glass with hot water.

"Will you be here when I wake up?" she asked, sipping.

"Told you I'm not going anywhere," he said, and slipped into bed beside her.

Beth went to sleep. Later she was awakened by his hands stroking her thighs. They moved up to her stomach, stroking slowly, then her breasts, then back down again. She rolled over and turned to him, put her arms around him and exchanged a long kiss.

"Oh, Lloyd," she said, "I've missed you so much."

"When we're married," he said, taking her face in his hands, covering it with little nibbling kisses, "we'll never have to miss one another again. We'll have each other all the time. Every night. Every day. Say that's the way it will be."

"That's the way it will be."

"I almost lost you tonight. Do you know how scary that was? I'll never leave you. I won't let you leave me."

"I won't leave you," she said.

"Oh, Lord—it's been so long," Lloyd said as he entered her. "This is like coming home."

"Take me home, too, Lloyd," Beth said.

And he did, with great certainty and tenderness. They had been apart nearly a month, but they had not lost their intuitive knowledge of the right touch and the right rhythm. Their bodies still remembered each other and fit each other perfectly.

"Did I hear you propose to me just now?" she asked when she had gotten her breath back.

Lloyd turned on her small bedside lamp. "No, you heard me state a fact. We are going to be married, and that's that. Too many things can go wrong if we aren't married. Single people have far too many options, too many chances to make mistakes."

She yawned. "Sounds like you've given this a lot of thought."

"I have, indeed. That means you don't have to think about it at all."

"Don't I have the right to refuse?"

"No," he said. "This is a Mafia proposal. Nobody refuses our offers."

Her nose began to run. She sniffled. He passed her the Kleenex and said, "Blow."

"Just one question," she said when her nose was clear. "About all those options. I came by your house the other night and saw you come out with a white woman and ride off in her car."

"Was that Thursday night?"

"I think so. Yes."

He was ready with an answer. "That was the assistant station manager. She came to pick me up because my car wouldn't start."

"Why didn't you call me?"

"I tried, but you weren't in your office. You must have already left."

"What about my cell phone?"

"I forgot the number." Now he looked uncomfortable—not as if he were lying, but as if he were getting close to a lie.

"Did she bring you home after your show, too?"

"Sure," he said easily. "And called her auto club and got me a tow to her garage. Is this the third degree?"

"No," she said, turning away from the sudden closure in his face. "As my niece said to me once when I was about to spank her, I don't have papers on you."

"You could have them any time," he said quietly. "Did you spank her, anyway?"

"Of course, and I'm going to buy you your own auto-club membership for your birthday."

What a mess I must be tonight, she thought as he held another Kleenex up to her nose. *If he wants me when I look like this, he must mean it.*

"Now cover up," he ordered. "I'll turn on your electric blanket. Where's the control?"

While Lloyd was fumbling under the bed for the little dial, her phone rang. He lifted the receiver and held a finger to his lips while he listened. "Uh-huh," he said when the party at the other end had finally stopped talking. "Now tell me where you are, motherfucker, so I can come over there and tear you a new asshole. I thought so. You stinking coward. If you call here again, I'll find you and kill you." He hung up.

"That was some of your bad people," he said. "I don't think they're as bad as they think they are."

"Lloyd?" she asked, suddenly chilled, and not just by the water she'd been in. "What do I do when I'm here alone? You have to go to work sometime."

"Don't worry about it right now," he said. "Told you I'm not going to leave you alone. Get some more sleep."

In the morning, he hung around the apartment, doing laundry, playing some of her records and humming along, even taking down a book from her shelves and dipping into it. It was, she saw, *The Fire Next Time,* by James Baldwin.

"This guy was some kind of prophet, wasn't he?" he said, looking up from his reading. "He wrote this stuff just before the rebellions started in the sixties."

"Yes, he was a prophet," she agreed. "I think many writers are. I think their work opens up their minds and lets the ESP in."

"Interesting theory. What other writers would you call prophets?"

She yawned. "I can't think of any right now." For once, she had no desire for intellectual activity. It was too bad that she felt so weak and languid just when he was getting on her wavelength.

"Are they really trying to kick you out of your job?"

"I've had a stern warning." She felt too lazy at the moment to deal with that, too.

"I have a relative who might be able to help you."

She was surprised. "Who's that?"

"Senator Walter Bostwick. He's my uncle, sort of. I don't like to bother him unless something really important comes up, but if I do, he usually comes through."

Beth was impressed. She was not a political person, but even she had heard of Senator Bostwick. He was a power in state politics, a senior senator who chaired important committees. He was also a rich undertaker. "What do you mean, sort of? And how come you never mentioned him before?"

Lloyd laughed. "My proper family doesn't recognize him because he doesn't have their precious name. He accepts their foolishness and doesn't claim the relationship. But he and my father are brothers, even though they have different names, and he and I have always been tight. I'll make an appointment with him for you."

She yawned. "Next week, maybe."

"Okay. Get some more rest." She stayed in bed because she could not seem to get warm, and watched game shows on TV. He brought her a bowl of soup at noon. Late in the afternoon he rummaged in her refrigerator and brought out ingredients: garlic, tomatoes, some frozen beef, some mushrooms, and an old forgotten bottle of Chianti that had been pushed to the back.

Soon the heavenly aroma of simmering garlic filled the apartment. He was making sauce for pasta. He was also showing her, as if she had any reason for doubt, that he would make a superb husband. She just wished she could get the image of that white woman out of her mind. In time, she supposed, it would fade. Somehow she didn't want to bring the issue up again.

Lloyd turned on the oven to get her thoroughly warm when she got up. After they ate, he gave her the last piece of garlic bread, which he had grilled himself in the broiler, and the drippings in the bottom of the Chianti bottle, strained through cheesecloth to catch the dregs.

Life went on like that, safe and lazy, caressed by the increasing spring sunshine through her east windows, for three or four days. They watched reruns of old TV shows and played old albums and prepared cooperative meals, Lloyd grilling the meat, Beth fixing the vegetables, both of them washing dishes. Blessed spring break.

Just before the break began officially, though, Beth remembered that she still had a job, and called the department. She wanted her mail sent to her, and she needed a couple of phone numbers, Natalie Hinton's and Vincent's, because she couldn't find her school directory in the mess on her desk at home. Before she could make her requests, Eloise said, "Dr. Barnes? Thank God. We've been trying to reach you. You haven't been answering your phone."

After that call in the middle of the night, Lloyd had left it off the hook. "What's up?" Beth asked.

"Your work-study student, Patrick Mukamba. Did you give him a key to your office?"

"Well, yes, I did," Beth admitted. She wasn't supposed to give out a key, but she had told Paget that he could use her office to sort articles and letters for her on the days when she was not in. When she did come in, she would find them waiting for her in neat folders, with summaries and comments attached. If Paget also availed himself of her phone and her computer while he was there, she didn't mind.

"Well, someone got in there yesterday and beat him up."

"What?" Beth cried so intensely that Lloyd heard and came out of the bathroom with half his face shaved and half still lathered with shaving cream.

"He's in the hospital. I heard he was in pretty bad shape, but at least he's out of Intensive Care now. He's in room five twenty-three."

"Oh, my God," Beth moaned. "Listen. Get me Dr. Henry Butler's number."

"Yes, Dr. Barnes. One more thing. There were swastikas all over your office, some written on the wall with markers, some printed on pieces of paper and stuck up on the walls. I heard they also carved a swastika in that poor student's arm."

"Dear Lord. Poor Paget," she said aloud, and wrote down Henry's number and dialed it.

"Dr. Butler? This is Beth Barnes—"

He cut her off. "I have something for you," he said. "Are you wearing underpants?"

"Henry," she screamed into the phone, "I simply do not have time for your nonsense this morning! Somebody broke into my office and beat up my work-study student. He's over there in room five twenty-three. His name is Patrick Mukamba. Please go and take care of him."

"I'm on my way," Henry said. "But if I find that this young African has been cutting in on my time with you, I will beat him up some more."

"Thank you, Henry."

"About that present I have for you, my dear. It's hard and hot and throbbing."

"I already have one of those, Henry, thank you very much. Please go and see about Paget."

"I'm going, but with a sad mien and a broken heart. My congratulations to the lucky man, whoever he is."

Lloyd listened to her repeat the story with concern on his face. When she finished, his forehead was corrugated with worry. "That does it," he said. "No more campus activism for you."

"Lloyd, don't you see? I'm committed to this fight. I can't stop now."

That was when Lloyd told her that his post office job was no problem, his cronies there had covered for him and would continue to do so, but he had to show up at the radio station. "They're too cheap, they won't hire any backup guys," was his explanation. They were also too cheap to pay him a salary that would allow him to quit the post office, but, next to her, that radio job was the love of his life, she knew. He would have worked at the station for nothing. The trouble was that the station management knew it.

"Take me with you, Lloyd," she said. She put on a black turtle-neck and black pants. He remarked that she appeared to be hiding from someone, and that she didn't need to hide, since she would be with him. She agreed, but tied a black scarf over her hair anyway and put on dark glasses.

"I have to stop by the hospital first," she told him. Lloyd swore softly, made a U-turn, and pulled up, screeching, at the visitors' entrance. Pointing to the parking lot across the street where he would wait, he said, "You have fifteen minutes."

Beth stopped in the gift shop and bought a half dozen milk chocolate Hershey bars, Paget's favorites. She could always tell when he had been in her office from the wrappers scattered everywhere. Paget, it seemed, had not yet grasped the concept of a wastebasket.

The little fellow did not look as bad as she had feared, though there was a hideous bruise and swelling over his right eye, and a bandage around his head. There was another bandage on his arm where she presumed the swastika had been cut into his flesh.

Beth pulled up a chair and patted his hand. "How are you feeling, Paget?"

He turned his head toward her on the pillow. Now she could see that his entire forehead was grotesquely swollen.

"Oh, Miss Doctor Barnes," he said. "Thank you for coming. Please excuse the way I appear."

"I am so sorry this happened to you, Paget. It must have been dreadful," she said.

"You have some strange people in this country, I think. They came charging into your office hollering, 'White power! White power!' I ask myself, why do they do this, when whites already have all the power? Then they were knocking me around. I think they were looking for you, Miss Professor, to hurt you. I think it was better that they found me."

"I will never forgive myself," she said.

"Please," he said. "I am tough. I have survived worse." He smiled, revealing a newly chipped tooth. "They tell me I was knocked out for two hours, and that I have some broken ribs. They want to watch me for a few days, I guess to make sure I do not go out of my head and become as crazy as my attackers."

She handed him the candy bars. He immediately unwrapped

one and bit into it. She asked, "What else can I bring you? Do you want TV?"

"No TV, thanks. I would rather sleep. You might bring me the book I am studying, *The Decline of the West,* by Oswald Spengler."

She laughed. "You don't go in for light reading, do you, Paget?"

"I don't have time," he said. "I am not a young college student, as some people think. I am thirty-four years old, Miss Doctor Barnes. I have a wife and four children at home. I was going to send for them soon, but I think now I shall wait until I learn more about this strange country." He looked at her with deep-set eyes full of pain and history. "You be careful, Miss Professor. Do not go out alone, especially at night. Not even for such an important mission as visiting me."

She was surprised at his revelation. But then, it was hard to tell the age of someone so small and dark and foreign.

"I'm not alone," she said. "Someone is waiting for me."

"Good," he said. "There is no hurry for the book. Sometimes I think I can read, but then the flashes start going off behind my eyes, and I think maybe I cannot."

"You should rest," she told him. "Are they treating you all right here, Paget?"

His room was small but seemed adequate. She had seen the spare remains of a supper tray outside. He must like the food.

"Oh, yes," he said. "I saw your Dr. Butler this afternoon. He is quite a jokester, but I think he is a good doctor and has much influence in this place. He taped my ribs and arranged for me to get all the pain medicine I need, and assured me that I would not be neglected during my stay here. He also offered me the services of a plastic surgeon to smooth my face and remove this tribal mark from my arm. I said I wanted to think about all of that beautification before I agreed to it. I think it would be quite a distinction to be the only black member of the Aryan Nations."

Beth laughed. On impulse, she bent and planted a light kiss on his forehead before she said good night.

She was over her fear now, she announced to Lloyd when she got into the car. Now she was just mad. Someone innocent had been hurt just for being her associate.

"That's too bad, baby, but what can you do about it?"

"Put me on the air," she told him. "I want to be on your show tonight."

"No way," he said, but she continued to demand and insist. "People don't tune in to my show to hear about problems."

"Well, maybe they should. Maybe it's time they heard about something besides music on your show. Maybe it's time they heard about terrorism, and learned who the real terrorists are."

"What are you trying to do, straighten out the world all by yourself? It's dangerous. I won't let you." He groaned, he grumbled, he complained that she was just as stubborn and hardheaded as his mother. Worse. But in the end, he gave in.

Chapter Twenty-two

Solomon's method of dealing with nuisance callers was cooler than Lloyd's. He was extremely polite on the phone, and therefore more chilling. He would listen patiently, letting the caller spew his threats and his venom, and then say calmly, "It is clear to me that you want to die. You have choices. Would you prefer shooting, asphyxiation, or stabbing? I recommend asphyxiation. It is uncomfortable, but it is less messy and does less damage to your possessions. Our knife men tend to get sloppy, but our stranglers are extremely skillful and efficient. One must think of one's heirs, after all, and of whoever will be cleaning up after us."

Then, if the caller had not hung up, he would ask, "Does your family have a favorite undertaker? We need to know whom to call when we are finished with you." By then, the line would usually have gone dead.

In hope of tracing the calls, Lloyd had installed caller identification on her phones, but there was always newer technology to defeat the latest innovations, and the calls always came up PRIVATE or ANONYMOUS. She thought of changing her number, but it was unlisted, and her harassers had it, anyway—so, she reasoned, why bother?

Solomon and Sherri were installed in Beth's bedroom, with the bedroom phone on his side of the bed. Beth slept on her sofa bed in the living room, with that phone unjacked.

Her friends arrived every night before Lloyd left for work. The four of them would take turns preparing tasty dinners, mostly vegetarian because of Solomon. They would eat their salads and beets and pasta with much witty conversation and laughter, but there was always an underlying tension at the table. They knew the grim nature of the reason they were together, and that put a damper on their fun.

Things were also tense between her and Lloyd. For one thing, because of the crowding at her apartment, they were back to forced celibacy, except when she could meet him at his house. For another, he had come in the day after their joint broadcast and thrown an audio tape at her. It was his show of the night before.

"Listen to it," he had snarled. "Then tell me why I should not have us both committed."

She played it after he left, while Sherri and Solomon listened.

The woman on the tape sounded reasonable and coherent at first. "A young foreigner lies in the hospital today," she said, "the latest victim of the organized forces of racism at our university. There is every indication that he was attacked by the same group that insulted four black female students with the epithet 'water buffalo.' Some people say that 'water buffalo' is not an insult. Water buffalo are black animals that live in Africa and do all the work. Draw your own conclusions.

"If the phrase 'water buffalo' is not racist, what do you say about 'dumb black bitch'? That was the phrase used to address a university instructor of whom the racists do not approve. They were, it seemed, angry with her support of the insulted girls and with the content of her teaching. But they were really angry about her very presence at the university. These people do not want any black presence there at all. They are violent, they are organized, and they are growing—because they have the tacit approval of many of the people in charge. But public money helps to support this place, people! Your taxes and mine go to support institutional racism!"

Then she began to rant. That was how Beth thought of the voice as it got louder and shriller and higher in pitch, as belonging to another person, *she,* someone Beth did not want to know.

"And if 'water buffalo' is not racist, people, if 'dumb black bitch' is not racist, either, what do you say about crippling blows to the head and cuts in the shape of a swastika on the arm of a poor man who had done nothing more than work for the threatened instructor? What do you say about an institution that allows such incidents to take place? Are we in America now, people, or are we in Nazi Germany? Is there any difference?"

On and on she went, comparing student skinheads to Hitler Youth and the school administration to the Reichstag and the city to Selma, Alabama. She sounded like a woman who needed to be injected with tranquilizers and flung into a rubber room. She sounded totally deranged.

She sounded like Harriet.

No wonder Lloyd had gotten dozens of complaining phone calls and a warning from the station manager. He was supposed to be "Lloyd Bounds, the Man with the Sounds," not a community leader or a political activist.

"Whew!" Sherri said when Beth turned the tape off.

Beth was appalled at her own excesses, but she asked, "Well, did I rouse the rabble, or what?"

"You roused me," Solomon said. "Where are the evil forces, so I can go and destroy them?"

"Girl, that was over the top, even for me," Sherri said. "You sounded like the late Brother Khalid Muhammad in a dress. You sounded like you were foaming at the mouth and had smoke coming out your ears. Any minute I thought you were going to say that the little brown men in space ships were about to land and rescue us."

"Word," Solomon said, and chuckled. The rescuing brown spacemen theory was one of Elijah Muhammad's wilder fantasies, part of the mythology he had created for the Nation of Islam. She hoped Solomon was not a Muslim, because they had medieval ideas about women. She hadn't had a chance to ask Sherri about his religion.

"See, Solomon," Sherri said, "this is what happens when you shelter a person for most of her life and then shock her with reality. No wonder it's driven her crazy. The horrible thing about our alma mater is not the hostility, though, it's the coldness and indifference. I can deal with hostility; anybody can." She put up her fists and danced backward on her toes. "You don't like me, I don't like you, so come on, come on, let's have a fair one. But what do you do with a stone wall of indifference that smiles in your face and then sneaks off and does you dirt behind your back?"

"Untangle that metaphor," Beth said.

"Okay. But you know what I mean. How can you fight your enemies when you can't even find them? Beth is having a job problem, Solomon, but she doesn't know who's behind it, and she doesn't know the reason."

"I think we just heard the reason," Solomon said as his long arm snaked out to pick up the phone on the first ring.

"Psychic Hotline," he said after listening for half a minute. "You have cancer."

There were babbling sounds of protest at the other end.

"Sir, I am a psychic, and I tell you, you have cancer. I strongly recommend that you see your doctor right away."

He put the receiver down gently.

"Clever," Sherri said, and applauded. "That was really clever, Solomon. Wasn't it, Beth?"

"Very," Beth said, suddenly irritated at these constant presences in her life, even sick of their protection, though she had asked them to move in for that purpose. She went to the kitchen and started banging things. It was her turn to cook.

A couple of days later, Beth moved in with Lloyd, just in time to save her friendships from being soured by close quarters and possibly turned into enmity. Her toothbrush now sat beside Lloyd's toothbrush; her printed robe hung on the hook beside his gray velour one. It should have been cozy, but it was not. Lloyd's house howled "lonely bachelor" from every empty, echoing room. He disliked matched sets of furniture, as did she, but he had much more tolerance for empty space, and added a piece only when he found something he liked. His bedroom had a low bed. Period. One room contained only a rug and a chair. Another had shelves of tapes and CDs, a wall of stereo equipment, and only two brown floor cushions for comfort. She yearned to add curtains, pictures, pillows, and lamps, but she knew too many women who had decorated men's houses only to break up with them.

"You know," she said to him, "if you had to move, you could put all your stuff in one small truck and have space left over."

"That's good, isn't it?" he said with a grin.

"I suppose so." Sitting in one of his two leather and chrome living room chairs, Beth looked across the room at his only calendar, which was illustrated with African animals, zebras for April. Spring break was almost over. She had to teach again in two days, but she didn't feel like preparing for class. She was completely lacking motivation. It didn't help that she had been threatened with the loss of her job.

"Did you call your uncle for me?" she asked Lloyd.

"I'll do it now," he said.

"Please."

After a ten-minute absence, he came back and said "Senator Bostwick is very busy, but he will see you on Friday at three. He'll be at his funeral home."

"Thanks," she said with a sigh. She still had no interest in getting ready for her classes. At least, she thought, she could organize her briefcase.

She knew it was messy, but she hadn't known how badly it needed organizing. Notes and books and papers, including some from the previous term, were jammed into it without any order. Working her way through them, she found plenty to toss into the trash. She also found the job announcements from Yale and Berkeley and from the historically black colleges in North Carolina and Texas.

"I've got to go and get some things from my apartment," she said to Lloyd.

He looked at her. "Want me to go with you?"

She shook her head. She was tired of needing as much baby-sitting as a child under ten.

"Well, be careful."

"Of course."

This back-and-forth living arrangement was not going to work for long, Beth thought as she climbed the stairs and unlocked her apartment door. She felt safe at Lloyd's and happy to be with him, but her life was still here—her clothes, her books, her notes, her computer. At Lloyd's, she was always missing something she needed and making a note to pick it up: her hairbrush, some earrings, her old address book, her favorite pen. A man who lived as simply as Lloyd would not understand, but these things were important to Beth. She needed to be able to see and select from all her stuff. Almost at random, she grabbed some hair bows, some stockings, a couple of scarves, and some texts to stuff into her near-empty briefcase. Then she sat down at her table and turned on her computer.

After a moment's thought, she printed out a cover letter and two one-page resumes to be sent to the two Southern colleges and then tossed the notices from the elite schools into the trash.

Then she set to work on the long curriculum vitae Dr. LaRosa had requested. One page for her background and training. Another for her employment history. A third for her publications and honors— fewer, as Irene had said, than they should be at this stage of the game. On the same page, her volunteer work as a tutor at her church and as guest editor of a literary magazine. There was plenty of white space on that page, but her professional history was still respectable.

Last came her courses, each described in detail, one to a page. She printed up three copies of the twelve-page CV and put one in her briefcase to be copied for the committee, and one in each of the envelopes that were addressed to the Southern schools.

Chapter Twenty-three

The undertaker's establishment was a maze, a series of underground rooms and long passages with dim lighting overhead and red lights over interior doors. To get to his office, Beth had to pass through a set of garage doors and a vast main room that was a sort of receiving area. As she entered, a gray hearse pulled up beside her and she heard the driver's amplified voice. "I've got Maceo Walker from Old York Road, boss," it said. "Where shall I put him?"

"See if Prep Room Three is empty," a voice boomed back. "If someone's in there, take them out and put them in the cooler. Maceo Walker has A-priority. And for God's sake, Gordon, tag them both. We're still trying to live down that last mixup."

As her eyes adjusted to the cool dimness, she saw that she was stumbling past a number of very quiet people lying side by side on gurneys that were parked like cars on a lot. She brooded on how the great and the humble found themselves equal at this, their last stop. But maybe not; maybe that was just a bookish sentiment. People who lived too much in books were always misjudging reality, she often thought. The voice had said that someone had A-priority. Perhaps, even in death, some people were more important than others.

She found her way to a corridor and opened several wrong doors, each leading to a room in which someone lay very still on a wheeled cot. The sweet, tinny sounds of Muzak accompanied her on her journey down this maze of blind alleys.

Finally, a door opened at the end of a corridor, and a small, beige-skinned man waved her into his office. He had a sweet face like a Kewpie doll's and a soft, cultivated Southern voice. "Come in, Dr. Barnes," he said. "Have you been getting an accidental tour of our operation?"

"Yes, Senator," she admitted. "It's impressive."

"Someone should have met you when you arrived and brought you here to my office," he said, frowning and showing her to a seat. "I don't like it when visitors get lost and have to stumble around. I'd rather give you a guided tour, if I may. I like to show off our premises to people who aren't in immediate need of our services. That way, our visitors don't feel any pressure, but when the time of need comes, they may think of us. May I show you around?"

Beth hesitated. The last thing she wanted or needed today was a tour of a funeral home. But she was about to ask a great favor of this man, and he seemed very proud of his business and eager to show it off. She nodded.

"We are professionals. We take great pride in our work," Senator Bostwick said as he knocked on one of the doors she had passed. A scorched odor came from the room. The door was opened by a woman who had been curling a dead woman's hair.

"This is Miss Bessie Akers, our hairdresser and cosmetician, Dr. Barnes. Have you finished the makeup on this client, Miss Akers?"

"No," the hairdresser said. "I like to do the hair first."

"Bessie is a genius," the senator said. "Sometimes she's able to work with a person's actual hair, but often our clients require wigs.

She can match any color and texture of hair within a fraction of a shade from her wig collection."

Bessie silently flung open a closet door and revealed several shelves of wigs on stands.

Unconsciously, Beth raised her hand to her own hair, which was piled abundantly on her head. The Undertaker chuckled softly. "Don't worry, young lady, no one is thinking of making any changes in your hair. It's perfect."

Was he flirting with her? In this dreadful setting? Beth hoped not.

"May we watch you do this lady's makeup, Bessie?"

"I guess so," Bessie said. She put down her curling irons and selected a jar from a row of cosmetics. "Her skin has a few red blotches, so I will even them out with this yellow concealer and use a bronze foundation."

Beth watched with horrified fascination as the woman's skin became smoother and more even and her lips were tinted a bright red.

"The families are happier when their loved one has a lifelike appearance," the undertaker said as Bessie applied mascara to the lashes on the closed eyes.

Beth thought there was nothing lifelike about the form on the table, but she said nothing.

"Bessie's been with us for an eternity. What is it, Bessie, fifteen years?" the Undertaker said.

"Twenty."

"She must like her job," Beth commented.

"I don't have to listen to any complaints," the woman said.

The undertaker laughed. "I will spare you a visit to our preparation rooms. They are very modern and hygienic, but they make some people squeamish." He knocked on another door. It opened, and the pungent odor of formaldehyde rushed out and almost knocked her down. A tall, thin man who was dressed like a surgeon stood up from behind his desk.

"This is Mr. Saint," the senator said. "He's the best embalmer in the business."

Mr. Saint merely bowed when they were introduced. He did not say a word from behind his surgical mask, nor did he extend one of his rubber-gloved hands. Beth, thoroughly frightened and repelled, did not offer her hand, either.

"Now let me show you our slumber rooms." There were four of them, each with collegiate names. Each had patterned wallpaper, plush carpets, and rows of gilt chairs with seats upholstered to match. The Howard Room was white with blue accents, the Hampton Room was all blue, and the Morehouse Room was maroon. In the Tuskegee Room, where the carpet was red and the draperies gold, a woman lay in state in a long lavender lace gown, an orchid in her hand.

"Isn't she beautiful?" the undertaker asked.

Beth, who did not think a corpse could ever be beautiful, murmured something noncommittal and observed, "I see you're a fan of the black colleges."

"Absolutely," he said, his voice louder and stronger. It was, after all, the booming voice she had heard over the intercom. "They've educated some of our best people. I went to Morehouse, myself. Splendid school."

An organ at the back of the room began to play softly. "Some establishments use taped organ music. I'm proud to say we have a real organ in every slumber room. We only use tapes when our organist is absent." He nodded to an attendant in a black suit and then led the way out of the Tuskegee Room.

"Her viewing is about to begin. Come, let's return to my office."

A tea tray had materialized on his desk. He poured tea for them both into elegant porcelain cups. "Ah," he said, after a sip. "Tea time is one of the few British customs I like. Otherwise, they are barbaric people, no matter how civilized we Americans think they are."

"You've been to England?"

"Several times. The most prejudiced place I've ever seen."

Most of Beth's colleagues were crazy about England. It was another reason why she would never fit in.

The senator looked at her intently over his cup. "Dr. Barnes, my nephew told me about your background and your situation. I feel it's too bad that a talent like yours cannot be utilized at one of our black schools, to inspire and uplift our young people. But they can't afford you, of course."

"Maybe they will be able to soon," Beth said. "Something is always better than nothing."

"Do you anticipate a problem?" he asked.

"I've been warned," she said.

"That's a terrible, prejudiced place where you work, Dr. Barnes. I understand that you have just found out how bad it is. They are in my district, you know. I do what I can, but sometimes I despair of teaching them to be tolerant. Let me tell you a little story."

He folded his hands. "I wonder," he said, "if you have noticed the service employees at the university. The cleaners, the janitors, the maintenance people and so forth. They are mostly African American."

Beth nodded. She felt guilty that she had never really gotten to know any of the support staff, merely spoke when she noticed them and went on about her business.

"A lot of those people work there for only one reason, Dr. Barnes. They want the educational benefits. Year after year, they slave at those wretched jobs because they will have free tuition for their children. You know how we have always believed in education as a way out for our youth. It's almost a second religion with black folks."

She nodded her understanding.

"But, Dr. Barnes, those little people almost lost their jobs a couple of years ago, and with them all hopes of higher education for their children. The Mafia moved in and attempted to replace them with one of their unions. I am proud to say that we nipped that takeover in the bud."

"Did you sue?"

He smiled slightly. "We didn't have to, young lady. We chair the appropriations committee that votes on a hefty portion of the University's budget. About half a billion dollars."

We meant *him.* Beth was bowled over. He was—well, so old. And so small. Yet this little man was a giant, a superpower in the state. And he was a fighter.

"I'm proud to know you," she said. "And I feel privileged to have heard that story."

He inclined his shiny head. "I am proud to have met you too, Dr. Barnes."

"Please call me Beth."

"Well then, Beth, if you find that you really have a problem, just call us. We don't like to get out our big guns until the other side fires its artillery, but in that event, we will put in a call to your provost. When he finds out that he is not going to get his money on time, that should put an end to your problem.

"In the meantime," he cautioned, "don't mention this visit around your place of employment. It wouldn't win you any popularity contests there, I suspect."

"Do you always work behind the scenes?"

"It makes me more effective, I've found. In some quarters I am known as the Shadow Senator."

" 'Who knows what evil lurks in the hearts of men?' " she quoted from the introduction of a popular old radio show.

" 'De Shadow knows,' " he said, completing the quotation.

They shook hands, laughing. She stumbled out of the undertaker's subterranean territory into the light, weaving her way between the rows of parked bodies.

Beth had never thought much about death. She had especially

not thought about the procedures surrounding the end of a life, the embalming, the decorating, the dressing, all the expense and industry devoted to preparing a corpse for its final public appearance. It might make the survivors feel better, she supposed. At least the final viewing would make them know for sure that so-and-so was gone for good, give them closure, let them begin the healing process. But she thought the show was more repulsive than dying itself. Death was necessary, if only to relieve the overcrowding of the earth. Funerals were not.

Still, somebody had to do the undertaker's job. Black people were Africans, after all, and Africans thought that a funeral was the most important event in a person's life. It commemorated and celebrated the time when they entered the spirit world and rejoined the ancestors. And the money he made from his occupation had put the Undertaker in a position to help many of his people.

Gratefully, she had taken his private telephone number and put it in her purse. Just having it gave her a wonderful new sense of security.

At her place, too, she felt safer as her visits to collect texts and clothes lengthened, and she began to work there undisturbed for longer hours. Emboldened, she told Lloyd she was moving back to her apartment. She needed, she said, to be there to work. By now the understanding between them was so deep he needed no other explanation.

"I'll move back there with you for a while," he said quickly. "You mustn't be alone."

At night, after he left for the station, she would turn her radio on just to hear his reassuring voice and go to sleep with a chain lock on the door and a pistol he had brought for her under her pillow. The chain lock had some slack and opened with a key. He had one, of course. She hadn't wanted the gun, but after he showed her how to use it and took her out for target practice, she felt safer having it handy.

One night she was having a nightmare, which happened frequently now. In this one she was fleeing in her car, but pursuing men on motorcycles were gaining on her. She could hear the roar and whine of their engines and see the white glare of their headlights behind her. All of the riders were faceless. Two motorcycles flanked her, keeping pace with her on each side, while another moved in front of her, making a formation like a diplomatic escort. The rider in front swerved and was about to cut her off when the phone rang.

Beth sat up in bed with a jolt and fired her gun at the moving shape in the mirror, which turned out to be herself. The mirror shattered in a hundred pieces. She picked up the phone and growled, "Yes?"

"Hey, Bust-head," a soft voice said. "It's me. Your sister."

"Hey yourself, Twerp. How ya doin'?"

She tried to sound normal for Bonita, even though she was shaking both inside and out at the damage she had just done.

"Oh, nothin' to it. Just checkin' on you. Thought it was time we had one of our heart-to-hearts. You sound funny. Is something wrong?"

She couldn't fool Neet. They were too close, too tuned in to one another. "Something unusual happened just now, yes. I'll tell you about it some other time. We'll have a good laugh."

Neet let that one pass, thank goodness. "I called you a week ago, and some gruff-voiced man answered. It wasn't Lloyd. Have you changed up on me?"

"No, that was just a friend of a friend."

"Well, he didn't sound very friendly. I hung up. You sure have been hard to catch lately. Still chasing buffalo?"

"Yes. Still suing sexists?"

"Oh, I've moved on to bigger things. There's a corruption probe coming down from on high. I'm cooperating."

"Neet! Are you crazy?"

"No crazier than you. You inspire me, big sis. Besides, I'm sick of my precinct captain. I'm sick of the way he puts his hat upside down on his desk every night, expecting us all to put something in it when we come in. Even sicker of seeing the brothers get profiled just 'cause they have nice cars and watching them get beat up if they object.

"The last time that happened, we were out on 295, and my partner started chasing a brother in a nice Saab 900. No reason, no speeding or anything, just mad cause he had that expensive car. When he finally pulled the brother over, my partner said, 'Watch me teach this smart coon a lesson.' He must have forgot who was riding with him. By the time I got that gorilla off his victim, Brotherman was bleeding from the head and in no shape to drive. I called an ambulance for him and insisted on waiting till it came. My partner said something smart like, 'Just take him home with you, why don't you?' And I pulled my gun on him. Held it on him, too, till we got back to the precinct. Next day, I told the Justice Department investigators, 'Here I am, I'm your girl.' "

"Neet, you scare me. It even scares me to hear you talk about this on the phone."

"Why do you think I called you this late? I know our wiretap people and their habits. They knock off at twelve."

"Twerp. Bonita. Baby girl. What can I say to make you stop getting all up in those people's faces, and just do your job?"

"Nothing."

Bethesda, knowing she was licked, let a big sigh escape her. "How's Della?"

"She's great. She adores you. That's why, if something happens to me, I want you to take her. Delores might give you a fight, but I've got it all written down, and there's a copy in my lawyer's office. Frank Jerome is his name."

Beth remembered Frank. He had been one of the smartest people in her high school class, and also, memorably, one of the ugliest.

"Della needs *you*, not me, Neet. You ought to think about that before you go jumping bad on the job and blowing whistles."

"This is just in case. James doesn't care, he's long gone to Chicago and he isn't interested. But I make him comply with his support order, and so should you."

"Twerp, Bonita, baby sis, I can't believe I'm hearing this from you. What are you trying to do, reform the whole world all by yourself?"

"That's what Lloyd thinks *you're* trying to do. He calls me when you have him totally frustrated, you know. He hasn't been able to make you stop your crusade, has he?"

"Nope." Beth felt herself giving way, giving in to her stubborn little sister.

"Then don't expect me to be any different. I'm just like my big sis."

She had just one arrow left in her quiver. It was an important one. "I'm free to take risks if I want to, Neet. Unlike you, I don't have a child to raise."

"Not yet. But you might. You oughta marry Lloyd. That man really cares about you. So do I. G'night, Bust-heada."

"Good night, Twerp. Please be careful. I love you."

"Love you, too," said the sobbing voice before it faded away into a sigh.

Chapter Twenty-four

Word of her possible firing had spread, Beth realized when she returned to campus. Before, her colleagues had simply ignored her. Now, uncomfortably, they seemed all too aware of her, but unwilling to admit it. They dropped their eyes when they came face-to-face with her and danced away from her in the halls, mumbling incoherent excuses about appointments and meetings.

Only Irene Levinson spoke to her in the department office and asked, "How are you?" while searching her face intently.

"I'll just say 'fine,' because I don't know what else to say," Beth replied.

"Got time to stop by my office and talk?"

"Not now," she said. "Later, maybe." Actually, she had a couple of hours to kill. She hated lying to Irene, but she didn't want any sympathy, and she certainly didn't want any I-told-you-sos.

When Vincent Addison stopped and greeted her warmly, she was so grateful she wanted to cry.

"Got a minute? Let's go get a cup of coffee," he said, and tucked her arm into his. Bolstered by this show of support, she sailed out of the building.

They went to Le Bistro, a commercial imitation of a French café a half block away. It had outdoor tables, and the day was warm enough to sit out in the early spring sun, but she refused, preferring to go to a dark booth inside and sit with her back securely against a wall.

Vincent went to the coffee counter and came back with two tall mugs of American. "Hey," he said, as she tried to stir hers and her spoon rattled against the inside of her cup. "What's making you shake like that? Whatever it is, it ain't worth it."

"Just this place. These cold, heartless bastards. They think they're apostles of liberalism and civility. That's why they're so scary."

"I know. Can I get you something else? Doughnuts or crois-sants?" She shook her head. He brushed the crumbs of a croissant off his lap and buttered another. Vincent was one of those people who could eat anything he wanted and not gain weight. The way he scarfed food at department parties and kept his trim build was criminal. So were his good looks, especially the hazy gray eyes that lit his tan face.

"I was going to call you today. While you were at home, er, rest-ing, I took the liberty of telling the Gamma women to call me if they had anything to discuss," he said. He was referring, delicately, to her almost-suicide, her near-drowning. Apparently word about that had gotten around, too.

"They've come to a decision. They're meeting in my office today at four."

"I'll be there," she promised.

For some reason she trusted this man alone among the faculty, except for Irene. Though his was a perfect package, he was begin-ning to let his humanity show.

"It's been rough, hasn't it?" he said gently.

She let herself lean momentarily upon that trust; let her shoulders sag and then shake. "Yes," she admitted, and dug in her huge purse for some Kleenex. "I just realized something, Vincent," she said. "They don't really want us here."

"Of course they don't. Why did it take you so long to catch on?"

She hesitated. She had to sniffle and wipe her eyes. "Because— because I haven't had any problems until recently. And I guess because my parents sheltered me from racism."

She was beginning, at some deep level of consciousness, to get angry about that sheltering. Her family's censorship about black history. The move to that smug little all-black town where everyone thought they had it made because a couple of centuries ago, their ancestors had escaped from slavery. Where the civil rights struggle had been only a muffled drumming in the distance.

"Tell me something, Vincent. I suppose I sound terribly naïve, as usual when I ask you a question—but if they don't want us here, why do they let us in?"

"Public relations again. The need to look good. Even the most conservative people and institutions don't want to look like hard-core bigots. It's much better to appear to be liberal."

She had to blow her nose. "Please excuse me for getting weepy. I'm sorry."

"Please don't be. I'm honored that you feel safe enough with me to let your feelings come out. You're a lot of woman, you know that, Beth? I wish I'd gotten to know you long ago, some time before . . ."

Startled, she looked up at him. He had gotten married only last year, she'd heard. His fabulous cloudy eyes were serious and troubled.

"I hope you're happy, Vincent."

"I am. Just the thought of getting out of here makes me feel like flying. I have this great sense of freedom and possibility, like I'm only twelve years old again. Why don't you follow my example and get the hell out of here?"

"I just might," she said.

He escorted her back to the Humanities Building, where they parted. At the doorway, she slipped her arm free of his.

"I want to thank you for something else, Vincent. Today, for the first time in a long while, I'm going up to my office. You've given me the nerve to finally do that."

Taking a deep breath, she left him and went upstairs and unlocked the door onto the scene of recent carnage. Someone had scrubbed the room and tidied it so thoroughly she didn't recognize it as hers. It was too neat and clean; it even smelled too clean, redolent of fresh citrus instead of its usual musty library odor. Her papers were neatly stacked instead of tumbled all over her desk, which would make it harder for her to find things. Her books were now arranged alphabetically by author on her shelves. She had kept them shelved by course and by their order in each syllabus, which made more sense, but only to her.

She looked around. Something was missing. Ah—there were lighter squares on the cream-colored walls where her William Johnson reproductions had hung. She searched and found them on the floor, leaning against the wall. She had been evicted. The room had been bleached and restored to blank whiteness, awaiting a new tenant. This was no longer her home.

There was no sign of Paget's ordeal or of the recent desecration of her academic cell. But there was a folder he had left there. Apparently, judging by its contents, the furor over the speech code and the rebellion against what the writers termed its political correctness continued unabated. Every article and letter opposed the black women and their cause. The writers sounded like a lynch mob. Whoever would have thought that the small act of demanding respect could lead to such an uproar? Beth thought of Aretha's song about respect and went on reading. She highlighted one letter that read, "I have finally concluded that I can no longer direct financial support to the University. This decision is not made without sadness, since I have contributed to the University every year since my graduation."

The president of the University noted below it, "This letter is fairly typical of many I have received in recent months."

This, of course, was the factor that was deciding the issue, making Backus waver and Bartlett postpone hearings, reinforcing LaRosa's prejudices and putting her reappointment at risk. Beth underlined it, then dropped her pen and bent to pick it up. A yellow Post-it note that the cleaners must not have noticed was stuck to the inside of one leg of her desk. A swastika was drawn on it in heavy black marker. Someone had left it there, she decided, just in case she ever forgot and got comfortable again.

The meeting was in the History Department, in a small conference room near Vincent's office. As Beth entered she saw him, sharp in blue blazer and khakis, sitting with Natalie and three of the Gamma sorors around a large round table. To her surprise, Harriet leaped up and gave her a warm, affectionate hug. She looked rested and attractive in a dark red dress with a navy scarf.

"Keep wearing wine, Harriet, that's your color," Beth said.

Harriet gave her a quick smile. "Dr. Barnes," she said, "you the best friend I ever had at this backward place."

"Word," said Dana, meaning that she felt the same way.

At that moment, Cynthia Forrest flounced in wearing a low-cut black satin dress. She had gained a few pounds, and the fabric was stretched too tightly across her curves.

"Looks like you didn't have time to go home and change this morning," Rhonda said to her. "Business must be brisk on your corner."

Cynthia bared her teeth and lunged at the taller girl, but Dana put herself between them. "Sorors, please. This occasion calls for unity. Let's put our differences aside."

"Yeah, leave Cynthia alone," Harriet said. "She probably just got dressed up hoping to get on TV."

Harriet was probably right, Beth thought. Cynthia loved profiling and being the center of attention. She could not help comparing the two. Cynthia was unwilling to stay the course, but had been heard to brag about her plush new job in the provost's office and the free computer she had been given to compensate her for her ordeal. Whereas Harriet had hung in there with them, in spite of her fragility, received no reward, and seemed to have grown stronger in the process. Beth was very proud of her.

"That's enough, Harriet," Dana said. "Cynthia came to stand with us, and we should all be glad that she's here. Now that everybody's present, let's get this meeting started, shall we? Our press conference has been called for five P.M., so we all need to be agreed on what we're doing by then.

"First, let me fill everybody in. Professor Barnes, a hearing was set for Monday night at midnight. They woke us and our roommates to tell us. We couldn't reach you to tell you. We figure they picked that time to avoid press coverage and in the hope we wouldn't show up. Professor Hinton objected to the short notice anyway, so none of us went. Now Bartlett has scheduled a new hearing for May twenty-fourth," Dana said.

"May twenty-fourth?" Beth said in surprise. "But that's—"

"Long after commencement. I know," Natalie said. "After everybody has gone home. That means no campus demonstrations, no press attention, and maybe nobody showing up. I know I won't be here."

"Neither will I," said Dana. "I'm graduating and getting out of here."

"Attagirl," said Beth. "Get your diploma and leave this place as far behind as you can, as fast as you can."

The girls looked at her in surprise and then smiled.

"Word," said Harriet.

"Bartlett has also refused to lift the rule of secrecy he imposed on us. That means no talking about the incident, not to the press, not to our classmates, not to anyone. We have honored it until now."

Beth turned to Natalie. "I should have asked this before, but isn't that illegal? Doesn't it take away their freedom of speech?"

"Sure it does," Natalie Hinton observed. "Besides, it's one-sided. Corrigan isn't sticking to it, not that he ever has. Look."

She spread open an issue of *Newsweek* in which the white boy's advisor was the subject of an extensive interview. "This hit the stands today. He had to have done it last week, in spite of the gag order."

She passed the article to Harriet, who read it over and said, "This just the same old retarded stuff. We supposed to put up with all kinds of insults to protect that white boy's precious freedom of speech. Meanwhile, we supposed to keep our mouths shut."

"Will somebody please tell me what they're trying to do?" Beth asked. It seemed as if the administration was trying to walk like a crab, sideways and in several directions at once.

"They're hoping our case will go away," Natalie said. "If it won't, they want to postpone it as long as they can, probably till fall."

"Starkey Backus has resigned. He has been appointed to a job in Washington," Vincent told them. "Head hangman or something at the Library of Congress. He wants this thing to wait until his confirmation hearings are over."

"Forget it," Harriet said. "I'll be at Howard by then, finishing up and trying not to get distracted." Because of the classes she had missed, Harriet would have to repeat part of her junior year. She had chosen to transfer her credits.

"I'll be in grad school at Georgetown," said Rhonda.

"Looks like you'll both be in the right town to haunt and embarrass old Starkey," Beth said. She looked around the table at the familiar faces she'd grown to love—Natalie's: dark, chiseled, severe;

Vincent's: equally chiseled, medium tan, handsome; Harriet's: broad, brown, and worried, with permanent frown lines etched in her forehead; the other young women: pretty, angry, impatient. Except for Irene, there were no other people at this school whose faces she cared to remember.

"Oh, one more thing, Professor," Rhonda said. "The chief of Security has been fired because we complained about getting roughed up. They're really trying to appease us, without giving us what we want."

Once more Beth was out of the loop because she had failed to read *Letters*. "So, what are we doing here today?" she asked.

"We are dropping our charges," Dana said, and passed out copies of several typewritten sheets. "We are stating that we despair of ever receiving justice at this institution because our case has been tried and decided in the media. And we are ignoring Bartlett's gag order. We are telling everybody who will listen."

Beth opened her mouth to say, "But—," then closed it. These young women were adults now, in charge of themselves and their decisions. The transformation from adolescent to adult always happened in the senior year, and it was always miraculous.

"Please read it aloud, Harriet," Dana said.

Harriet read the document, which described the incident that had humiliated the Gammas and their subsequent harassment.

> *We filed a grievance with the Judicial Inquiry office with faith that the judicial process would run its course.*
>
> *The respondent, Otto Jurgen, and his advisor, Dr. Corrigan, chose to circumvent the judicial process and try this grievance in the national media, making it an issue of freedom of speech and political correctness instead of the real issue, racial harassment. Because we honored the University's confidentiality policy, the cov-*

erage of this case, thus far, has all been slanted in favor of the respondent. The media coverage deprived us of our right to an impartial panel and, therefore, of a fair hearing. Realizing that justice cannot be served, we have decided to formally withdraw our complaint.

We were victimized on January 13, further victimized by the media, and thereafter by the judicial process and agents of the university. Based on our experiences while in pursuit of justice at the university, we have concluded that the system is not designed to protect our rights.

Signed,

Cynthia Forrest
Rhonda Harris
Dana Marshall
Harriet Taliaferro

It was honest. It rang with authenticity and stark truth. It was effectively written. It was beautiful. And it was unspeakably sad.

Beth gave her approval to the document and then retreated to Vincent's office to help draft a supplementary statement by the Gammas' advisors, in case anyone was interested.

It said, in part, that free speech and offensive conduct were different things that had been deliberately conflated by the press; that calling African American women "water buffalo" and telling them to go to the zoo took away their humanity and turned them into beasts of burden, which was the same rationale that had been used to justify slavery; and that the media blitz occasioned by the other side's breach of confidentiality made it impossible for the complainants to receive justice. Beth signed it, along with Vincent and Natalie.

Then they went outside and stood just behind the young women

as Dana, the official spokeswoman for the group, read their statement to the gathered media in front of the History Building. All that
was missing was the funeral music.

Those poor, well-brought-up, obedient girls, she thought. Law-
abiding products of the black middle class, they had done as they
were told and obeyed the gag order, and the press had tried and
convicted them in absentia.

Sometimes she thought black parents disciplined their children
too much. They had a tendency to beat all the rebellion out of them
lest they incur the master's wrath—whether they used switches or
psychology.

Afterwards, walking across the campus, a luxury in which she
had not indulged for a long time, she saw about fifty students clapping and hopping gracelessly to the noise of a rock band. It was
the beginning of Spring Fling, an almost exclusively white festi-
val featuring noisy, dissonant music and the consumption of large
amounts of beer. The black students unanimously ignored it, preferring to party on the weekend of the annual relay carnival, which
brought track athletes from all over the nation to the campus and
had inspired an elegant dress code, several formal dances, and
dozens of house parties. Here as in every other area of choice on
campus, the separation of the cultures was marked. Arguments about
whether this was a good thing or a bad thing were irrelevant. It was
a fact, and likely to remain so.

It was a pretty campus in spring, though it presented a blank,
ugly, inhospitable face to the street. Once you got inside, you saw
that the Green was indeed vividly green, as were its numerous
trees. Everywhere she looked, azaleas and other shrubs flowered.
An aria drifted from an upper window in the Music Building. A
Confederate flag hung from a top-floor window in a dormitory.
Beth quickened her steps.

As she continued to walk across campus, her heart was briefly
lifted by the appearance of a large crack in the ivy-covered stone

facade of the Administration Building. She thought it was symbolic. The president had resigned. The chief of Security had been fired. The Gamma women may have lost their case, but they had certainly succeeded in shaking up the University.

Her pleasure lasted just about a minute. She pictured the young women reading their statement with their trio of faculty supporters backing them up, and the few press people in attendance listening, and wanted to cry. Such a small, brave, pathetic group. Beth was somehow reminded of her family.

She was also reminded of herself. Like the Gammas, she was a well-behaved child of the black middle class, behaving herself, doing her job, obeying the white folks' rules as if they were designed to protect and save her. She wished she had told the girls to ignore the gag order. Now it was too late for them to get their story told.

The Gammas were doing the only sensible thing. They were giving up a useless effort, getting back to their work and getting on with their lives. Then why did she want to sit down on one of the slatted benches that lined the campus walks and cry?

She didn't, of course. She waited until she got home and closed the door behind her before she flung herself on her rough tweed sofa and bawled.

"Hey, baby, what's wrong?" Lloyd was solicitous.

"They gave up," she said, sobbing and sniffling. "Those poor girls. After struggling most of the semester, they dropped their charges. They're such good girls, so obedient, so well-raised. They were told to keep quiet, so they did."

His voice was very gentle. "Did they have a chance of winning?"

"They thought so. I thought so, too, for a while. It's not fair!" Uttering the favorite phrase of disappointed children, she kicked the couch and pounded its cushions and howled like a toddler having a tantrum. "It's just not fair!" Not fair, she was thinking, for our families and our communities to make us such good, law-abiding members of society, when they know all along that society will not support us and its laws will not protect us. She was glad the Gammas had committed and enjoyed at least one act of rebellion. They did steal those newspapers.

"Take it easy, Beth," Lloyd said, and patted her shoulder. "Those kids will survive, you know. They've got time and youth on their side. Sure, they had a rough experience, but they've learned from it, they learned it's tough being black in America, and they're moving on. You have to let them go, and move on, too. As for me, I'm glad they finally dropped their charges."

She pulled away from his hand and sat up indignantly. "How can you say that, Lloyd?"

"Their case had become an obsession with you. It put you in harm's way."

"I think," she said very seriously, "that black folks in this country are always in harm's way." After a moment, she added, "I'm getting the hell out of there, Lloyd."

"Fine. There are over sixty institutions of higher learning in this city. I bet any of them would hire you."

"They aren't far away enough." She had been crying, she realized, not just for the Gammas, but for all she had been through and all she had lost, including her innocence. She turned her tear-streaked face to him. "Lloyd, if I got a job out of town, would you come with me?"

He didn't answer right away. "I'd want to. But, hey, that would be a pretty big step," he said. "I'd have to think about it."

It was a reasonable answer. Then why did it make her feel hot with anger and impel her to move away from him on the couch?

Because love was not reasonable and sensible, never had been and never would be.

Chapter Twenty-five

E valuations are in, Dr. Barnes," Eloise said breathlessly on the phone. "Do you want me to open yours?"

Eloise always sounded hurried and out of breath, but what was the rush this time?

"Why should I want you to do that?" Beth had called the office to check on the time and room assigned for her final exam. She was annoyed with the presumptuous secretary, and also by the strands of her long hair that refused to stay trapped in a scarlet scrunchie so that she could finish getting dressed.

The girl sounded hurt. "Well, you haven't been in all month, and they're pretty important, since you're trying to—"

"Trying to save my job. Yes." There really were no secrets on the campus. "Go ahead, open them," she said wearily. "Tell me what they say."

Eloise responded with a speed that told Beth she had already opened the envelope and scanned its contents, "You've got mixed reviews, I'd say. I haven't had time to do a tally, but it looks like about half of your students give you top marks, and half of them flunk you."

"Any comments?"

"Let me see. One major says, 'Best class I've had all four years.' That's great. Another, a non-major, says, 'An engaging, stimulating teacher.' Then, let me see here—oh, Dr. Barnes, I can't read this out loud."

"Try."

"It says 'N-word b-words should confine themselves to cooking, cleaning, and laundry. They don't know s-word about literature.' "

Beth hated the student evaluation system because it was anonymous. It allowed the kids to say vicious things about their teachers without having to acknowledge or justify them. "Charming. Any more like that?"

"Here's one that says 'Affirmative Action 1, Students 0. When they hire losers like this woman, *we* lose.' That's awful.

"Here's another one. It says, 'N-words should dust Faulkner's books, not read them.' Oh, Dr. Barnes, I'm sorry."

"Don't be. There's a pattern here, Eloise. Can't you see it?"

"Yes," the secretary said. "It's"—she dropped her voice to a whisper—"it's racial."

"I always knew you were a smart girl, Eloise," Beth said. "When are you going to take some courses?" She said it lightly, but she was serious. Wild partying was not helping Eloise, but a degree, which she could pursue for nothing as long as she kept her job, just might. "Leave the evaluations in my mailbox, please. I'm coming in this morning. I'll collect them when I get there."

"Nobody blames you for not coming in all month, Dr. Barnes. I don't see how they could. What happened to your work-study student was terrible. I don't know how he can stand to be up there."

"I imagine some of the things he went through before he got here make him able to stand a lot more than we can. See you later."

What Eloise meant, of course, was that Beth *was* being blamed for not appearing at her office. An officer never abandons her post. Don't give up the ship. Keep a stiff upper lip, and all the rest of that British Army–officer shit. Like all English departments everywhere, hers adored the Brits. She was willing to bet that they ran from danger as fast as anybody else, though. Cornwallis surrendered, didn't he?

Once in her office, Beth made sure that her door was locked. Feeling silly, but preferring that to feeling unsafe, she also shoved the back of a chair under the doorknob.

The phone rang before she could take a look at her evaluations.

"Good afternoon, Beth," said the chairman's falsely jocular voice. "I'm lucky to have caught you. Would you have a chance to stop in and see me?"

"Say, in about half an hour? At three o'clock?"

"That will be fine," Dr. LaRosa said.

Her phone rang again as soon as she hung up.

"We heard you raving on the radio," a young male voice said. "When will you learn, bitch? When will you shut up?"

Beth gently laid the phone down in her desk without interrupting the connection and let the caller spew his vomit into her blotter. She took a few minutes to go over her evaluations. Eloise had been kind. A lot more than half of them were negative. Might as well go and face the music.

She went downstairs, pausing automatically to check her mailbox before she kept her appointment with LaRosa. There were no papers in her box. There was, however, a small dark object pushed way into the back. She reached in, felt it, found it to be soft, and pulled it out, only to cry out at its ugliness and drop it.

"What is it, Beth?" Eloise had been so roused by her cry she forgot and called her by her first name, a familiarity Beth actually welcomed in this cold, impersonal place.

Wordlessly, she held up the object. It was a small black cloth doll with button eyes and large red lips, the kind of demeaning soft sculpture that used to be called a golliwog. In its heart, head, and back, someone had inserted hatpins. It was disgusting.

"Someone left me a present," she said, and dropped it into the community trash can, and walked straight into the lion's den. She went through the ritual of shaking hands and allowing herself to be seated at the chairman's table so that he could devour her for his lunch. She did not take her eyes off him.

"That was a fine CV you prepared for me," Dr. LaRosa said, "but I noticed that you did not include any references."

"I don't have any," Beth told him.

"That is most unfortunate," the chairman said, and clucked like an old hen. "They might have made all the difference. I won't beat around the bush, my dear. I have read the analysis of your evaluations, and they were unfavorable."

"Not all of them," Beth said.

"No, not all, certainly. But enough of them are negative that I do not see how I can recommend your reappointment to the committee. Good references would certainly have helped you. Pity."

Beth felt strangely detached, like an observer at her own execution. *He really said "Pity,"* she thought. *I thought they only said that in books, but there are people who really say it. Amazing.*

"What do you suggest, then?" she asked him.

"Are you, er, still advising those young women in their case against that freshman?"

"Yes, I am."

"I see. I did hear about your recent radio broadcast, but I was hoping that you might have decided to be reasonable."

"Dr. LaRosa," she said, "it is not I who am being unreasonable. It is the university that is out of line in failing to back up its students or enforce its policies."

"Well." He hemmed and began assiduously polishing those eyeglasses. "I suggest that you attend the next meeting of the Modern Language Association. You are a member, aren't you?"

She wasn't, but she nodded as if she were. She belonged only to the National Council of Teachers of English, a down-home group of teachers, mostly at state schools, who were bent on keeping it real, but she could easily become a member of the communion of saints who canonized writers. All she had to do was send the MLA a rather large amount of money, which she had never been able to spare even back when she knew she could expect another pay-check every month. She would rather attend a convention of under-takers than one of theirs, she thought, and that thought reminded her of her other line of defense.

She had probably been here too long, but she remembered something that Curtis, who had taught her many card games, used to say when they played bid whist. "Always bid from a strong hand, Bethesda."

She was not sure she wanted to move to a new job, though she recognized that the terror she felt in her constricted chest and the closing up of her throat were nothing but the phobic's irrational, consuming fear of going anywhere—but if she did, she did not want to start out under a cloud, with people thinking that she had been let go from her previous position.

Her chairman was droning on with his useless advice. "All the important job openings are announced at MLA, you know, and many interviews take place on the spot."

He rose. "Well, I guess that's all I have to say for now, unless you have questions."

"I do have one. Who, exactly, is behind this campaign of harass-ment and persecution against me?"

"I am not aware of any campaign, Dr. Barnes. Do you have evi-dence of a campaign?"

"I threw it away," she said, feeling foolish.

He grimaced. "Well, I, of course, will write you a favorable letter of recommendation, as I said I would. Good day, Dr. Barnes. Good luck."

She remained rooted to the spot. "They have to send me a letter, don't they?"

"Ah—yes. It's a mere formality, of course, but you should receive your notification of nonrenewal within a week. I am truly sorry this has happened, Dr. Barnes. Of course, there is still a chance that if you, ah, cease the activities that disturb some of our administrative people . . . but I can't be certain of that. The main problem is your classroom performance, as perceived by your students."

No, it isn't, she knew, but it was too late for him to retreat from his phony position. Besides, she had no reason to believe this sugarcane-sucking good ole boy wanted to retain her on his faculty.

Moisture sprang to her eyes. How could they do this to her, after all her efforts? She thought of the many nights she had stayed up past 1 A.M., reading texts and grading papers. Of all the social events she had missed while meeting with students and counseling them, giving them every spare minute of her time, every ounce of her energy. How could they? She stood up and left the chairman's office in a blind rage, squeezing her eyes tight to keep the tears from spilling over.

It was time to call the undertaker.

Chapter Twenty-six

A few days later, as Beth was coming out of the department office, Vincent Addison grabbed her elbow and led her outside to a bench. He had been turning up so often lately that she suspected the dear man was watching over her.

As soon as she sat down beside him, Vincent turned a face to her that was bright with merriment. "Ever gone fishing?" he asked.

"No."

"Then you don't know what a worm looks like when it's wriggling on a hook. Too bad. That's what your chairman looked like at the department meeting this morning. It was all I could do to keep a straight face. Girl, you really messed with them. How did you do it?"

"What are you talking about, Vincent?"

He took a deep breath, expanded his chest, leaned back, and hooked his thumbs in his striped suspenders. He was clearly going to enjoy telling this story.

"Well. Seems the provost called and asked what the hell was going on with your appointment, and told LaRosa to stop holding it up. If he didn't, the provost said, there would be no money for computers, no money for visitors, no money for the rest of his faculty, let alone new hires, and maybe none for light or heat, or even water to flush the toilets. Everybody was on LaRosa's case. You should have heard the uproar. They really had him on the hot seat. Tell me how you did it."

"I went to see the undertaker," Beth said. "Senator Bostwick, that is. He said he would hold up the university's state appropriation till I got reappointed. Half a billion dollars."

"I wish we weren't in a public place, Beth," Vincent said. "That news makes me want to shout and dance. I think I will, anyway. Hooray!"

He rose, but he did not exactly dance. Vincent was too intellectual to know how to dance. What he did was perform a funny, sedate little hopping movement in place while pumping his arms. She laughed, and he sat down again, breathing hard.

"Thank you, Jesus. Thank you, Beth. We really needed that victory. May I tell Natalie?"

"Of course," she said.

"God is good, isn't he?"

"All the time."

He laughed in pure joy. "May I congratulate you by buying you a drink?"

She glanced at her watch and said, "I'd love it, Vincent, but my office hour is starting, and then I have a class."

"I'll give you a rain check this time, Beth. But remember why our ancestors on the plantation stopped being conscientious about their cotton-picking. The wages and working conditions were not right."

"I know conditions haven't gotten much better, Vincent, but old habits die hard." Ruefully, she recognized that she was still the Maid of All Work, but it was hard to change. So, after she and Vincent exchanged high fives, they parted and went in different directions.

Beth had decided to avoid her office for the rest of the semester. She tried various spaces for meeting with students and finally settled on a lounge on the first floor of the black residence, Evers House. There was a TV in the lounge, and the receptionist had the annoying habit of watching soap operas all day, but after Beth asked her sweetly and bribed her with cookies, she reluctantly turned the volume down on her "stories."

Two months ago she never would have admitted it, but Beth felt safer in a place where black people were always around. Their speech, their gestures, and their constant comings and goings were reassuring. Evers House was funky, raggedy, and ill-kept, like any other ghetto, and sometimes it was noisy, but it felt safe. The only disadvantage of using its lounge as her office was the lack of privacy, especially the lack of a private phone, but she carried her cell phone with her in case she needed to make a call. Anything to keep from going back to that room where Paget had almost been beaten to death.

The little man was coming along fine. His swellings had gone down. His dark skin hid the worst of his bruises, and long sleeves concealed the slashes on his arm, which he called "tribal marks," and said he had decided to keep. Once he was discharged from the hospital, he asked permission to go on using her vacated office.

"I do not think those terrible people will try to strike again in the same place, Miss Doctor Barnes," he said, "and it is better than my room. More space, more heat, more everything—and more convenient, since I do not yet own a computer or possess a telephone."

She would feel horrible if anything more happened to Paget, but she accepted his rationale and let him use the place. Paget was always cold. Even during that mild spell in March, he had kept both the heat and her space heater going. She shuddered to think of what the temperature in her office must be now, in early May. It must be like a sauna. She worried about him, but she had learned that he was more than old enough to be responsible for himself.

Besides, though it made her feel guilty, it was convenient to have him drop off and pick up her mail.

Between the two of them, the University was going to have its hands full, which gave her much pleasure. Paget had been in touch with his embassy, and they had lodged a formal complaint. His embassy had also released the story of his sufferings. CBS wanted to do a story on one of its news magazine shows, but Paget said he wanted to keep a low profile and refused the interview. Beth was still trying to talk him into it.

She had moved her classes to Evers House, too. She had taught here once before, years ago when she broke her ankle, and there had been no problems or complaints then about her move to the first-floor Multi-Purpose Room. She would not mind if she never again set foot in the Humanities Building.

For the first week after spring break, mindful of Dr. LaRosa's warning, she tiptoed on eggshells in both her classes, trying to offend no one without compromising the integrity of her teaching. Sometime during the second week she said to hell with it and stopped trying to please her students, abandoning restraint and flinging challenges at her classes. After she relaxed, she thought she had never taught more brilliantly.

Remembering the chairman's remarks, one of the first things she did was tell both her classes, "There are no special admissions students in here. If affirmative action had anything to do with your presence, you have certainly justified it. All of you have first-rate minds and are fully qualified to be here."

The days of classes always flew by after spring break. Regretfully, she realized that she would not have time to cover Walker and Wright in her Women and Literature class, and she dropped them from the syllabus. She was able to wind up her Political Fiction class with *Native Son*, though. The group met for its last session at ten o'clock in Evers.

Bigger Thomas was a sensitive subject. Nobody in her class,

black or white, seemed to like him. When Beth, trying to spark discussion, suggested that Bigger might be instructively compared to O. J. Simpson, Witmayer bravely spoke up.

"This novel shows us what types like O. J. feel and think, Professor. It gives us insight into the heart of a murderer."

The girls in the class were ready for him. "O. J. was acquitted, you idiot! Didn't you hear the verdict?" cried Dana. "And why is he a type? What type?"

"Jock, impulsive, short fuse, no self-control," Witmayer replied coolly. "That's his type. We all know at least one like him."

"He was found not guilty! How can you call him a murderer?" came from someone in the back of the room.

"Oh," the white boy said, "everybody knows O. J. did it."

"Everybody white, you mean," growled C. T., who had become more forthcoming lately.

"Speak for yourself, *Mr.* Witmayer," Dana added. "You don't know what everybody thinks."

"Can we agree," Beth interjected, "that Wright's novel was so successful because it reinforced certain stereotypes in the white psyche?"

"That must be right," Witmayer said, "because it was a bestseller, and black people don't buy books."

C. T. was on his feet, fists balled and at the ready. "Say that again, will you, man? Step to me and say it. My parents have a library of five thousand books."

"Good for them," the white boy said. "I was speaking of the majority of your people, of course, not your parents."

"Mr. Witmayer is a very brave young man." Beth said. "He seems to have forgotten where he is, or not to care."

Throughout the room, there was laughter. Her remark had broken the tension, as Beth had hoped. The boy's scalp turned deep red around his ears and under the stubble of his blond hair. He was a spy, she had become convinced. A plant, put there to find out just what she was teaching in her classes. He slunk out of the class-room, to hide his embarrassment, she thought.

She went on, "O. J. is a figure in the recent news, of course, but I want you to think about the possibility that he may have also entered into the realm of literature by becoming a myth. O. J. may be no longer merely a man, but a legend who is bigger than life, like Paul Bunyan or Samson. He might profitably be compared to Othello as well as to Bigger Thomas—a suggestion for those of you who are writing papers for extra credit.

"To bring the discussion closer to home, O. J. Simpson is viewed as a superman of great strength, like Joe Louis or John Henry, and also as an antisocial hero, like Jesse James, Clyde Barrow, and Stagolee. O. J. has become a mythical figure because people have created him out of their needs, the way Bigger Thomas attracted so many readers because Richard Wright met their needs for a violent black scapegoat. The time may come when people wish they could get rid of O. J. and turn him into a footnote in history."

"I do already," said Cynthia, eliciting laughter.

"Why, Cynthia?"

"Because I'm sick of hearing people argue over whether he did it. The verdict is in, the man was acquitted, case closed, so let's forget it."

"I share your sentiments," Beth said. "I was also going to ask what you think some of the stereotypes that are reinforced by Bigger Thomas and the O. J. myth might be."

Hands shot up. Beth called on C.T. But she never got to hear what he had to say. His comment was interrupted and obliterated by a dull thud that was followed by a series of reports and then crashing sounds, and a loud racket like helicopters landing on the roof.

"Get *down*!" C.T. yelled. "Down!"

Something sharp struck Beth in the nose. Somebody pushed her, and she landed underneath the table where her papers had been spread. Others were down there already, huddled in rude proximity. Dust and smoke were rising all around them, making it difficult to breathe or see. Through the thick curtain of dust, she heard screams and the muffled sound of weeping.

When the noises stopped, Beth crawled out from beneath the table and was suddenly blinded by harsh daylight coming through a space where it had not been before. There was a hole as big as a garage door in the wall opposite the place where she had been standing. She saw smoke and debris pouring from the ceiling above the hole. She heard yelling and screaming in the confusion. Somewhere nearby, someone was still weeping. A moment later, she heard sirens.

Others were crawling out of the places where they had hidden or been thrown. Her students all looked like ghosts with their coverings of thick gray dust. Beth reminded herself that while this group was assembled here, she was in charge. She would have to pull herself together.

"Take your time getting up, everyone," she called. "Check yourselves for broken bones and concussions." She had no idea what she would do if anyone reported either.

She stood up shakily and then, finding it difficult to see or breathe, sat down, this time on a chair coated with gray powder.

A strong hand seized hers.

"Excuse me, ma'am." It was C. T.'s voice. "We have to get out of here now. This building might collapse."

"Oh," she said. She hadn't thought of that.

Even as he spoke, a couple of bricks fell on the other side of the room and bounced off a detached cinder block. C. T. had Dana by the other hand, and was dragging them both toward the lobby. She wondered why he did not lead them to the hole through which she saw daylight, since it was closer. Then several very large chunks of debris fell from above it, and she appreciated his wisdom.

"Go on outside," he directed as they reached the lobby, where an alarm was sounding and people were pouring in from upstairs. He pushed their hands forward, released them, and said, "Get as far away from this building as you can."

And he went back to get others.

By the time the medics arrived, her small seminar group of twelve students was huddled under an oak tree across the Green from Evers House, brushing dust off themselves and checking one another for damage. One girl was weeping quietly. Others were cursing loudly, which Beth thought was healthier.

She looked around, counting heads, attaching names to bruised and dirty faces. Everyone was present except Witmayer. "You're bleeding," she observed to Dana, who appeared to have a small cut on her wrist.

"So are you, Professor," said Dana, touching her own top lip to indicate where the blood was. Beth rummaged for and found a tissue to wipe away the moisture. "So I am," she said, wondering where that calm voice had come from. "Thank you."

It was Rhonda who had been crying. "Why did they do this?" she asked with large, staring eyes. "We dropped our charges. Why now?"

Beth did not have a ready answer, except that feelings on campus were high and the backlash they had unleashed might not be spent. "Those crazy people are still angry, I guess. When something has been set in motion, it's not always easy to stop it," she told Rhonda.

Only two of her students went with the medics, one a boy with an ugly gash on his arm, the other a girl with a bad headache and a possible concussion. Though she tried to persuade the others to go and get checked, they protested that they were okay and had only surface scrapes and bruises. But shock and pain, she knew from her sketchy first-aid training and her one automobile accident, might set in later.

Campus police moved them back a few feet, to the other side of the tree, and set up barricades around Evers House. A city bomb squad began poking around the building. She heard more sirens. A city fire truck came screaming around the corner. The University preferred to police itself, but this disaster was more than its Security force could handle. *Good,* she thought. She didn't trust the campus police. They, too, might be in the public relations business.

"Where's that ugly baldhead white boy? What's his name. Witmayer?" Dana asked suddenly.

"I don't know," another student said.

"He walked out just before it happened. I'll bet he did it," Dana said, hands on her skinny hips, elbows jutting dangerously.

"You can't prove that, Dana," Beth said.

"Well, at least he knew it was going to happen."

"You don't know that for certain, either," Beth said.

"No, but I can have my suspicions," the girl replied. "He's one of those nasty skinheads."

"Listen, everybody," Beth admonished her students. "These people, whoever they are, are trying to start a race war. Let's not oblige them. You may have to talk to the police, but you don't have to talk to the press. Just report the facts as you observed them. Please keep your speculations to yourselves. Okay?"

"Here comes Security now," said C.T. as a blue Jeep drove up with a campus cop at the wheel. "I'm not hanging around to talk to them. Professor, Rhonda, you-all be careful, hear? Coming, Dana?" Dana and several others followed his lead and ducked across the grass and between some buildings.

To the battered group that remained, Beth shouted over the incessant sirens, "I guess those policemen will want to talk to some of us. After that, let's just go home and go quietly about our business. And *please* don't let me hear about any of you trying to retaliate."

She heard rumblings of disagreement. She ignored them and went on, "We don't even know who did this awful thing. Let the police find out."

The remnant of her class was beginning to disperse. She raised her voice. "One more thing," she said. "There will be a final exam." The groans of discontent were louder this time. She was known to assign take-home final exams or final papers, which gave the students more time. But this time she wanted samples of all of their handwriting to compare with the writing on those horrible threats.

"There will definitely be a final," she repeated. "Check at the Humanities Office for the time and place."

She gave a brief, factual statement to the police and walked to her car among students who were running away from Evers House. She drove home feeling oddly calm and composed, and remained so even when she saw her dirt-streaked, scabby face in the mirror. There was no need to be afraid now. The other shoe had dropped. The worst had happened. She washed her face, dabbed peroxide on her nose, poured herself a drink of gin with lemon, and sat down to watch the news broadcast that was preempting the afternoon soaps.

Lloyd had left for work, but he came home as soon as he heard, and watched the broadcast with her, hugging her close and swearing softly under his breath. It looked as if the campus Nazis had gotten their wish, and the race war had begun. The cameras captured a melee on the green, showing a montage of black boys throwing rocks, white boys throwing bottles, and a group of unidentifiable people taking part in an all-out, hands-on brawl. Her words counseling restraint had had little effect. She recognized C.T. and two of his friends among the rock-throwers. She saw Harriet with a microphone stuck in her face, telling the camera about the white conspiracy to annihilate all black people.

Oh, God, she wondered, *do those children know what the*

far-reaching consequences of their speech and actions might be? Did they care that they were being videotaped and telecast and that their futures might be affected? After all that had happened, *should* they care?

Next, the screen showed the damage inside Evers House, a sickening view of the room where she had taught, and said that no one there had been seriously hurt.

Beth's lips moved silently, thanking God.

The cameras cut to the Hillel Foundation, which had been hit at the same time. Medics were carrying several students out of the Jewish student union. The camera moved in for a closeup of a crude swastika that had been smeared on the building's door. It would have to be rebuilt, the reporter said. Four people had suffered serious injuries. No group had claimed responsibility for the attacks, the commentator continued, but campus and city police were both investigating.

Someone would go after those skinheads now, Beth thought, especially if one of the kids who had just been carried out of Hillel died. There was plenty of money represented among Hillel's alumni. Then, ashamed of herself, she began to pray that everyone would survive.

The camera cut to the Evers housemaster, Joe Morgan, who had suddenly become an angry race man. Maybe the bandage above his eye had something to do with it. She laughed as the mouse roared about dangerous bigots and the need to restrain them.

There followed a clip of Starkey Backus declaiming silver-tongued platitudes that were as worthless as the Confederate money his ancestors had issued.

Beth always had a delayed reaction to bad experiences. Now, she felt herself shaking inside. Shock was beginning to set in. Her elbow was stinging, too. She examined it and found a scrape she had not noticed. It must have happened when she was knocked under the table. Her bruised body had begun to ache all over. She took three ibuprofen, then went to rummage in the vanity under the bathroom sink for Epsom salts. She found none.

"Lloyd, do we have any Epsom salts?"

"I'll look in the kitchen," he said. In a minute he came to her empty-handed. "We're out."

"Would you go to the store and get me some? Please? I'm starting to hurt all over." She recognized the delayed reaction as the same one she'd had after her auto accident three years ago. It had been half a day before she knew she was hurt. Then, it had been her back. Now, she felt sure, it was only her psyche. The physical pain was probably temporary. But the rage and anxiety that were coursing through her might last a long time.

After Lloyd left for the drugstore, she dialed the number in North Carolina and talked to Mrs. Lorraine Houston, secretary to the president of Baldwin College, who had left her a message. Mrs. Houston had a sweet, refined Southern voice that put Beth immediately at ease. She managed to sound as if there were nothing she would rather do that day than talk to Beth.

Beth pictured a small violet-scented person with dainty features, wearing gold-rimmed bifocals, an old-fashioned print dress, and sensible low-heeled shoes. Mrs. Houston assured her that the personnel committee wanted her badly. Her interview would be strictly pro forma.

They set a date in the third week of May, two weeks after Beth would finish her present duties. They talked briefly of salaries and course loads. The former were much lower, the latter heavier than in the Ivy League, which she had expected. Then Mrs. Houston ventured a question.

"There is one thing, though. We have been wondering why you would consider coming to us, since you now hold such a prestigious appointment. I hate to ask an intrusive question, Dr.

Barnes, especially since we haven't even met, but are you having problems?"

"Not of the sort I think you mean," Bethesda said. "I'll have to explain that later, perhaps when I come down."

"I understand completely, Dr. Barnes. We can wait. Till the twentieth, then."

"Till the twentieth."

Chapter Twenty-seven

S tretched out on her bed a week later, listening to the "Midnight Hour" segment of Lloyd's show, Beth read the blue books she had collected at the end of her exam period and tried not to think about the devastation or its aftermath. The police had detained C.T. and his friends for throwing rocks, but they had not yet arrested anyone for throwing bombs. C.T. was released the next day, but that fine, heroic fellow would always have an arrest on his record, she thought bitterly, while the really dangerous perpetrators of violence still went free.

Almost all her students had passed, though not with distinction. Witmayer's exam book troubled her the most. He had answered one question brilliantly with an essay on Sinclair Lewis, whose book was probably the only one he had read; left another question blank, and written only vague, incomplete responses to the other three. His grade was either a borderline D or an F.

She spent half an hour trying to compare his handwriting to the writing on the threatening notes, but could not be sure whether they were the same. She was no handwriting expert, after all. Giving up on that task, she considered his grade. Should she be generous or strict?

Usually she was generous in borderline cases. She thought about it and then said aloud, "Flunk the Nazi."

Later, after a long soak to relieve her lingering aches, and ten minutes of deep breathing for her still-frayed nerves, she went online to check the accuracy of her grade reporting and to see if she had any e-mail. There was one new message from an unknown correspondent: patriot@yahoo.com.

> *Dear Big Fat Boss Black Buffalo: You and your people were not meant to associate with your betters or judge them. You have no business examining us or grading us, only serving us. Get back down in the mud where you belong. Go wallow at the zoo, you cow.*
> *—Aryan Prince*

That was Witmayer, she thought, reacting to his F. Online grades were transmitted instantaneously. She deleted the horrible message. She didn't want any souvenirs of the recent ugliness. Later she thought that perhaps she should have printed a hard copy to save for legal purposes. But what avenues of legal recourse were left? Charges had been dropped. There would be no hearing. Already, the silence around the girls' case was profound.

Beth decided to go to bed. But her body was still sore, and there were still tremors in her muscles, and even though it was just an e-mail message from a kid, she was scared. She turned Lloyd's radio voice down to a loving murmur and pummeled her pillow into submission, but she was not meant to sleep tonight. She lay awake until her visions of bald boys in camouflage shirts and high-top boots were interrupted by the ringing telephone. She picked it up with trepidation, expecting the familiar threat.

But it was only her mother. "Are you all right, Bethesda?" Delores asked feebly. "I heard about the explosions at your school."

"That happened a week ago, Mother. Surely you're not calling to check on me after all this time."

"No," Delores admitted, and cleared her throat. "It's your sister, Bethesda. They found her in her Jeep, her Trail Blazer or whatever it's called. I told her not to buy that ridiculous car, especially in that color. I said no one would take her seriously, that it looked like a toy, like she was playing soldier. That's what she's been doing all this time, you know, playing soldier. Trying to be a boy, just to frustrate me. Knowing how I prize femininity."

If only Delores could be made to stop placing herself at the center of everything, if she could be made to stop believing for just one minute that the entire world was engaged solely in a conspiracy against her, Beth might be able to get some sense out of her. But she had a sickening knowledge already of what that sense would be. Something final, something dreadful.

"Start over, please. I can't understand you. You know Neet always loved police work. It started out with her reading Nancy Drew mysteries. Maybe you shouldn't have bought her so many of those books. Then you let her take karate. She loved it, she was good at it, she earned a black belt. You remember. What's her car got to do with anything?"

"I told you, Bethesda. They found her in it, shot. They're calling it suicide. She wouldn't commit suicide, not Bonita. No child of mine would commit suicide. She had too much to live for. I know that man gave her trouble, he was never good enough for her, no good at all, really, but still—"

Beth interrupted her mother's rambling with an urgent question. "Where's Della?"

"Right here with me, of course, sleeping. Bonita was working one of her late shifts, and her baby-sitter was sick, so she asked me, and

I said, of course I would keep my grandchild till it was over. Well, it's over."

Maybe, but you're not going to keep her, Beth said to herself. "Have you told Della what happened?"

"Of course not, Bethesda. But the child is terribly perceptive. Smarter than you, and you know how bright you were at that age. Reading encyclopedias and Shakespeare, and oh, my, we were so proud of you, we couldn't resist showing you off, making you read out loud for our friends. I think she knows somehow."

She would, of course. Nevertheless, Beth said, "Don't tell her till I get there."

If her mother sounded like she had finally gone over the edge into total, babbling insanity, well, she had plenty of cause, Beth decided as she threw some things into an overnight case and ran down to her car.

She had no memory of crossing the bridge, and only noticed that she had done so when a Delaware River Port Authority cop pulled her over at the foot of it.

"You were doing ninety miles an hour, ma'am."

The face she turned to him would probably have frozen mercury or melted steel, judging by the sudden way he stepped back. He let her go.

Suicide, my fine black behind, Beth thought as she sped away, pedal floored, watching him in the mirror. *One of you swaggering fuckers shot her. Murdered her. Murdered my sister. My only sister. Because she had the goods on you and was sick of you and was vomiting all of it up.*

Zipping onto a wide highway that usually scared her, but that gave her no problems tonight because she had more urgent things on her mind, she rehearsed what she planned to say.

Like the younger women she taught, she had given up trying to change a hard-nosed institution and its ideas—especially when the institution was as dangerous and ungoverned as the police force.

She would say, *"It was not suicide, Mother, it was murder. Another in the long, dreadful list of police homicides. But we will not call it murder, Delores, and we will not call for any investigations."* Her students had taught her what was possible and what was not. *"We will not call it self-murder, either. We will call it an accident. Accidents happen. Even in the best of families."*

"Have you talked to anyone?" Beth asked as soon as she slammed on the brakes in front of her mother's house and ran inside and caught her mother by the shoulders.

"No, of course not, Bethesda. Just you." Delores was calm, but she was wearing pearls and a pink pinafore-style apron over a green sweat suit, a combination that suggested she had gone over the edge.

"Good." Beth tried, then, to fold her mother into an embrace, but they had never been much for touching, and she soon gave up and settled for brushing Delores's papery cheek with her lips.

Della came in then, barefoot in a long white nightshirt covered with printed pink lipstick kisses. She gave her niece a long, strong, satisfying hug, and got one in return.

"Go back to bed now, bunny rabbit," she said, and then remembered that she had often called Bonita that when she was small.

"I'm not sleepy, Aunt Beth," Della said, her amber eyes brightening. Hungry for information, she looked from one of them to the other. "Why did you come here so late?"

"Your grandma and I have a lot to talk about," Beth said. "Be a good girl and go back to bed so we can have our talk."

"You can talk with me right here," Della said with indisputable logic. But she went padding obediently back to her room, anyway.

Beth and Delores went to the kitchen and closed the door, where Delores postponed their talk by putting water on for tea. Beth really wanted an alcoholic drink, but she did not ask for it.

"Ready for some tea?"

Beth shook her head. There was no easy way to launch this discussion. "It wasn't suicide, Mother," she announced abruptly. "She was shot by one of her fellow officers. I'm as sure of it as if I were there." Those cyclists in her terrible nightmare had been cops, she realized suddenly. Motorcycle cops. Her dream had been precognitive.

"Why on earth would one of them do such a thing?"

"Well, you know she had charged some of them with sexual harassment."

"I knew nothing about it. You know, Bonita always wore her skirts too short. She liked to show off her legs. I told her to stop shortening her hems, but she wouldn't listen."

"It was not her fault, Mother," Beth said sharply. "Some of those pigs would have hit on her if she'd worn burqa"

"Well, I don't think women should dress provocatively," said Delores. "We bring some of our troubles on ourselves."

"Just a few days ago," Beth said, trying not to let her mother get her angry so early in the visit, "she told me that a state investigation of police corruption was under way, and that she was cooperating. Mother, some of those guys she worked with were up to their eyeballs in stealing and brutality."

"It was never the proper sort of work for a woman," Delores said. "I told her that. But she didn't want to teach, didn't even want to go to college. She broke your father's heart by becoming a cop."

Why, oh, why, was her mother always so off the wall? Why did she always respond to a serious remark with something trivial and irrelevant? Was it her way of avoiding unpleasantness, or was she really a dipstick?

Beth went on relentlessly, "She fell in love with police work when you and Daddy encouraged her to join the Explorer Scouts, remember? She always wanted to be a detective. She loved doing undercover work and investigations. You remember.

"I tried to talk her out of cooperating with the state investigation.

I didn't get anywhere. I think she almost expected something like this to happen."

"Why do you think that, Bethesda?"

"Because, when she called, she asked me to take care of Della if anything happened to her." Beth felt the tears flooding her eyes. One started down her cheek. She dug frantically in her pocketbook for a Kleenex and finally found one that was crumpled and gray, as usual, and filled with cracker crumbs. Beth was not the kind of woman who routinely replaced things like tissues in her purse. She put in fresh ones only when she changed handbags, if she remembered to do it then.

Her mother, who always noticed things like that, passed her a box of clean tissues. "I don't think that would be a good idea," Delores said. "Della has always lived in this community and gone to the school down the street."

"That's not what Neet wanted," Beth said.

"So you say," said her mother, and began rocking back and forth in her chair, moaning. "What do you know? Oh, Lord, what have I done? Lord, why are you taking my whole family from me?"

There was no point in saying that the tragedy was not aimed at Delores. No way her mother would believe it.

"I'm still here," Beth said, and got up and went around to hug her mother, who stiffened and pushed her away.

Beth decided that she was not going to argue with her mother about Della's future. She would simply get her sister's will from that lawyer, her homely, skinny classmate. What was his name? Never mind. She would remember it in time.

"So that is what I think happened. I think she was killed by another cop. But we're not going to call it murder. We're not going to stir things up by calling for investigations and demanding justice. I've already been involved with enough quests for justice this year, and I'm sick of them. It's not just that you and Della can't stand all the notoriety. It would put you both in danger, and I know we can't get justice, anyway. It's pointless to ask the police to investigate the police. They're a law unto themselves. Neet was pretty sure she wouldn't get away with what she was doing. That's why she called me."

"Then what do you propose to tell people?" Her mother suddenly seemed small and helpless, as if she had become the child and Beth was now the mother. But under that helplessness, Beth knew, was a spine of steel.

"That it was an accident. She was cleaning her gun, or doing something else to it without checking whether it was loaded, and it went off. I'm sure the boys in blue will be happy to let us say that. It lets them off the hook and makes her seem inept, unqualified to be on the force, which is what they want to say anyway."

"I'm not sure that would be helpful to your sister's memory, especially since she leaves a child."

"It's better than saying she committed suicide."

"True."

"It's the only way to handle it."

"All right," said her mother. "An accident. That would be best."

Her face lit up suddenly. Beth, her back turned to the door, did not know why until she heard Della say, "I'm thirsty."

"Come to Grandma, Della," Delores said while Beth got up to get the child a glass of water. She wrapped the girl in a tight embrace and said, "You're not going to ever leave your grandma, are you, sweet thing? You want to stay with Grandma forever, don't you?"

The child answered with a mumbled syllable and began twisting her body and shifting her feet in an effort to free herself.

Frank something was Neet's lawyer's name. Frank Jerome, that was it. Beth would go and see him after she called the undertaker.

"My poor sweet baby is an orphan," said Delores in her honeyed baby-talk voice. "Don't worry, Della, Grandma will take care of you."

"Let her go, Mother," Beth said sharply. "Come back to bed, Della. Come with me."

She led the child back to the room that was once her own and Neet's and sat on one of the pink twin beds, holding Della's shoulders firmly, looking her straight in the eyes. "Della. Do you understand what's going on?"

"Is my mommy hurt?"

"Yes."

"Did she die?"

"Yes."

"Did the bad people get her?"

Beth continued to look into the blazing beauty of her niece's eyes, and renewed her silent commitment never to lie to her, not that it was possible with those golden searchlights trained on her face. "Yes, Della. But we have to be strong. We have to pretend it was an accident."

The girl nodded. "My mommy told me once she was a soldier fighting a war, and that soldiers' families have to be brave. She fought very hard, didn't she?"

Beth nodded, unable to speak.

"Do I have to go and live with my father now?"

"I don't think so," Beth said, and paused before asking gently, "Would you like to come and live with me?"

"I'd like that a lot," Della said. "I want to go to the zoo again, and go look at the ancient jewelry."

"Would you like being with me even if we can't go to those places?"

"Yes, Aunt Beth," said Della. She was suddenly very serious. "I think I need to cry now."

Beth closed the door softly and went back to the kitchen.

"Did you tell her?"

"Yes. I had to. You practically told her yourself."

"How is she taking it? My poor baby," Delores said, and stood up and started off in the direction of the girls' bedroom.

Beth's firm hand was on her mother's shoulder, pushing her

back down into her chair. "Leave Della alone, Mother. She'll be all right. We have some things to talk about."

Delores rubbed her eyes. "You know, Beth, I'm tired. All this has worn me out. I think I want to go and lie down."

"This will only take a minute," Beth said. "Mother, I know you've always used Morton's, but there's someone else I'd like to call this time, someone who might handle things the way we want them done."

Morton's was the local funeral home, the one everyone used after their loved ones had failed to be helped by the feeble efforts of the local doctor.

"I was not satisfied with Morton's," her mother said. "They charged too much to take care of your father. Do what you want, Bethesda. Just remember our funds are limited." She got up and went to a kitchen drawer and drew out a parcel wrapped in plastic. "Here. Bonita left this with me. I believe this is all the insurance she had."

It was pitiful. Neet had a ten-thousand-dollar life insurance policy, and had borrowed half of it. As far as Beth could tell, the amount had not been repaid. She was angry. Not at her sister, who had done the best she could, but at those who had burdened and handicapped her people. Black folks were pathetic. With all the work they had done, they should own half the country. But they had only enriched white people. They had nothing.

"Try to get some rest, Delores, while I call this person. If you can't sleep, look in your closet and see if you can find something dark to put on in the morning. A suit or a dress."

"I have nothing," her mother said.

"What about the dress you wore for Daddy's service?"

"That was a winter dress. It was wintertime."

"Look in your closet anyway. Maybe there's something in there you've forgotten. It doesn't have to be black. We have to find something for Della to wear, too."

"I doubt that the child has anything suitable. Her mother always bought her things in such gaudy colors."

"Well, then, you can take her shopping tomorrow." That was a good thought. Give her mother something to do. "Again, it doesn't have to be black. Black is old-fashioned, and besides, she's too young for black, don't you think?"

"In the old days, children wore white to funerals. Or is that old-fashioned, too?"

"I think white would be wonderful on her. It's just old-fashioned enough to be new again. I knew I could count on you, Mother." *For any material thing, anyway.*

"Haven't you always?" said Delores, and retired to her room.

Chapter Twenty-eight

S he had been lucky enough to get the undertaker himself on the phone. He had been extremely courteous and accommodating. Yes, he was licensed in both states, and in several others, as well. He would arrange for the body to be released to him, and the family should not worry. The medical report would list the cause of death as an accident, just as they wished. He merely had to make a phone call to someone who owed him a favor.

"Why make life any more difficult than it is already?" he questioned philosophically. "Or, to put it differently, why make death more complicated than it is? We are lucky when we can smooth things over and keep them simple. An investigation will not bring your sister back, Professor Barnes. It will only bring you and your mother more grief."

Beth knew the Undertaker was right. Look what had happened to her and the Gammas, and they had only been opposing a college administration, not a police force. She thanked the undertaker for being so understanding.

"We have a lot of experience in these matters, Dr. Barnes. We are always glad when we are able to help, only sorry that you waited for such a sad event to get in touch with us again. You have our sympathy on the loss of your sister, Dr. Barnes."

Maybe it was an act, maybe it was years of practice, but he really did sound sympathetic. "Please call me Beth, Mr. Bostwick."

"Beth it is. Ah, your other situation, your employment problem—has that improved?"

"Yes, from what I've been told. I haven't heard from my superiors directly, but the rumor is that I will be retained."

"You can probably believe the rumor, Beth. We made that call. Again, we are always happy when we have an opportunity to help. Now, please tell me when is not too early to visit you in the morning."

Anytime after nine, she told him. She hung up and began moving restlessly around her mother's house, turning out lights in the living room, grabbing some juice in the kitchen, adding some vodka to it from the dining room cellarette, and finally settling in her father's den.

She turned on the brass light with the green shade and sat at his desk, a massive piece of dark mahogany. It had seemed huge when she was a child, but now it fit her. They did not make solid pieces of furniture like this anymore. She decided to tell her mother that she wanted this desk. It had a vast working surface covered with black oilcloth, which of course she would remove, and six drawers, including a file drawer.

The upper right-hand drawer had always been locked. It was locked now. She searched through the wide, shallow center drawer for the key and found none. Frustrated, she yanked at it, and it came open easily. She had found the secret. It was simple. Opening the center drawer unlocked the upper right drawer; closing that drawer locked the other. As a child she could never figure it out because, back then, she was not supposed to. Her father had not wanted her to open the drawer then. Now, she felt sure that he did.

Beth felt him blessing her as she searched the contents of the drawer. It had three compartments. The front one held only impersonal items like the others: paper clips, brass paper fasteners, file cards. In the middle compartment were clips of ammunition for his gun and the gun itself, a .38. There was also an awesome arsenal of knives that he had taken away from his school's combative students: everything from switchblades to X-Acto knives and stilettos. Mindful of Della and even of her mother when she had her tantrums, she dropped all the weapons in a paper bag that she would discard tomorrow.

Beth felt around in the back of the drawer and found a thick parcel. She drew it out.

At first she was disappointed. The thick manila folder contained nothing personal. It held only piles and piles of clippings and a few notes in Curtis's handwriting. But then she began to read the clippings and became absorbed. Soon she discovered their common theme, which was racial prejudice and its harsh effects on the parts of Curtis's life that were most important to him: education, the naval service, and baseball.

Some of the clippings were very old and fragile. One set, which was dry and yellow like autumn leaves, dealt with the entire history of blacks in baseball, starting with the Negro Leagues. Her father, a pitcher, had spent a year on the road with the Baltimore Elite Giants. She picked up one of the illustrated articles and was amazed to see a picture of him in baseball uniform, handsome and young and squinting into the camera. Beside him, she recognized Roy Campanella, the great catcher.

Her father's presence was palpable now, quivering with an excitement that sped up the pace of her own heartbeats. He was credited with the invention of something called the Barnes Buzz-Ball, a fast pitch that batters never seemed able to connect with. His team's travels and triumphs were documented here, as was the entire career of Jackie Robinson.

At first, Curtis had seemed impressed with Robinson's achievement. Then he began to underline places in the stories that mentioned the insults and slurs Robinson had received from teammates and fans. "He deserves this!" her father wrote in one margin. "This will kill us," in another. The last article in the series told, with mute eloquence, of the collapse of the Negro Leagues in 1960.

Her father also seemed unhappy with the efforts of the children at Little Rock, or at least with those of their parents, and with the Supreme Court decision of 1964. "We are taking too many chances with our children," he had written under an article about Little Rock, adding, "We will lose more by this than we gain. Children will be harmed. Jobs will be lost." He had written, when the Supreme Court decision on school integration was announced, "On this date I end my membership in the NAACP," and signed it with a flourish. "Bravo!" she cheered aloud, not sure she agreed with his action, but proud of his decisiveness.

The last clipping on school integration, dated several years after his retirement, was an article on the school where he had worked, the one she always thought of as "Daddy's school." It still mainly served black children, but now a white man occupied the principal's office that had been his, and the teachers were all white or Asian. He had filed it without comment. She was heartbroken for him.

There were times, Beth remembered, when her father came home, spoke to no one, and retreated to this room. She had overheard her parents' late-night conversations at these times and knew that he was struggling with a prejudiced school board and an intransigent superintendent. She had not known the details, but he had ended by taking early retirement, which put the family in a tight financial bind until Beth finished school. At work, Curtis had probably been under tremendous pressure, but he never let it show in front of his girls. He always smiled for them, was always funny and cheerful, never admitted that anything was wrong. Probably, she decided, her father's circumstances at work were something like her own. It might have helped her if he had not kept them to himself.

Beth read on. This was a man she had never known. Her father was angry with white people, furious with blacks who sought to integrate with them, and despairing about the future. He had saved a virtual history of the civil rights struggle and its aftermath, and sprinkled it with the ironic, frequently impolite comments he dared not make out loud in his house.

There were other things in that drawer—clippings about other athletes, from Jesse Owens to Tiger Woods, mainly featuring not their triumphs but their humiliations and sufferings. There were clippings about the brutality of life in the segregated Seventh Fleet, the so-called Texas Navy, with its Southern officers and outlook, which he had experienced. There was an account of the horrendous Port Chicago disaster in Long Beach, California, in which almost four hundred men were killed in an explosion of defective ammunition, for which the black sailors who had been loading the shells were blamed. There was a horrifying file on lynchings, from Emmett Till, who was lynched for looking at a white girl, to James Byrd, who was dragged to his death behind a truck in Texas. "Should not have trusted those crackers" he had scrawled in a newly shaky hand beside the account of Byrd's death.

There was very little in that drawer that did not have something to do with race problems and prejudice. It was mostly a file of horrors, a testament to his suppressed rage.

There were also some souvenirs of Curtis's early teaching days, shots of him standing in front of what appeared to be an unpainted board shack. A sign on the door of the shack declared it to be THE MANUAL TRAINING INSTITUTE FOR COLORED YOUTH, COLUMBIA, SOUTH CAROLINA. Bethesda found it hard to believe that such an institution ever existed, or that she and her father had even lived in the same century.

She needed to mourn her sister, but Bethesda felt herself drawn into mourning instead for the father she had never known and now would never know. She would have liked to know more about that institute. He could have told her how, with his Howard degree in hand, he had managed to serve out his time there, as all black teachers did in his day, and how, while pretending to live up, or down, to the institute's menial mission, its hardy faculty had stealthily shaped it into a college.

But he never had told her those things, and now he was gone. It must have taken an enormous effort for Curtis Barnes to hide his real thoughts and concerns from his children. The father she had known had been a funny, tender, smiling, easygoing fraud. This locked drawer was where her father really lived, the only place where his angry heart and troubled soul could be found. The poor man, smiling and pretending everything was fine until the end. No wonder he had a stroke.

It was after four in the morning when she finished going through the file. It left her saddened and angry that he had kept his most important experiences secret from her. He sent her to white schools, but he did not believe in integration. He told her, "You can be anything you want to be," when he knew her future was limited. He implied to his children that everything was all right with the world, when he knew how much was wrong with it. He talked often and intensely about the importance of being prepared for a career, but he had deliberately omitted the most important part of her preparation: Never trust white folks.

Her parents and their peers believed that the Ivy League was the pinnacle, the absolute peak of any black child's aspirations. "So-and-So goes to Brown," they would say in hushed tones, with a reverence once reserved for Holy Communion. "So-and-So was accepted by Harvard." Once you had arrived in the Ivy League, you had really *arrived*. And you were safe. The Ivy League was the next best thing to resting in the arms of Jesus. You were at the top, securely ensconced in a place that was presumed to be civil and reasonable because it based its very existence on the concepts of human civility and reason.

What was it Malcolm had said, in that sonorous voice of his that was bright as a trumpet's, beautiful as a mockingbird's? "Ah, my friends, you've been had. You've been hoodwinked. You've been tricked." You've been bamboozled.

You've been buffaloed.

Studying the contents of her father's secret file made Beth remember things that had never been explained, like her parents' sudden departure from Philadelphia's Mummers' Parade, dragging her small unwilling body along, when she was about five and a group of clowns jigged toward them. Her mother had clapped her hands over Beth's eyes, but Beth had peeked through and seen the white men in blackface. Dragging her by both hands, her parents couldn't give her a reason why she had to miss the other clowns and the string bands.

At their house, the newspaper usually disappeared before dinner. She didn't read newspapers often, they were mainly her father's reading material, but her parents were taking no chances. At least twice she saw her father furtively carrying his newspaper to the trash. There were other times when the paper was full of holes where there had been stories. Their TV viewing was full of holes, too: plenty of comedy but no *Eyes on the Prize*, no *Tony Brown's Journal*, no *Both Sides with Jesse Jackson*.

There was the family's refusal to discuss slavery, an insistence that it was an evil thing that happened to some other people in a faraway place long ago and had nothing to do with them. But among the papers Beth had found in her father's drawer was a family tree showing that his great-great-grandfather had come from a plantation near Charleston, South Carolina.

Once, Beth had asked her mother to explain slavery. It had been mentioned casually in her fourth grade class one day, along with a few other snippets of history. But she somehow knew it had something to do with her, mainly because Miss Stone was looking everywhere but at her black students. Her mother simply told her that it was a bad thing that happened a long, long time ago, and refused to say more. Later, Beth overheard Delores on the phone to her teacher, complaining about her shocking the children with material unsuitable for tender ages.

"No, I didn't accuse you of discussing sex, you idiot! She can handle sex, she knows all about sex, she's known about it since she was five. I don't want you talking to my child about s-s-s-slavery!" It had taken her mother forever to push out the distasteful word, and when she turned, red-faced and panting from the effort, Beth was standing there.

"Were you eavesdropping on my conversation?" her mother demanded.

Beth knew, as children always do, that it was one of those times when she had better lie. "No. I just came inside from jumping rope with Nadia. Are there any cookies left?" And her mother, who usually forbade sweets before supper, had reached gratefully for the knobby blue cookie jar and let Beth help herself without counting how many she took.

It must have taken tremendous effort to shelter her and Neet from the truth when the sisters were young and curious and history was happening everywhere around them. But her parents had managed it, keeping from their daughters the news of the jailings and beatings and bombings of the civil rights struggle, hiding the horror stories of people like Autherine Lucy and Emmett Till, sharing with them only the victories, like the appearance of black stars on television and black columnists in white newspapers, and the accommodations newly to be had at Holiday Inns.

Then a wonderful time arrived when Black was Beautiful, and she was young, gifted, and black, and the sky was the limit. Her parents encouraged this way of thinking, even let her tease her straight hair into an Afro, with egg white whipped into it to give it more texture. Daily she and her friends slapped palms, hummed "Land of a Thousand Dances," and celebrated their blackness, but they had no idea, really, what they were celebrating.

Beth had entered the seventies at thirteen, a bright, confident teenager, and exited them at twenty-three, an assured young woman starting graduate school. By the time she was twenty-eight, she had her Ph.D. in hand and believed that any door on which she knocked would open.

But there was so much she did not know. She had no idea, even at seventeen, that little brown Bethesda Barnes was any less welcome in the world than a white Beth would be. She had worked all four years on the high school newspaper, where they were happy to let her slave like a good darky, but never made her an editor. She was passed over, they told her when she asked, because she could not do art or layout. She had believed them.

She had been turned down for a part in a play because, they said, she did not have a good singing voice. She had accepted the decision without a murmur.

It was not a musical.

Once, she remembered, her father seemed about to blow the family silence on racism when she brought home a high school boy who appeared to be white. "Daughter, I need to talk to you. Now!" he had thundered.

Her mother quickly shushed and soothed him. "It's not what you think, Curtis," she said. "I know his parents. He was in Jack and Jill with Bethesda."

"Oh," her father said, and went back to his reading. Beth had been almost sorry. Her father had been about to launch into a spectacular eruption worthy of Vesuvius, she could tell, and she would have been interested in seeing and hearing it.

Later her mother had said, "Beth, I lied for you today. Don't ever make me do it again." She got the message. To avoid upsetting her father, she never invited Maurice Lavelle or any other white boy home with her again.

It was her father, hoping she would become or marry a doctor, who had named her Bethesda, after both the pool of healing in the Bible and the hospital where they had drained his sinuses and saved his life and also his teeth. He loved to tell of the exquisite agony of that operation, of them going up into his skull with steel picks and hammers, and the filth that came out. All without benefit of anesthesia, as were his root canals. "Only good thing about being in the navy," he always said. "If I hadn't joined the navy I'd have been dead. Dead and toothless."

"If you were dead, you wouldn't mind being toothless, Daddy," she always pointed out.

"True," he said. "But you and Bonita and Delores might be embarrassed."

Along with his humor, why had he not shown her his pain—not just his toothaches and his horrible sinus headaches, but the emotional pain of his real life?

Instead, he had moved her and Neet to the cocoon of this all-black town, where prejudice was only a distant, muffled rumor and they could grow up sheltered and safe, protected from the pain of racism.

The conservative people of Refuge, New Jersey, were red, white, blue, and black patriots who had refused to change their Fourth of July celebration to a Juneteenth one. They celebrated their ancestors' escape from slavery but did not talk about that condition— just felt smug and faintly superior to their Southern cousins because the escape had been made.

No one in this community talked about the lynching of Emmett Till or the deaths of the four little girls in Birmingham, and yes, by God, it must have been a sweet relief for Beth's parents and the other adults to be away from that sort of conversation, that sort of agony, but the ignorance was dangerous for their children, and, somehow, those events and the white attitudes they expressed were in the very air they breathed. They were like an invisible poisonous gas, a subtle, toxic fog that stung the skin and closed up the throat, kept the tongue under restraints and inhibited risktaking.

Nothing threatened them in the safe, all-black territory of Refuge, but Beth and her friends knew, without discussing it, not to behave exuberantly in the rich neighboring town of Wakefield or to "show out" (raise their voices, get emotional, act *colored*) at the high school they attended in white Crescent Heights.

But like Zora Neale Hurston, who was a product of all-black Eatonville, Florida, the Barnes girls were mostly unaware of racial restrictions and thought they could get away with anything. Bonita had grown up fearless and free, as her parents wished, and had died young as a result. Armed with her childish belief in her omnipotence, she had pulled the tiger's tail once too often, and it had turned on her with hot breath and sharp fangs.

The lesson that Beth learned from the town's conservatism and her family's scary silence on racism was not the one Delores and Curtis had wanted her to learn. With no guidelines and no map for her behavior except strange, symbolic statements like "Don't go where you're not wanted," she decided early that white folks had the power and the way to survive among them was to avoid making waves: Keep your head down, don't upset people, stay out of their faces and out of trouble. Just do your job extremely well, better than anyone else, work very hard, and you will be fine. That had been her policy. Look how it had failed her.

Beth sucked her breath in sharply. In a sudden, head-tightening rage, she knocked the ornaments off her father's desk and broke the glass on a framed photo of herself and Neet. It was the middle of the night, but she could not wait until morning.

Chapter Twenty-nine

Beth burst into her mother's room yelling, "Why did you and Daddy lie to us?"

Her mother was not asleep. She was sitting at her vanity table, brushing her long, thinning black hair. "Lie to you about what?"

"About our history. About the horrible part of being black. About slavery, and lynchings, and segregation, and the rest of it."

"Don't blame your father. If you were boys, he might have told you about all that. But you weren't, so he basically left your raising up to me."

"Were you ashamed of what we were? Is that why you never told us the truth?"

"No, of course not." Delores calmly put down her hairbrush and picked up her cold cream. "I wanted you to be proud of yourselves—proud, confident little girls. That was why I never talked about those horrid things. There was no need—"

Beth interrupted her. "So, for the sake of pride, you let us grow up without a history, without identities, without even knowing that life would put limits on us?"

"But that was the point, dear," Delores said. "We didn't want you to know you had limitations."

"That was wrong, Mother. Ignorance isn't bliss, it's dangerous."

"How can you say that? Just look at what you've accomplished! Look at all you've done!"

Beth brushed that aside. "And why did you tell us our ancestors were all born free—like Elsa the lioness, or something? I should have seen through that one, it was so ridiculous. Why did you lie to us?"

"Could you have done all you have if you knew you were descended from slaves?" Her point made, Delores turned back to her dependably consoling friend, the mirror, and began creaming away the layer of ivory powder that had settled into the creases of her face. "—On your father's side, of course," she added under her breath.

"Maybe I'd have done more things. Or different things. I stuck out my neck this year at work, Mother, not knowing white people would be happy to chop my head off. I could have died last week when they bombed the black dormitory. Bonita *did* die."

She looks like Morticia, Beth thought, observing how her mother's harshly dyed black hair contrasted with her near-white skin and came to a widow's peak in front. The character from the creepy Charles Addams cartoons. *I always thought she was a silly idiot, but she's not; she's a monster.*

Shaking with fury, Beth went on. "Neet's death is on your hands, Mother, and mine might have been. She never learned she had limitations, poor baby. She believed in fairy tales. She thought she could fight the evil giants and win. I couldn't help her. I was over forty before I knew that I had a place and had better stay in it if I wanted to survive. Forty-two fucking years old! Christ!"

"You don't have to be vulgar, Bethesda," her mother said, wiping off cold cream. "Why can't you ever talk about pleasant things? I was thinking, maybe I could find a nice navy blue outfit for Della, something in cotton plissé or that new crinkled rayon, maybe. That would be suitable for the service, and it would be a dress she could wear again this spring."

There's no point in arguing with her, Beth realized. *She's in total denial. She'll never see that she was wrong. She'll never change.*

"I could use a nice navy print dress for myself," Delores went on. "I'll wear it again. I have a couple of fashion shows in June."

"I'm going down there, Delores," she announced. "I'm going down there, and I'm taking Della with me."

"Down where?" asked Delores.

"Down to South Carolina, to the plantation where Daddy's people were. I want her to know her family history."

"You can't do that!" her mother screamed, and threw the hairbrush at her. It was full of tangled black hairs with white roots. "You can't expose my grandchild to all those horrors."

"I can and I will."

"Why don't you go on and take her to Mississippi while you're at it?"

Mis'sippa, her mother had said.

With a dropped syllable and a short ending.

"Why? Is that where the slaves on *your* side of the family were?"

It had been a terrible argument, one that escalated from screaming to cursing to threats to throwing things. It seemed likely to escalate even further, but suddenly they were both exhausted. Dead tired, wrung out, empty.

Beth was the one who gave up first, realizing that her mother would never understand why her daughter was so upset. Delores had worn rose-tinted glasses for so long that she could not see shadows. Her life was one long garden party, a parade of luncheons and fashion shows at which everything was delightful. She steadfastly refused to look at anything ugly. She had joined two clubs of like-minded women who sought to hide from reality and provide equally pleasant hiding places for their children.

At seven and eight years old, Beth had learned to curtsy and pour tea at Miss Briscoe's Charm School, which also taught social dancing. Her most vivid memory of Miss Briscoe, a small, twiglike woman, was her insistence that they keep their knees together: "Sit up straight, young ladies, and remember, I don't want to see any space between those knees!"

Every birthday, her mother gave her a new box of stationery with which to write thank-you notes for presents, and supervised her writing of them. And at sixteen, a skinny, scared Bethesda was presented at one of Delores's club cotillions. She had learned to waltz in a long white lace skirt, she had walked in on the arm of a buck-toothed boy with bad breath, and she had hated the entire evening. To their mother's frustration, and to her eternal credit, Neet had managed to avoid all that.

Near the end of their argument, her mother declared, "I have paid my dues and then some, Bethesda. I dealt with things like that for most of my life so that you wouldn't have to."

And that, at last, gave Beth pause. It made her wonder what ugly ordeals her mother had once faced to make her duck behind those rose-tinted glasses. It also set Beth to wondering whether she herself had failed to confront reality. Nasty memories began to surface, one by one, like bubbles of odorous gas rising to the top of a stagnant pond.

In her early twenties, she had gone out to lunch at an elegant tearoom with her aunt Kate and her cousin Leslie, to celebrate Leslie's eighteenth birthday. All around her, she saw people being served before them. She was not blind. Yet, when Aunt Kate rose to object, she pulled her back down in her seat and tried to shush her, saying, "They're just busy. This is a nice place. They'll take our orders soon." She had believed that.

Another time, at lunch with Sherri, she had been just as accepting of a delay in service. But Sherri, being Sherri, had not let her get away with it. She had stalked out, loud-talking the management, and insisted on going instead to the soul food joint up the street. Beth had been embarrassed. At the time, she thought her friend was too angry and oversensitive.

She had thought Lloyd backward and conservative because he did not want to go to resorts inside the United States—only abroad. She had called herself opening up his world by dragging him to places like Tanglewood and Woodstock and Virginia Beach, when he would rather have gone to American Beach, Florida, or Peg-Leg Bates's resort in Kerhonkson, New York. But he remained stubborn. In the Poconos, in spite of her wish to try other hotels, they stayed at the black-owned Hillside Inn. It was the only place he would go. She enjoyed herself, but chafed at being so limited.

Denial had been so much a part of Beth's upbringing, she realized, that it was a part of her. She did not always know insults when she heard them, or understand rejection when it was aimed at her, or even feel the sting of half the arrows she caught.

Before teaching, there had been interim jobs, but Beth had failed to get the ones she wanted. At least two prospective employers had been thrilled with Beth's credentials—until the interview. They had practically hired her on the phone. Face-to-face with her, they retreated into nervous mumbling and the recitation of almost identical speeches about how the position had already been filled. Beth had accepted this news without question. If something else were involved, she did not want to face it.

She had told herself over the years that she was happy at her place of work—when, most of the time, she was scared to death. She felt like an eternal outsider at the university—uncertain of how to behave, not understanding these assured, superior white folks or knowing their rules.

Beth loved contemporary black writers, but preferred not to

read slave narratives. She had objected to the grimness of black history and to being confronted with so much of it during what she called Black Misery Month. The previous condition of her people depressed her, she had said. She didn't see the reason for immersing herself in the horrors of the faraway past.

Who the hell was Beth, free, black, and over twenty-one, warm, well-fed, and well paid, to complain of depression? Slavery was not as distant as she had thought. She felt ashamed.

At that point, she stopped hurling accusations at her mother. It was time, she knew, to start working on herself. Time to understand why a shadow fell so often between her and her desires. To know the source of that shadow and stare it in the face. To understand the limitations that still circumscribed her life, her work, and her pleasure, without ever believing they were right or insurmountable. To grow wise and aware. To become deeply black.

The argument between Beth and her mother had produced a catharsis of sorts. Afterwards, though nothing was settled or resolved or ever would be, they were able to be civil, even kind, to one another. Delores's wonderful talent for irrelevance and non sequiturs helped. Five minutes after they had been hurling threats and abuse at one another, she said, "I wonder if Bonita kept her sewing machine. There might be time for me to run up a couple of dresses for Della and me to wear to the funeral. We will have to watch our pennies now, you know."

Beth resisted the temptation to ask who she meant by *we*, and replied, "I think she did keep that machine. By the way, I'd like Dad's desk. Maybe you could turn the den into a sewing room after I take it."

"That desk is probably worth a lot by now," her mother protested feebly. "I don't think I can afford to let it go." But later she admitted that she would be glad to get rid of "that big black ugly thing."

Talking about things, having decided by silent accord to make no more mention of feelings, they made a fragile peace and were back on common if shaky ground by nine, when the undertaker came to call in a silver Lincoln with a driver who waited at the curb. Beth introduced Senator Bostwick to her mother and her niece; then she sent Della out in the yard to play while they discussed the grim details.

"Our cosmetologist is a great artist, and she has done her best," he said, "but it has been difficult. She decided that it was best to have your sister sleeping on her left side."

He went on, in a gentle voice, "The injury was to the left rear portion of her head, you see."

"So I was right. There was no way that it could have been suicide," Beth said.

The undertaker nodded. "Not likely, at any rate, if she were right-handed. It would have been too awkward to get her hand around there."

"She was right-handed," Delores said.

He went on, "There's no way that it could have been an accident, either. But, out of respect for the family, and to return a favor he owes me, your county medical examiner has signed a certificate of accidental death."

"Would it be best, do you think, not to have a public viewing?" Beth asked.

"I think so. That way, you see, no one will have reason to question the ME's finding. However, if you feel strongly about following tradition, the young lady is presentable. You may, of course, come and see her yourselves to say a private good-bye."

"I don't want people looking at my mommy!" Della screamed through the screen door.

"They won't, dear, I promise," Beth said. "Delores, isn't it time you and Della started for the mall?"

"Yes," Delores said, and knocked her chair into the cupboard in her haste to get to her feet. She seemed awed and unnerved that such an important man as the senator had come in person to help them. She peered out the window at his fine car for the third or fourth time, as if to make sure she had not imagined it, and then said, "Thank you for coming, Mr. Bostwick. I'll let you take care of the rest of the details, Bethesda. I'm sure whatever you two decide will be fine. Just remember our little budget. Come on, Della, you're going for a ride with Grandma."

In the end all three of them went to see the prettily painted thing that was not Neet stretched out gracefully in the Fisk Room, and Della covered it with its white satin blanket, and the Undertaker closed the lid on Neet's short, lively life, placing her photograph on top of it. An invisible organist played softly, somberly as a few more people filed in.

Then Della said, "I think I need to cry now," and ran to find the ladies' room. She and Beth would say that phrase a lot to each other in the days and weeks ahead. They would use it to begin a tradition of respect for one another's privacy. Beth always left the room when her niece said, "I think I need to cry now," and when her aunt was the one to say it, Della would leave. Beth said it now right after her niece, and proceeded to soak three Kleenexes as well as Lloyd's lapel, for he had quietly joined them, was silently and solidly there for her, as he had said he would always be.

Chapter Thirty

Two letters came from Beth's employer on consecutive days. The first one terminated her contract. The second one renewed it and asked her to disregard all previous correspondence.

She and Sherri laughed hysterically for half an hour when Beth showed her the letters. Beth explained about Lloyd's sending her to the undertaker, and how the second letter showed the powerful man's hand at work. One call from him had probably done it. They would keep a chimpanzee on the faculty if it would save their half-billion-dollar appropriation.

"Guess what my chairman did? He called me and asked how he could make a contribution to the senator's next campaign."

"What did you tell him?"

"I told the little creep where Senator Bostwick's office is and said he could take it there himself. I hope he meets Mr. Saint, the head embalmer, and gets scared shitless."

Sherri laughed heartily and then returned to her task of going through Beth's closet to help her pack. "What kind of clothes do you want for this trip, girlfriend? Work or play? Is this trip business or pleasure? And what's the weather like down there?"

With Sherri's help, Beth was finishing her packing for a ten-day trip South. Her argument with her mother, Beth now understood, was necessary to break the eggshell that confined her. Now she was able to be pleasant and civil with Delores, because she was free to fly far from home.

"Both business and pleasure," Beth said. "And the weather will be warm and then warmer. First there's the conference in Ocean City, Maryland."

Sherri plucked a long red chiffon dress with a silver lamé bodice from Beth's closet. She held it up to herself and took a few turns on an imaginary dance floor. "You'll want this, then. Conferences are for fucking."

"Not this time," Beth said, and took the gown away from her friend and replaced it on its rack. She had agreed last winter to present a paper on surrogate mothers in the fiction of, among others, Ellease Southerland and Toni Cade Bambara at the annual Women Writers of Color Conference in Ocean City. It would give her a chance to make some contacts at other schools. More important now, it would give her and Della an apartment on the beach for four days. "This time I'm taking a chaperon."

Sherri raised a quizzical eyebrow. "Who?"

Della was still at her grandmother's, packing her own stuff and keeping Delores pacified, but Beth would be picking her up later that day. "I'll need some conservative things for presenting my paper and schmoozing with people from other schools, and some play things to wear on the beach with Della."

"Oh," Sherri said. "Gotcha. Your navy dress, your purple bathing suit, your matching terry caftan."

"That's a good start. I'm really looking forward to this trip, Sherri, but I don't mind telling you I'm scared to death. Della is a great kid, but she's a big responsibility. I don't know a thing about being a parent. My mother was not such a great model, you know. Do you think I can handle it?"

"I do, absolutely," her friend said.

"Well, then," Beth said, "I guess Lincoln and Edwina saved my life for something."

"Lincoln and *who*? Did *what*?"

"Edwina. You remember, the sister who used to take care of us at the pool. She and the guard, Lincoln, saved me one night last month when I almost drowned myself."

"Girlfriend," Sherri said, putting her hands on both of Beth's shoulders and gently pushing downward, "I think you'd better sit down."

Beth obeyed, sitting on the edge of her bed and looking up at her friend questioningly.

"I don't remember Lincoln, but Edwina died about ten years after we graduated. Don't you remember? We took up a collection for her flowers. You contributed to it."

It took a few minutes for Beth to digest this information. "I'd forgotten," she finally said. "I guess sometimes God sends angels to look after fools who won't look after themselves." She paused for a long time and then added, "I wish he'd sent a couple to Neet."

"Yeah," Sherri said, trying to zip her friend's overstuffed travel bag. "I remember Lincoln now. He was the old guy Edwina lived with, or maybe married. He'd be nearly a hundred by now if he were alive."

Beth took a look at her bulging bag. "Hey, what have you got in there? Let's take out some of those play clothes. There's no room left to hang another business outfit in there. I need something super-conservative for an interview in a super-hot climate."

"They got English departments in hell now?"

"No, in North Carolina."

"Same place," said Sherri.

"I hope I like it," Beth said. "Della will be ready for college in ten or eleven years. I do not intend for her to suffer the way I've seen black kids suffer where I teach now. If that college in North Carolina won't work for us, I intend to keep on looking. The South is full of schools."

"I see your point," Sherri said. "But if you move down South, girlfriend, you'll have to come back here to see me. This Negress has never set a foot below the Mason and Dixon line, and I do not intend to start now, at the ripe old age of forty-three. I am not convinced they have abolished slavery yet down there."

"You sound about ninety. Provincial as hell, and set in your ways."

"Maybe I am," Sherri admitted. She looked away shyly. "Solomon finally got his divorce, you know. I was afraid he never would, but now we are making plans. Then I'll *really* be set in my ways. What about you and Lloyd? If you leave town, what happens to him?"

"I don't know," Beth said. She winced. Sherri had touched on the flaw in her happiness, and like any sensitive spot, it hurt. "He'll have to adjust, I guess. Della comes first now. He'll have to accept that."

Chapter Thirty-one

Somehow, in spite of everything, Beth and the two Gammas who were graduating made it to commencement. She decided to go, and to take Della. It was a fine, bright day, and while the speeches were dull, they enjoyed the music and the marching students, especially the ones who were bravely flaunting their kente stoles. Some of the white males were drunk and rowdy, pouring beer and wine on one another and displaying the underwear that was all they wore under their black gowns. Beth was embarrassed, but at least she was not a parent to any of them. She sang the one school song she knew and taught it to Della, and hummed the others, and cried when she saw Dana and Rhonda because she was so proud of them. They came up afterward and hugged her, and met Della, and called her the Little Professor. When they left to be with their parents, she cried some more.

"Are you sad, Aunt Beth?" Della asked.

"No, baby, I'm crying because I'm happy."

"I do that, too, sometimes."

Then, with the top of the Mustang down and scarves and sunglasses firmly on, Beth and Della flew down the highway, sometimes singing "The Bear Went over the Mountain" in loud inharmonious voices, sometimes silent because the wind kept taking their breath away, and munching the popcorn and potato chips they had not spilled in the car.

After the forlorn little private funeral, she had kept an appointment with Frank Jerome and acquired the document that made her Della's guardian. There was no chance, he told Beth, of anyone's legally disputing it except the father, and James Bowen, who had flown in for the funeral and flown right out again, had signed over his parental rights temporarily for the attorney who waited quietly in the back row. He might change his mind later, he said, when he was better situated—but for now, he felt, he could not raise a girl, and only wanted visits. Frank Jerome believed that James would never be "situated," whatever that meant, and that Beth could confidently make plans for Della.

Document in hand, Beth visited Della's school and asked permission to take her out of school for two weeks. Her teacher, a faded blonde named Miss Oliver, said, "Of course she can go. A trip is a wonderful idea. It might take her mind off her recent ordeal. What a tragedy. Our poor little Della. I feel so sorry for the precious child."

Afterward, at the ice cream shop, she asked Della, "How do you like your teacher, Miss Oliver?"

"She's a smacked ass," Della said, and slurped soda through her straw.

"Watch your mouth, young lady." The woman *had* been a gushing fool, though, Beth thought. "She gave you some homework to take on the trip. Make sure you do it."

Delores would be all right without them, Beth felt. She had left her mother with an assignment that made her comfortable. She would spend her days in Bonita's apartment, sorting her younger daughter's possessions, shedding a tear now and then, but mostly humming happily as she decided which of Neet's things to sell, which to give away, and which to keep.

Fortunately, Delores told her surviving daughter in the course of one of her nightly calls a week or two after the funeral, she and her deceased child had worn the same size. She only needed to let down hems and make a few other alterations, which would be facilitated by Neet's sewing machine. The things which were too young for her she would give to her church's free clothing program. Did Della want her mother's typewriter or her small TV?

"Maybe," said Beth, conscious of the quavering in her mother's voice, knowing she was using the gambit of talking about things to keep her emotions from coming through. "Store them. We'll decide later, unless you want them."

"We-ell," her mother said, "I was thinking they might be useful here."

"Then take them, Mother. Take anything you want. I know Neet would want you to have them."

"I don't want anything, really." Delores sounded suddenly weak and pathetic. "I just want some of Bonita's things because they were hers. What I really want is my baby back."

An image of Neet flying around a corner on skates flashed into Beth's mind, and her eyes filled. "Oh, so do I, mother. So do I." Neet had always been in motion. On skates, on her bike, in her Blazer. It was awful to think of all that energy stilled.

The Ocean City conference on Women Writers of Color turned out to be a blast. Every morning she and Della had breakfast brought in by room service, and then they opened the sliding glass doors of their beachfront apartment and ran to the sea. Afternoons they spent in the air-conditioning, reading and watching TV, while hordes of nearly naked white college students took over the beach. In the late afternoon they dressed and drove over to a small town called Crisfield that had a supermarket in which ample farm women sold wonderful, wholesome home-cooked meals. These they took back to their room and ate greedily. Then they sat on the emptied beach and watched the sun set and the moon rise, and listened to the waves until Della got sleepy.

The hotel had a day camp for kids, but Della refused to attend it. She said she wanted to come and hear her Aunt Beth speak. Beth was both concerned and gratified that her niece seemed not to want to leave her side. She didn't want to be too heavy-handed with her authority at first; she wanted to keep their relationship fun right now. So, wearing the denim dress Beth had bought her, a princess style with a pin-tucked front embroidered with red cherries, Della sat in the front row surrounded and petted by female academics, and listened to Beth deliver her paper on surrogate mothers in black women's fiction. Minnie Ransome, the healer in Bambara's *The Salt Eaters*, and *her* surrogate, the spirit called Old Wife. The midwife in Southerland's *Let the Lion Eat Straw*, and the plantation midwife in Walker's *Jubilee*. The pair of aunts in Naylor's *Mama Day*. Aunt Jerutha in Hunter's *The Soul Brothers and Sister Lou*. Aunt Cuney in Paule Marshall's *Praisesong for the Widow*. This time, Beth decided, she would take Irene's advice and try to publish her paper.

Listening with apparent interest, not squirming at all, Della heard her own surrogate mother ask why black women's heroines were in need of so much extra mothering. Was it a yearning to be nurtured that had persisted since slavery, when their natural mothers worked in the house or the fields? Or was it simply a device the authors used to pass on wisdom from the ancestors, since so much of the past had been lost? Beth leaned toward the latter explanation.

Afterwards, she found that the child had not merely listened, she had understood, as well. "The girls in those books need those extra mothers to teach them old stuff, like I need Grandma—right, Aunt Beth?"

"Right," Beth said. "Would you like to go and see the wild ponies?" There would be a bridge to cross, but she started off toward it without a second thought. Driving down to Maryland had been a release and a miracle. Beth had no problem negotiating the bridges and highways. The terrible argument with her mother had cut the cord that had kept her tethered within ten miles of home.

But the bridge to Assateague Island, where the wild ponies were, was one of those terrible constructions that loomed up in front of her suddenly and appeared to rise straight up in the air. Beth stopped at the foot of it, suffocated by the old fear.

"Why are you stopping, Aunt Beth?"

"To pray. I need to pray now."

"I think that's a good idea," the child said solemnly, and closed her eyes. *Remind me to tell you sometime who you are named for,* Beth thought. *Not just your grandmother but Della Reese, an eternal diva and a deeply spiritual woman.*

Della's blindly trusting face gave Beth the strength she needed. Her foot hit the accelerator, and she ascended the bridge easily, like a bird on an updraft of wind. It turned out not to be so terrible after all.

"Look, Della! The ponies!"

It was fine to be wild and free and surrounded by other wild, free creatures.

All those years at the university had been spent drawn up in tension, with her shoulders hunched in fear and her arms tightly pressed to her sides. Now the restraint seemed to fall off her shoulders and release her. Beth felt younger, and as if she could raise her arms like a pair of wings and fly. But she would not be free as a bird, at least not until her new fledgling was launched, and probably not even then, because by then she would be responsible to and for yet another person. That was how Beth saw her future, and she liked it fine.

She called Lloyd every night to report on their whereabouts and their day's activities, to share telephone kisses and count the days till they would be together again. On the phone, they were like a pair of teenagers instead of aging adult lovers, playing guessing games ("Guess what I did today?" "Guess what happened today that reminded me of you?") and even using baby names for each other. (She was Juicy, and he was Horsie.)

She and Della traveled on to North Carolina without incident, stopping at a chain motel where they both swam in the small pool. It was Beth's first swim since the one that had almost killed her. She was hyperalert when she first slipped into the silky water and then relieved to see that Della already knew how to float and kick. She taught her the elementary backstroke, and was happy that she had not forgotten her own aquatic skills. But it would be a long time, she knew, before she could surrender completely to the water's caress again.

Baldwin College was not paradise, and they would never be rich on the salary it offered, but it was better than Beth had expected: a pretty campus with a rich curriculum in what appeared to be an enlightened college town. The student body was composed almost entirely of girls of African descent who smiled warmly at Della and bent their knees to greet her. Two of them were delegated by the department secretary, Mrs. Houston, to take her to lunch while Beth went into an old, shabby building and met the English faculty.

The chairman seemed warm and wise, as did Mrs. Houston, who was neat and dignified, just as Beth had pictured her. But the junior secretaries had greasy Jheri curls, and one of the professors who were gathered to interview her stuck out his little finger while sipping tea and pronounced *literature* with a hard *t* and a long *u*. "Litera-toor." Dear God. Where had he learned to say that?

Dizzy after a tour of the other shabby buildings and dismayed by the low salary she was offered, Beth struggled with her decision.

Della was definitely college material. Since she was an orphan, she needed a college that would be like an extended family. This school would definitely offer her that, though, like any family, some of its members had serious flaws.

On the other hand, the besieged students back at the university still needed Beth. Her job there still awaited her. She would have to work twice as hard here for about half as much money.

There was a house available near the campus for very little rent, however, less than she paid for three rooms in Philadelphia. They would be safe there, she thought. Della needed her, and safety, most of all.

But Lloyd was back in the city she had left.

There had been nothing on her car radio since she arrived but country music and gospel. She had turned it off and persuaded Della to join her in some more off-key singing. The area could certainly use Lloyd, but she wondered if it had a place for him.

Before she and Della left, Lloyd had gracefully accepted second place on Beth's list of priorities. He would have to give her and Della time alone, she said; time to get used to one another. The child would need time to heal, time to form a new bond she could trust, and a space in which to feel safe before a third party came barreling into their shared life.

"I understand," he said. Then Lloyd winked and added with a wicked grin, "Of course, Della will be wanting to visit her grandmother and her father."

Beth frowned. "Not too often, I hope. And not for long visits."

"Still, I can look forward to those visits, and maybe to sleepovers at the homes of her girlfriends, and maybe even to a week or two at camp."

'I guess," Beth said. "But not too soon."

"It can't happen too soon for me," he said. Then his playful expression turned very serious. "Take all the time you need, Beth. I'll wait. I don't want anyone calling me Uncle Lloyd until I have a right to that title. Do you understand me?"

"Yes," she said, dizzy with a rush of gratitude. Too many children were confused by a succession of uncles. She would never let that happen to Della.

Now, in the course of her nightly phone call, she explained that she had a definite job offer. "It might be a better environment for Della, Lloyd. How would you feel about it if I moved down here?"

"The whole idea hurts. I'd miss you. But I couldn't love you as much if you made Della suffer because of me."

After a few minutes of serious thought, he added, "Let me know as soon as you decide. If you're going to move down there, I'll put in my application for a transfer. It's a slow process, but it usually goes through eventually."

She had almost flung the phone away from herself in her joy. "Oh, Lloyd, that would be wonderful. What about your house?"

"The world's full of houses, but there's only one you, woman. I'd sell it, I guess. That's probably why I never fully furnished it. I didn't want to get too comfortable, or too tied down by stuff. I've seen people unable to move because they can't leave their kitchens and bathrooms. Ain't that a sad situation?"

She agreed that it was. "What about your radio program?"

"It's not like I depend on the station to pay for my groceries, Beth. Most towns have radio stations. So do most colleges. I could send down some tapes. But we're getting way ahead of ourselves. All I have to think about right now is how I'm going to survive without you in the meantime."

"How on earth will we do it?" Beth wondered.

"One day at a time," he said. His love for her seemed unshakable. Beth said silently, *Thank you, Lord.*